The Perfect Mistress

Also by ReShonda Tate Billingsley:

Mama's Boy
Finding Amos (with J. D. Mason and Bernice McFadden)
What's Done in the Dark
Fortune & Fame (with Victoria Christopher Murray)
A Family Affair
Friends & Foes (with Victoria Christopher Murray)
The Secret She Kept
Sinners & Saints (with Victoria Christopher Murray)
Say Amen, Again
A Good Man Is Hard to Find
Holy Rollers
The Devil Is a Lie
Can I Get a Witness?
The Pastor's Wife
Everybody Say Amen
I Know I've Been Changed
Let the Church Say Amen
My Brother's Keeper
Have a Little Faith (with Jacquelin Thomas, J. D. Mason, and
Sandra Kitt)

And check out ReShonda's Young Adult titles:

Drama Queens
Caught Up in the Drama
Friends 'Til the End
Fair-Weather Friends
Getting Even
With Friends Like These
Blessings in Disguise
Nothing but Drama

The Perfect Mistress

ReShonda Tate Billingsley

G

Gallery Books

New York   London   Toronto   Sydney   New Delhi

G

Gallery Books
An Imprint of Simon & Schuster, Inc.
1230 Avenue of the Americas
New York, NY 10020

First Gallery Books trade paperback edition July 2016

GALLERY BOOKS and colophon are registered trademarks of Simon & Schuster, Inc.

For information about special discounts for bulk purchases, please contact Simon & Schuster Special Sales at 1-866-506-1949 or business@simonandschuster.com.

The Simon & Schuster Speakers Bureau can bring authors to your live event. For more information or to book an event, contact the Simon & Schuster Speakers Bureau at 1-866-248-3049 or visit our website at www.simonspeakers.com.

Interior design by Carly Loman

Manufactured in the United States of America

10 9 8 7 6 5 4 3 2

Library of Congress Cataloging-in-Publication Data is available.

ISBN 978-1-4767-1497-4
ISBN 978-1-4767-1504-9 (ebook)

PART I

1989

one

Lauren Robinson struggled to contain her excitement. Her daddy was going to be so surprised when he realized what she'd done.

As the pickup truck rumbled down the street, Lauren lay flat, trying to keep her body still so that she'd stay hidden. She brought her arm up close to her face and glanced once again at the Minnie Mouse digital watch her father had given her a few months before for her seventh birthday.

Just fifteen minutes had passed? It felt like they'd been in the truck for an hour.

Lauren deserved an award. Fifteen minutes of not moving or making a sound had to be some kind of world record.

She wanted to peek from under the tarp in the back of the truck, but if she did that, it would spoil the plan. She had to wait until her daddy came to a complete stop. Then she'd jump up and yell, "Surprise!"

At home, her father always liked when she jumped out of one of the closets. He always pretended to be so frightened, making a silly face. But she knew he put on that act just for her. Her daddy wasn't afraid of anything.

She couldn't wait to see his look of surprise this time, and the idea of that made her almost giggle out loud. It wasn't a closet this time. Plus, after the nasty argument he'd just had with her mom, she really wanted to put a smile on his face.

She felt the truck slow down and come to a stop. Were they really there or was he stopping because of a traffic light?

The breeze that had been tickling her cheeks since she'd snuck into the back of the truck had stopped, too.

This had to be it, where he was headed.

She edged up to peek out of the corner of the tarp just to make sure. That way she could set her timing so that she would get the surprise just right.

She heard the door of the truck creak open, and Lauren began to count in her head.

One-two-three . . .

When she got to ten, she would jump out.

Four-five . . .

"There's my baby." Her father's deep voice made her stop counting.

"Hey, Daddy."

That voice came from a female and the words made Lauren frown. *Daddy?* How could anybody else be calling her father daddy? She was his only daughter, not that she didn't want a baby sister. Or even a baby brother would have been great.

So why was some other girl calling Vernon Robinson daddy?

She lifted the tarp a couple of inches higher so that she could peek out. She had a sinking feeling that her chance to jump out was slipping away.

"You miss me?" her father said.

"I've been waiting on you all day."

All thoughts of her surprise were forgotten. The giggle-filled smile that she'd had since she'd jumped into her father's truck right before he left the house had vanished. Who was her father talking to this way?

Raising the tarp so her head stuck out all the way, she peeked over the roof of the truck cab and her mouth opened wide.

Her father and a lady were hugging. And it wasn't any ol' kind of hug like he gave the ladies in church on Sunday. No, this was the kind of hug that he gave her mother sometimes, the kind that brought on their adult smiles.

She was frozen in shock as her father embraced the woman even tighter. They were so busy with each other, Lauren had time to study the lady who had called her father the same thing that she did.

The woman was thick, a word that she'd heard her mother use when she described someone who was kinda on the chubby side. She had on a royal blue dress that rode up high on her thighs. It looked like it was a size too small, since Lauren could see every bump and curve on her body.

Lauren thought her father was going to step back and away from this lady, done with his hug, but instead he kissed her. One of those long, sloppy kisses Lauren sometimes saw on TV. The kiss went on and on and on, and Lauren wondered how they could even breathe!

The awful show got worse when her father moved his lips from her mouth to her neck. Lauren stared in horrid fascination as he licked that lady's neck up and down. Up and down. It was so bizarre and disgusting to Lauren, but the lady was smiling like this was the best thing that had ever happened to her.

Slowly, Lauren rose to her feet, her surprise to her father forgotten. Today he was the one with the surprise.

The tarp slipped from her shoulders and hit the bed of the truck with a soft thump. Only it wasn't quiet enough because the lady opened her eyes, and for a few seconds that were too long for Lauren, they locked eyes.

"Umm, honey," she said, tapping Vernon on the shoulder.

"Umm, yeah, babe?" her daddy moaned. He sounded like someone was hurting him, and Lauren wondered if maybe the woman's neck had cut his tongue. Maybe that's why he was groaning so loud.

"I think you'd better turn around."

The lady tapped him harder, pointing insistently toward the truck.

Her father eased his head around to follow her motion. His eyes blinked a couple of times as if he couldn't believe what he was seeing. Then he jumped away, putting a couple of feet between him and the lady.

"Pumpkin!" he yelled. "What are you doing?"

This was the moment when she was supposed to yell, "Surprise!" and her daddy would make a silly face.

But the image of her father and this lady and the slobbering they'd just been doing made her forget what she was supposed to do. Not that it mattered because she couldn't get her voice to cooperate anyway.

He marched over and pulled back the tarp completely. With the way he looked at her, she felt exposed, like she'd done something wrong. "What are you doing back there?" he exclaimed.

"I-I . . . I wanted to surprise you," she said to her father, though her eyes were still on the lady.

"Have you been back there the whole time?"

She could tell from his tone that he was mad at her. But usually Lauren knew why her father was upset. This time, though, she had no idea why. Maybe he wasn't mad at her at all. Maybe he was just mad that he had to break away from the sloppy-tongue lady. Or maybe he was mad because the sloppy-tongue lady had hurt him.

"Answer me," he said. Then he repeated, "Have you been back there the whole time?"

She nodded, her eyes still on the woman.

Her father fell silent, as if he was trying to figure something out. He looked slyly over at the woman, seeming to reach some decision.

"Ah, umm, this is Candy," her daddy said. "She's a friend of mine."

"Candy?" That name didn't make any sense to her. "Like M&M'S?"

"Yeah, yeah," he said, "just like that, honey."

At least that explained what her father had been doing. If the lady's name was Candy, maybe he'd been licking that woman's neck because she tasted good.

"So that's why you were licking her?" Lauren asked. "Because her name is Candy?"

Her father moaned, although it was a different kind of moan from the one he was making a few minutes ago. This was the moan he made when something went wrong.

He licked his lips, and she knew what that meant. He was trying to think of what he was going to say next. "Look, sweetheart . . . there are some things—"

The lady had come forward by that time. She touched

Vernon's arm, interrupting him. "Hi, precious." She grinned at Lauren, showing all of her pearlies. "Your daddy was just helping me get something out of my eye."

If Lauren hadn't been taught to respect her elders, she would have laughed out loud. Did this lady think that she was stupid? She'd watched enough TV to know what a kiss was. And she'd seen her mother and father kiss enough times, too, even though she hadn't seen them kissing in a long time.

But since she knew not to sass grown folks, she kept her eyes straight ahead and her mouth closed.

She must have shown some irritation in her face, though, because her daddy turned to the woman. "Candy, be cool. I got this."

The woman didn't like being dismissed like that, but she retreated to a distance that Lauren preferred. If she wanted to leave altogether, that would be all right, too.

Turning back to his daughter, Vernon said, much more brightly, "Come on, sweetie. You want to go get ice cream?"

Lauren frowned. He was offering her a treat? "So, you're not mad at me for hiding?"

"No, it's a nice surprise," he replied, smiling for the first time since he found her. "Any time I can spend an afternoon with my favorite girl is a good time."

Lauren took a deep breath and then let it out. Now she could smile, too. She was still his favorite girl, even though he'd been talking to that Candy lady that way.

"Come here." Vernon lifted Lauren out of the back of the truck. Her legs dangled in the air for a couple of seconds before he set her on the ground.

"Vernon!" He turned to Candy as if he'd forgotten that she was there. "We have plans," she whined.

He shook his head. "Sorry, but my princess comes first."

Those words brought a big smile to Lauren's face.

Then he added, "I'll call you later."

Lauren's smile dipped a little, but she was still the winner. When it came to her daddy, that woman was no match for her, even if she did taste like candy. How, though, could a person taste sweet anyway?

Her father opened the passenger door and Lauren hopped right in, not bothering to look at the lady as she got settled in the seat. Her father was thinking the same thing because he didn't look at Candy, either. He didn't even say good-bye. He started the truck and the two of them took off, leaving the lady standing there.

They drove in silence that lasted so long that Lauren wondered if maybe her dad was really mad at her. Because whenever they were riding together, they always talked and laughed. Sometimes they would even dance in their seats as they listened to one of her daddy's Marvin Gaye cassette tapes.

She was too afraid to say anything, though. She didn't even want to ask him to turn on the radio. After five minutes, he finally spoke up. "You know you can't do that, honey."

She was relieved when he said "honey." He was back to not being mad again.

He continued: "You can't hide in my truck. It could be dangerous. And I'm sure your mom is worried silly. In fact," he announced as he swung the truck into a gas station, "I'm going to pull up to this pay phone and let her know that you're with me."

Lauren felt every muscle in her body get tight. "Maybe

you shouldn't call Mom," she said, afraid of getting in trouble. Her mother was the one who did the disciplining in the family.

"Don't worry," her father said. "I'll make sure she's not mad, okay?"

That eased Lauren's fears a bit. Her father was always looking out for her. He pulled up in front of the pay phone, opened the door, but then paused before he got out. He said, "I'll take care of your mother, but you have to do something for me."

"What?" she asked, excited again. She would do anything that her father asked.

He leaned over the seat, looming in her face as he said, "You can't tell your mom what you saw, okay? You can't say anything about what happened."

Lauren frowned.

He added, "This has to be our little secret." His voice was soft, but stern when he said that last word.

Lauren folded her hands and shifted in her seat. Her mom had always taught her that she should always tell the truth, no matter what anyone else said.

Then he did one of those things that her mom and daddy did to her all the time—he read her mind. "Don't worry, you won't be lying. We're just not telling her because it would make your mom very sad." He paused to let those words sink in. Then came the words that would settle everything. "You don't want to make your mom sad, do you?"

Lauren whipped her head from side to side. Of course she wouldn't want to do that. Her mom was already so sad lately. Her mother wore a lot more frowns than she did smiles.

The door on his side of the truck was still open as he continued: "And if you told your mom this, she might get more than sad, she might get mad."

When she got mad, her mom yelled. Sometimes Lauren even got a spanking.

Her father said, "Your mom might get mad and leave. She might leave me and take you and your brother far, far away. And then, do you know what would happen?"

Lauren's eyes were wide and filled with fear as she shook her head, scared of what his next words would be.

"She might never let me see you again."

Inside, Lauren screamed. Never see her daddy again?

"Do you want that?"

"No, Daddy! No!" she cried, already feeling the loss. She loved her father so much and if she couldn't see him every day, she'd die for sure.

"So, do you understand, this has to be our little secret?" he asked.

Lauren could hardly breathe, but she nodded. "Yes, Daddy." There was no way that she would ever say a word about what she saw today. This day would forever be their special secret.

two

Please, Joyce!"

Her husband's words played over in her mind.

"Please forgive me!"

Joyce leaned back on the cushioned wrought iron patio sofa, and as she stared blankly at the thick woods on the edge of her backyard, she relived the fight she'd had with Vernon that morning.

"Please. Please. Please."

It seemed like Vernon was always begging. This morning he'd been trying to explain the hooker-red lipstick that she'd found on the edge of his shirt collar. She shook her head—he was a walking cliché.

"Mom, can I please go to the arcade with Sam and Terry?"

Joyce turned toward the sound of her eleven-year-old son, Julian. He and Lauren were the constants that made her heart smile. And while she adored her daughter, it was Julian, with his nurturing, loving self, who was her pride and joy. Maybe it was the way he wiped her tears whenever he saw her crying. Or the flowers he would pick on his way home from school for her, just because he wanted to put a smile on her face.

Vernon could learn a thing or two from his son.

"Please, Ma. Sam's mom will take us and pick us up."

She took in her rail-thin son, who had his father's curly hair and hazel eyes. She knew that one day he'd grow up to look just like his daddy. She could only pray that he didn't act like him, too.

"Yes, sweetheart, you can go. Just be careful and be back by eight."

He raced over and hugged her. "Thank you so much! I love you."

"I love you, too. There's a twenty-dollar bill in the jar on the kitchen table. Get that for the arcade."

"You rock, Mom!" he exclaimed before darting back inside.

Joyce watched her son take off. He and Lauren were the reasons she'd endured so much. She wanted to give them a good life. And Vernon had provided that. At least for the children.

With the remote on the table, Joyce clicked a button and the air filled with surround sound. She pressed the channel button, finally settling on a jazz station. Then she leaned back again, hoping that music would take her away.

But her thoughts stayed on her husband, and her mind wandered back through all of the years, back to the beginning, when she'd been filled with so much hope.

It had happened in a moment. That moment when she first laid eyes on Vernon Robinson. One of North Carolina's sudden summer rainstorms had thrown them together. One minute, the sky was that gorgeous shade of serenity, and the next, rain poured from the heavens.

Joyce had just paid Raven to have her hair roller-set. She was happy because she couldn't afford to have her hair done more than every few months. Spotting the diner right around the corner from the beauty shop, she dashed toward the door. But just as she reached for the handle, a man moved in next to her.

"Oh," she said, trying to get inside.

He opened the door. "You first," he said, though they both jumped through the narrow space and into the diner together.

They stood at the entrance, safe from the storm.

"What just happened?" he asked, looking out.

"Just one of our little rainstorms."

"Little?" He peeked through the window. "It looks like a little storm that plans to stay around a while."

"Yeah," she said absently, thinking that she really needed to get back to her dorm. Joyce had only stepped out to get her hair done before Raven left for her vacation, and she planned to get right back to studying for her finals. As the first one in her family to attend college, she had a lot of pressure on her to do well. For the first two years she had. But this junior year had been challenging, and she wanted to put in as much time hitting the books as she could.

"Don't sound so disappointed," he said.

Without looking at him, she said, "I just have so much to get done."

"Me, too," he said. "But there's nothing we can do unless we both want to get out there and fight the rain without umbrellas."

His sensible comment made her run her hand over her hair. He was right: there was no way she could go back outside. She sighed as she looked around the diner filled with students, college professors, and suited businessmen. They might have been a poster for the Research Triangle.

"I have an idea," the guy said. "Why don't we have lunch together?"

Joyce didn't know where that had come from.

He said, "I mean, since we're already here."

She looked him up and down. He looked vaguely familiar. But she said, "I don't know you."

He held out his hand and waited, forcing her to take it. "I'm Vernon Robinson," he said, chuckling. "I'm a student at Duke . . . Duke Law . . . and everyone says I'm a nice guy. Is that enough information about me to have lunch?"

"Yes," she said, thinking that he could have stopped with his name. No wonder he looked familiar. This was *the* Vernon Robinson, Valerie Abraham's fiancé.

As a waitress led them to a table, all kinds of thoughts floated through Joyce's head. She'd heard a lot of talk on the street about Valerie, the daughter of one of the most prominent doctors in Durham, and about the up-and-coming man who'd been featured on television and in all the major media when he'd been named editor of the *Duke Law Journal.*

Joyce was surprised that she hadn't recognized him right away, though she hadn't really paid much attention when he'd appeared on TV. But now that she sat across from him, Joyce saw why everyone was talking about Vernon Robinson. Not only was he smart, destined to be one of Duke's most acclaimed graduates, but this third-year law student was fine—Harry Belafonte sophisticated with extra-oomph fine. And he had class; she could tell by the way he held the menu, then asked her what she wanted before he gave both of their orders to the waitress.

He is exactly the kind of man I want to marry.

The thought of Valerie didn't enter Joyce's mind again. She didn't like thinking much about Valerie anyway. Back in high school, she'd tried to befriend Valerie when she'd worked at a church bazaar and Valerie had sauntered through. But Valerie and her snooty friends had dismissed her with their turned-up noses and sneers.

She'd felt like the lowest thing on earth on that day. Well, today, sitting across from Valerie's fiancé made her feel much better. And because of the way Valerie had treated her, it was game on!

She'd ordered a chef's salad while he'd had a cheeseburger smothered in mushrooms. Finishing their meals should have taken them fifteen, twenty minutes, tops. But hours later, when the sun had long ago emerged brightly and dried the city's streets, the two were still sitting in that booth, chatting and laughing as if they were far more than new friends.

Vernon's eyes got wide when he glanced at his watch. "Are you serious?"

"What?"

He looked at her with a wide grin. "We've been sitting here for four hours."

"No!" She glanced at her own watch. All that studying she was going to do . . . "It doesn't feel like that."

"I know! What's that cliché?"

"Which one? Time flies when you're having fun?"

"No. The one that says I want to see you again. I *have* to see you again."

"That's not a cliché." She laughed, flattered.

He shrugged. "But it's the truth. So when can we get together?"

From that moment, Operation Make Vernon Mine was in full gear. Actually, it had started the moment he mentioned his name, but now Joyce turned it up to level eleven.

Joyce accomplished her mission before too long. It was a bunch of ones: one discreetly forgotten pair of lace underwear at his apartment, one anonymous phone call, and one kiss that left lipstick on his collar. One month after Joyce and Vernon met, Valerie called off the wedding.

Of course, Vernon did all of his breakup crying on Joyce's shoulder. Not that he did too much of that. He transitioned from Valerie to Joyce quickly and smoothly, and right away the new talk around town was about Joyce and Vernon.

Although she'd schemed to go after him, it was Vernon who fell first and fell hard. A month after Valerie called off their wedding, Vernon asked Joyce to marry him.

"You don't even have to finish school," he told her. "You can drop out now so that you can plan the wedding that you've always wanted. It's not like you're going to work anyway. I want to take care of you while you take care of our children."

He didn't have to do too much convincing. The way she'd grown up—on the side of the tracks that people like Vernon and Valerie knew nothing about—she couldn't wait to live a different kind of life. And with Vernon, she'd be well on her way. He'd already been offered a position with one of Raleigh's top law firms at a starting salary of almost $150,000. If this was the beginning, Joyce couldn't wait to see the middle and the end.

So, against her father's will and with her mother's tears, she dropped out of North Carolina Central. A year after they met, Joyce and Vernon vowed to forsake all others for as long as they both lived.

But it took only six months for Joyce to find out two things: what went around came back around, and Vernon Robinson had no intention of forsaking all others. Before they even had a chance to exchange one-year anniversary gifts, another woman was doing to Joyce what Joyce had done to Valerie.

Vernon was so clumsy with his affair. Joyce hadn't gone digging; no one had left any unmentionables in their apartment. No, he cheated on her right in the open. Granted, Vernon and Alicia, one of the law clerks, probably thought they were in the clear since it was nine thirty at night, but still Joyce caught Alicia easing onto her knees in front of her still fully clothed husband. She had arrived just in time to catch more than an eyeful—she saw a mouthful.

Of course, just like those silly ladies in the movies, Joyce turned and bolted. Vernon took off after her, not catching her until she'd been trapped at the elevator banks.

"Please don't leave me," Vernon cried as Joyce sobbed.

He told her the whole story: how Alicia had been trying to seduce him for weeks. How he had resisted her all of this time, and no matter what Joyce thought she saw, what he'd really been doing was stopping Alicia.

Yeah. Right.

She called him a liar.

He begged her to forgive him.

She said she never would.

And he'd said please more times than one would think possible in twenty minutes.

In the end, she rushed home to pack her bags. She was still crying when he came home crying, too.

"I can't stay with a cheater," she told him, no longer shouting. Now her voice was soft, filled with pain.

"You can't leave me!" he cried, sounding like he couldn't imagine being alone. "Where are you going to go?"

His question made her pause. Where *was* she going to go? She'd dropped out of college to take care of this man, and they hadn't even made it one year.

"I don't know what I'm going to do." She stuffed as many clothes as she could into one suitcase. "I'm just so hurt right now."

"I swear I wasn't going to let it go there," he said again, as if repeating himself would turn his lie into the truth. "I should've stopped her when she came into my office and threw herself at me. I tried, but I was weak."

By this point Joyce was dumping her toiletries from the bathroom into her overnighter.

He said, "I'll make sure that she gets fired. I'll do whatever I have to do. I just can't lose you. You mean the world to me."

Joyce emphatically shook her head. She was not going to be one of those women who remained with cheating men. She zipped her suitcase and headed toward the door. Even though she was putting on a show of confidence, inside she was shaking. Where in the world *was* she going to go? What *was* she going to do? Besides her possessions in these two bags, she had nothing. No college degree and no money, because she hadn't done what her grandmother had always said—to build a stash for a rainy day or a quick getaway.

Of course, she did have one place to go—her parents'. But how could she face them after she'd disappointed them so much? How could she stand to hear I-told-you-so when she was hurting so much?

That's not to mention all the talk around town. Although Joyce had done her best to ignore it, everyone in Durham knew that she'd come between Valerie and Vernon. Now everyone would gossip about their breakup—and Joyce imagined how everyone would say that she deserved it. After all, if he'd cheated on Valerie, why wouldn't he cheat on her?

As she stood at the front door, contemplating her choices, Vernon pleaded, "This wasn't about you, baby. I just had a momentary lapse. Please don't leave me. I'm nothing without you."

She had her back turned to him when she felt his hand on her shoulder.

He whispered, "What about . . . our son?"

The word was barely out of his mouth before she covered her beginning baby bump with her hand.

Our son.

She'd hardly forgotten about being pregnant. She just couldn't think about her son right now. Because then she'd be more distressed, and she couldn't afford that.

But now Vernon had brought it up.

Our son.

They'd found out the sex of their baby a mere week ago, when she was at nineteen weeks. Vernon had been overjoyed that his wife was giving him what he really wanted. And he'd repaid her by cheating.

Whipping around, she faced him. "Don't talk about *our son.* You threw me and him away for your law clerk."

"Nothing. Happened." He emphasized those words. "But you can't leave me. Please don't leave me. And I promise, I will spend the rest of my life making this up to you."

She was about to ask him, which was it? Was it that nothing happened? Or was it that something happened and he'd make up for it?

But before she could challenge him with his inconsistencies, he dropped. Yes, right there in the entryway, he fell to his knees. With tears streaming down his face, the powerful Vernon Robinson humbled himself.

When he reached for the suitcase that her hand still gripped, Joyce allowed him to take it away from her. Then he buried his face in her stomach and professed his love again and again.

She'd let him make love to her that night, though it didn't feel the same. Not even the Tiffany signature pearl necklace that he brought home the next day could mend her heart.

"Hello, beautiful!"

Joyce took in the image of her husband, standing at the deck's entry. In his hand he held a gift box. He always brought a gift. Always a gift, always an apology.

"Are you still mad?" His tone was tentative.

"Where's Lauren?" was her response.

He motioned his head slightly to the left. "She went to her room."

"It took you this long to get ice cream?" Her tone was filled with suspicion.

"Yup. You know I don't like to rush my time with my princess," he said easily. "Plus, I had to make a stop. For this. For you." He held up the silver box.

She frowned. After all of these years Joyce had a hard time believing anything Vernon said. At first she'd thought that he'd left this afternoon, storming out after their argument, to go see some woman. Not until he called a couple of hours ago

to make sure she knew that Lauren was with him did she realize that 1) her daughter wasn't home and 2) another woman
wasn't on his agenda . . . at least not for today.

He said, "You didn't answer me. Are you still mad?"

Joyce didn't say a word; she didn't make a move.

"Bet this will get you unmad."

As he stepped closer, she could see the large white bow tie
on the box. Then he held out the package to her.

Still, she didn't move. And Vernon didn't back off because
they both knew she would take the box. Abusers always know
how to appease their victims. Yes, Vernon had never hit her.
Her skin bore no scars, but all kinds of tracks stretched across
her heart.

But just like the victim she'd been for ten years, Joyce finally took the gift the way she always did. And then one of her
favorite songs of the year filled the air out on the deck:

> *Compliment what she does*
> *Send her roses just because*

Vernon grinned. Joyce hated that this song would have to
play at just this moment.

Then James Ingram sang, *"Find one hundred ways."*

Vernon had done just that. He'd found more than one
hundred ways to manipulate her.

Together, they listened in silence to the song. And as she
held the box in her lap, with no plans of opening it yet, her
heart cried.

three

Lauren peeked around the corner. From where she stood, she had the perfect view into her grandmother's bedroom. Her grandmother sat at her vanity, putting on her makeup. Her Grandma Helen was the prettiest woman in the world. Even prettier than her mother, even though Lauren would never say that. Just like she would never tell her mother the secret she'd kept for the last two years.

She couldn't believe that she'd kept the secret that she shared with her daddy for all this time. She'd told no one, not even her best friend, Carly, though it had been so hard. She wanted to tell somebody. Just one person. But she had to do what her father had told her.

Suddenly, her grandmother whipped around, and Lauren hopped back into the hallway.

"Sweetie pie, are you out there peeping at me?"

She'd been caught! Lauren stood stock still, closing her eyes, hoping that maybe her grandmother would think that she hadn't been sneaking outside her bedroom. Maybe if she stood completely still . . .

"Lauren Louise Robinson!"

Uh-oh. When anyone in the family called her by her full

name, she was in big trouble. Opening her eyes, she took slow steps toward her doom. Her grandmother stood with her hands on her hips and a scowl on her face.

"Were you spying on me?"

"No, Granny. I wasn't spying. I was just watching you."

Her scowl became deeper. She wagged her finger at Lauren. "You know you're not supposed to do that, don't you? You're not supposed to sneak around on grown folks."

Lauren's head remained lowered. "Yes, ma'am."

"You know this calls for punishment."

Punishment? Only her mother punished her. She sent her to her room so that she couldn't watch TV, or told her that she couldn't have dessert, or said that she couldn't hang out with Carly after school. But now Grandma Helen was going to join in?

Her grandmother held her finger to her chin as if she were trying to think of a good punishment. "I got it."

Lauren looked up.

"Your punishment . . . come over here and give me a great big hug!"

Lauren's grin was so wide, the tips of her lips almost touched her ears. Even though her grandmother was only a few feet away, Lauren dashed to her like she was running around the track the way she did during recess in school. She wrapped her arms around her grandmother's waist, and her grandmother held her tight.

"I love you, Granny," Lauren said into her grandmother's bosom.

"I bet you that I love you more." She stepped back from Lauren to take a good look at her granddaughter. "Don't you look pretty?"

Lauren beamed and twirled in her pink taffeta dress for

her grandmother. They both laughed before Grandma Helen turned back to her vanity and sat down. "Well, since you're dressed for the tea, you might as well stand right here if you're going to spy on me."

"I wasn't spying on you, Granny. I was just watching you 'cause you're so beautiful."

"You think I'm beautiful, huh?"

"I think you're the most beautiful lady in the whole wide world. Everybody says so."

Grandma Helen laughed, but Lauren meant what she'd said. Everyone in Raleigh did say that about Helen Thornton. Folks said that she was as beautiful as Lena Horne. Lauren had no idea who Lena Horne was, but she bet that her grandmother was prettier than her, too.

Her grandmother dusted light brown powder onto her face, then took the black pencil and colored in her eyebrows. Granny spread more powder on her face before she got to Lauren's favorite part. She twisted open the tube of lipstick, and slowly, as if she didn't want to make a mistake, spread the color along her thin lips. She did that a couple of times until her lips were the brightest red that Lauren had ever seen. Grandma Helen smacked her lips together and cocked her head from one side to the other, studying herself in the mirror.

"How does that look?" Granny said.

"Fabulous!" Lauren clapped her hands as if she had just watched a performance and wanted an encore.

Grandma Helen laughed and hugged her granddaughter. "You sure know how to make an old woman feel good."

When Lauren leaned back, she said, "I can't wait until I can wear lipstick just like you."

"Oh, you can't, huh? Well, don't grow up too fast. You're

gonna look back one day and wish that you were nine years old again."

Lauren scrunched her face. She couldn't imagine ever wanting to be nine again. She wanted to grow up fast—at least get to be a teenager. She wanted to be old—like sixteen. "I don't want to be nine anymore," she said. "I want to be older so that I can wear lipstick like you!"

"Oh, really?"

Lauren nodded.

"Well," her grandmother began, then lowered her voice. "What about if I let you wear a little lipstick to the tea today?"

Lauren's eyes widened.

"Yup," Granny said. "I think I can find a little something in this drawer here that a pretty nine-year-old can wear."

As her grandmother fumbled through the dozens of lipstick tubes, Lauren's heart quickened. This was something she'd dreamed of, something that she and Carly talked about.

"We'll try this one," her grandmother said. She twisted open one of the tubes. It was beige, kind of clear. Lauren was a little disappointed. She wanted the red, like her grandmother, but she was willing to start anywhere.

"Okay," Granny said. "I'm going to put just a little dab on your lips. But first I need you to promise me something."

"What?" Lauren said.

"You have to promise first," her grandmother said with a wide smile.

"I promise!"

Granny laughed out loud. "You have to promise that this is our secret. You can't tell anyone that I let you wear lipstick. Can you keep a secret?"

Lauren nodded.

"Are you sure?" her grandmother asked with an expression that made Lauren think that her grandmother doubted her.

She wasn't sure if her grandmother was teasing her or not. Grandma Helen loved to play teasing games. But Lauren couldn't take the chance that her grandmother was serious. If she thought that she couldn't keep a secret, she might not let her wear that lipstick. Lauren knew of only one way that she could convince her.

"I can keep a secret, Grandma. I've been keeping a secret for Daddy for a long, long time."

Her grandmother gave her that teasing look again. "What kind of secret you been keeping for your daddy?"

Lauren bit her lip. She'd been dying to tell someone anyway; it was exploding inside. And if she told her grandmother, she'd get that secret out and she'd get to wear lipstick.

"Well," she began with a whisper because she knew that when you told a secret you weren't supposed to say it too loudly, "one night Daddy took me to this lady's house. And they were kissing and they were—"

The smile disappeared from Grandma Helen's face so fast, it seemed like someone had ripped it away. "I don't wanna hear no more."

She dumped the lipstick back in the drawer and slammed it shut.

"But Granny . . ."

Her grandmother put both of her hands on Lauren's shoulders and made her stand squarely in front of her. "I don't want to hear that secret."

"I was only telling you so that you could see that I could keep a secret."

Her grandmother shook her head sorrowfully.

"Are you mad at me?"

Lauren watched her grandmother's face soften before she pulled Lauren into her chest. "Oh, no, pumpkin. I'm not mad at you. You've done good, baby. You've kept the secret." She made Lauren stand back. "Now, I want you to keep that secret. You can't tell nobody. I mean, nobody, okay?"

Lauren nodded.

"Now go on back to the living room and wait there for me," she said.

Lauren didn't budge, wanting to remind her grandmother about the lipstick.

But when her grandmother added, "Go on," and then waved her hand, shooing Lauren away, she obeyed.

She left her grandmother's room the same way she had come in, feeling like she'd done something wrong. But she didn't know what.

Outside her grandmother's bedroom, she paused. Not because she was spying, but because her grandmother began talking. At first Lauren thought Grandma Helen was talking to her, but with the way she mumbled, Lauren could tell she was talking to herself.

But she mumbled loud enough for Lauren to hear. "Don't make no kind of sense, that man putting that little girl in that position." Then she tsked.

Lauren wasn't sure what her grandmother meant by that. Not that she cared. All she cared about was that now she wouldn't get to wear that lipstick.

four

This was the husband she loved. Joyce sat at the table as Vernon did the bird across the dance floor. The ballroom at the Embassy Suites hotel was decorated with Christmas trees in each of the four corners, and red and green lights shone from the chandeliers. The room was merry for the Black Lawyers' annual Christmas gala.

When he misstepped and bumped into the guy on his right, Vernon leaned his head back and released a Santa Claus laugh. Joyce laughed, too. She wondered why her husband couldn't be this way all the time.

She was still chuckling as he danced his way over to the table. "Come on, baby," he said flapping his arms like an eagle. *"What, have you heard? It's a brand-new dance and it's called the bird."*

Joyce laughed. The way he was moving, he could have been a member of The Time.

He grabbed her hand, but just as they got to the dance floor, the music switched from Morris Day to that old-school Al Green. Vernon pulled her closer.

"Yeah, that's what I'm talking about." He leaned in her ear and crooned, *"I'm so in love with you, whatever you want to do . . ."*

Joyce melted into his embrace. She wished that she could stay in this moment forever.

They'd had a rough beginning to the year. One too many late nights, stories that didn't add up, and a constant looming feeling that her husband was cheating, always cheating. All of that had made for a rocky marriage. But since July—since she found a birthday card from someone named Tammy—Vernon had been behaving like they were on their honeymoon. He was putting in as many overtime hours in their marriage as he was at the office; he was working hard to erase her concerns and let her know she was all he needed.

She took a good long while to believe it. Even longer to *feel* it. But here, in her husband's arms, she felt like they were finally headed in the right direction.

When the music ended, her heart sank. She wanted to shout out to the deejay and tell him to play "Let's Stay Together" again and again. She didn't want to let her husband go.

But Vernon pulled back, entwined his fingers with hers, and asked, "You want something to drink?" as he led her from the dance floor.

"We both do," Joyce's sister-in-law, Velma, said, approaching them.

"Hey, when did you get here?" Joyce hugged her, then stepped back to appraise her red formfitting one-shoulder gown. She nodded her approval.

"We just walked in." Velma embraced her brother, kissing Vernon on his cheek. "We're late as usual, thanks to Carl," she said, referring to her longtime boyfriend.

"I'll be right back, babe," Vernon said. He leaned in and kissed her passionately.

"Awww sookie, sookie now." Velma tapped Joyce's arm

playfully as Vernon strutted away. "My brother's got major game. I love black love." She sighed.

Joyce watched Vernon's backside as he walked off. "I love that man." She kept her eyes on him until he disappeared in the crowd surrounding the bar.

"I know you do. I'm really glad you two are working things out."

Joyce shifted uneasily, then walked Velma to their table. But as she led the way, her thoughts drifted back to that territory that she hated. Back to the women who'd invaded their marriage—by Vernon's invitation. Every time he said the same thing: each one meant nothing.

Alicia had been only the beginning. She was followed by Lois, a woman who he claimed was a pro bono client, and finally, the birthday card from Tammy had sent Joyce rushing over to Velma to cry on her shoulder.

"I'm never going back to your brother," Joyce had said to her sister-in-law.

Of course, once Vernon came begging and crying, that resolve lasted all of one day.

And those women—Alicia, Tammy, Lois—were just the ones she knew about. She wasn't dumb enough to believe that these were the only ones.

As she introduced Velma to the other couples, she searched for Vernon out of habit. She saw him standing on the outskirts of the crowded bar. Her eyes narrowed as she watched a woman laugh, then place one hand over her cleavage and the other on Vernon's arm.

But as if he knew she was watching, he brushed the woman off, taking a couple of steps away from her and shaking his head. That made Joyce smile. Maybe the last time had really been the last time. Just maybe Vernon was going to remain the faithful husband that he always promised to be.

"Hey, baby, here's your drink," he said, approaching her and handing her a red cup. "It's just punch, but I have some Jack Daniel's in the car. I can spike it if you'd like." He flashed a wicked grin.

"Punch is fine," she said. "The Jack Daniel's, maybe later." She rested her lips on the edge of the cup and looked up at her husband through her eyelashes.

"Where's mine?" Velma asked, making Vernon shift his gaze from his wife to his sister.

"Oops, I forgot you."

"Wow, so that's how you treat your sister?"

"Sorry, but I'm so blinded by my beautiful wife." He leaned over and kissed Joyce once again.

When they pulled apart, Joyce was breathless, but not overpowered enough to keep the words she'd meant to say from escaping. "I saw that woman flirting with you. She wants you."

"But I want you," he replied without hesitation. "Only you." He kissed her neck. "Now, let me go get my sister a drink so she can feel special since her man is over there telling lies to his friends."

"Whatever," Velma said, playfully pushing his shoulder as he walked off.

Velma smiled at her sister-in-law. Leaning over, she whispered so that no one else at the table could hear, "I'm so happy for you guys. You know I don't cut for some of my brother's ways. Our father was a dedicated family man, so I don't know where he got this gallivanting from."

"Well, hopefully, it's over." Joyce kept her voice just as soft.

"I have to give you your props, though, because you've taken more than most women. You've definitely taken more than I could." She eyed Carl across the room, talking to his friends. "Because I already told Carl, if he pulled some of the stuff my brother pulled, we're gonna be doing a remake of that Farrah Fawcett movie, *The Burning Bed.*"

Joyce chuckled, but her sister-in-law wasn't playing. Everyone knew that, especially Carl. And Carl wasn't crazy, so he remained faithful, at least as far as everyone knew.

Joyce propped her elbow on the table, then cupped her chin in her palm. Vernon was maneuvering his way through the thick crowd at the bar. Maybe that's where she'd gone wrong. She'd never shown Vernon her crazy side. Maybe if she yelled and threw knives, Vernon would have never strayed—at least not more than once.

She sighed. Why was she spending all of her time thinking about this? She and Vernon were on the right track. She really believed that. She'd never have to worry about unleashing her crazy side. That was good for her and that was definitely good for Vernon.

five

Keeping secrets had its benefits. Lauren couldn't help but smile as she sat down at the cafeteria table and twisted the glittering tennis bracelet around her wrist. She loved the way that it sparkled in the light.

Her father had given this to her this morning right before she left to catch the school bus. A Just Because gift. "Just because you're so special," he'd told her.

Because she was older, she knew that her father didn't give her gifts all the time just because he thought she was special. He did think that about her. But she knew that the reason was more that she'd kept his secrets. And the older she got, the more she understood.

Besides her grandmother, Lauren had told no one her father's secret over the past five years—she still had not said a word to Carly, her best friend. Or rather, make that her former best friend. They weren't as close anymore because Carly didn't like Lauren's new friend, Tanya.

"You guys act like you share a special secret and it's only for the two of you," Carly had said just yesterday. She'd said it with an attitude, like she was sure that something was going on, but she couldn't figure out what.

If only Carly knew. Lauren and Tanya did share a special secret. They were sisters. Well, not real sisters who came from the same mother and father. But they were sisters in a special secret kind of way. Because Tanya's mother was Miss Tammy, Lauren's father's girlfriend.

It was actually Lauren who was responsible for her father meeting Miss Tammy. She and her dad were out eating pizza when she saw Tanya, who she knew attended her school. When Lauren had spoken to Tanya, Miss Tammy immediately began making googly eyes at her father, and before Lauren knew it, her father had given Lauren and Tanya money to go play at the arcade, while he and Miss Tammy sat and talked.

Tanya was already thirteen, which made her extra super-cool to Lauren because she couldn't wait to be a teenager. And after that day at the pizza parlor, Tanya had started talking to Lauren every day at school.

Hanging around Tanya was like having the sister that she always wanted. And Tanya told her what it was like to be a teenager. She used her pillow to show her how to kiss a boy, and she taught her how to paint her nails and style her hair in all the hippest styles. She even helped Lauren create a Slam Book, which was a notebook that Lauren passed around school for all her classmates to answer various questions. It had taken Lauren's cool factor to a whole other level.

Lauren talked about her friend Tanya so much that her mother began to ask questions.

"Does she go to your school?"

Lauren wasn't quite sure how she should handle that. Should she tell her mother the truth? Because if she did, what if her mother came to the school?

When Lauren said no, her mother asked, "Where did you meet her?"

"Just around."

When Lauren didn't have any more to say, her mother insisted on meeting Tanya. "Invite her to come over one of these weekends," her mother said. "I want to know all of your friends. And I'd like to meet her mother, too."

That request made Lauren's stomach do flip-flops. But so far, every weekend, she had a different excuse as to why Tanya couldn't come over.

Lauren snapped out of her thoughts when she spotted Tanya crossing the cafeteria.

"Tanya!" she called out and waved. When Tanya ignored her, Lauren frowned and yelled out again, a little louder this time. "Tanya!"

Tanya finally stopped. But when she glanced back at Lauren over her shoulder, she had a face full of attitude.

"What?" Tanya snapped.

Lauren lost her smile right away. What was going on? "Uh, I-I . . ." That response had caught her completely off guard.

"Cat got your tongue? You shouting my name all over the place." Tanya marched over to where Lauren was sitting. "So what is it that you want?" Tanya's hand went to her hip.

It had to be Lauren's imagination. She and Tanya were practically BFFs, practically sisters. So, she tried a smile. "Um, I was just seeing if we were going to eat lunch together today."

Tanya rolled her eyes. "I don't want to eat with you." She came almost right up on Lauren, making her cower. "Matter of fact," Tanya hissed, "I don't want to talk to you, so don't you speak to me. I don't even want you to look at me. And if you see me coming, you'd better turn around and walk the other way."

Lauren shook her head. "Huh?" She did not understand at all. "Wh-what did I do?"

Lauren heard snickers around her, and she realized that other classmates were congregating around her, no doubt hoping to see a fight. Lauren's heartbeat quickened. She'd never had a fight in her life and she didn't want to start now. She didn't want to be seen getting beat up, especially not by a girl who just a minute ago felt like her sister.

"My mama said I can't be friends with you no more."

"Why?" Lauren whined, and then she caught herself, getting her tone together. "What happened? Why would your mom say that?"

"Your daddy is a dog," she said, loud enough for everyone around them to hear.

To Lauren, it felt like the whole cafeteria filled with laughter. "My d-daddy?"

"Yeah, yo' daddy. He broke up with my mama last night. Had her crying and yelling at me and everything. She said he was cheating on her."

Lauren's mouth opened wide. What in the world was Tanya talking about? Miss Tammy knew that her father was married. She knew that he was cheating *with* her. So, how was she gonna be mad if he started seeing somebody else, too?

Inside, Lauren sighed. Daddy's relationships were so complicated, but their friendship—that should be the same.

"B-but what does that have to do with us?" Lauren asked. "We're . . ." She paused, not wanting to say how she'd begun to think about Tanya. "We're friends."

Tanya waved her off like she was crazy. "If you mess with my mama, you mess with me. You lucky I don't kick your butt, so that you can go run and tell yo' daddy that."

More laughter erupted and Lauren felt heat rise beneath her cheeks. If she'd been thinking, she would have saved face in front of their classmates and told Tanya that at least she had a daddy. Tanya didn't even know who her father was.

But Lauren couldn't form any words. She just stood in the middle of the cafeteria, in the middle of her laughing class-mates, still in shock.

As if she were suddenly bored, Tanya turned to walk away. Lauren fought back tears. No way was she going to cry. But as she got up from the table and walked out of the cafeteria, she vowed that she would never let herself get close to a girl again. She'd never put herself in the position where a friend like Tanya could humiliate her.

six

Life wasn't fair. Joyce had heard that from people all of her life. But usually when she'd heard one of her elders saying that expression, they were talking about life in general. They were wrong. It wasn't life that was unfair, it was love.

She glanced down at the receipt in her hand and realized that she'd been clutching it so tight, her nails were digging into her palm. She released her grip and read the information on the paper for what had to be at least the tenth time:

```
October 3, 1993
Marriott Hotel. Durham, NC
```

That was just two weeks ago, when Vernon had told her that he was out of town on business for a legal conference. In fact, he'd been laid up in a hotel twenty minutes down the road.

Love wasn't fair.

Everything had been going so well for the past few years. She'd been absolutely sure that his cheating days were behind them. For the last three years he was always in her sight, or at least he was someplace on her radar—at work, at a church meeting. Not to count all those times when he took Lauren out.

She'd been thrilled that he was spending so much time with their daughter, and so much time with her. Joyce thought they'd been building their marriage, making it stronger.

But she was wrong.

Vernon was a low-down, cheating liar. That's who he was and who he would always be.

With tears in her eyes, Joyce laid the receipt on the nightstand and pushed aside the suit jacket inside which she'd found the evidence of his infidelity. She hadn't been snooping. She was getting his clothes ready for the cleaners, cleaning out his pockets, and found the receipt. He'd tricked her into becoming complacent and he'd gotten sloppy.

He'd never been good at cheating, though. She'd always caught him, or at least she liked to believe that she did. She was sure that the romp he'd had two weeks ago wasn't the first in the last three years.

She lay back on the bed as a headache suddenly overcame her. How had he done it when he spent all of his time with her, and Julian and Lauren? When had he found time to cheat?

Maybe what he'd done two weeks ago was just an aberration. But a second after she had that thought, she doubted it.

Once a cheat, always a cheat. He'd been cheating on her; she just didn't know how.

Now she had to figure out what to do. Was she really ready to do something this time? In the early years when she'd stayed, she blamed her weakness on her children. Raising young children was always better with both parents. But Lauren was thirteen now, Julian seventeen. What was her excuse now? Why couldn't she find the strength to leave?

Because when he's good, he's so, so good.

Plus, she'd tried leaving before. Twice. She squeezed her eyes shut at those memories, but still her mind took her back to the first time she tried to love herself more than she loved Vernon.

Joyce had been suspicious, since Vernon had never fired the law clerk like he'd promised, telling her that he was new at the firm and he couldn't make hiring and firing decisions. But he made other promises.

"I promise that nothing will ever happen with me and Alicia again."

"I promise that I will never hurt you again."

"I promise that I love you."

She'd tried her best to believe his promises, but then when Julian was only six months old, Alicia had been bold enough to call their home.

"I want to inform you that Vernon and I are in love," she said with the assurance of a woman who was having a torrid affair. "He's only staying with you because of the baby."

Alicia described their trysts, all the different times that she had been with her husband, in lurid detail.

"He told me that if it weren't for Julian, he would marry me."

Joyce was sure that Alicia had embellished the facts, but at the core of Alicia's story was the truth—she was having an affair with Vernon. Joyce's bags were almost completely packed before she hung up the phone. She wasn't going to give Vernon a chance to charm her this time. She wasn't going to give him a chance to sway her with another one of his sad apologies. This time when he came home from work, she and their baby would already be gone.

The only thing was, Joyce didn't really have anywhere to go—except back home. She'd showed up at her parents' door without any warning, praying that they wouldn't ask any questions.

She'd showed up just after five, and both her mother and father had already come home from work. Of course, they'd let her in with their arms wide open. But while her mother gave her the space she asked for, her father wasn't having it. As soon as she laid Julian down to sleep, he grilled Joyce to the point of tears, asking, "What are you doing here? What did Vernon do to you? Does he know you're here?"

He shot questions at her rapid-fire, ignoring the fact that he had reduced her to tears. That made Joyce's mother finally step in.

"Leave her alone, Charles," she said. "Joyce, go to your room and pull yourself together. We'll take care of Julian."

She didn't have to tell Joyce twice. Joyce bolted from the room and headed to the place that had given her childhood solace. Her room was still the same, as if her parents had expected her to return home someday.

She lay down on the twin bed that she'd had since she was six and closed her eyes. She slept for long hours, and when she awoke, the clock on the nightstand told her it was close to midnight.

Her stomach growled and she rolled over and out of the bed. As her feet hit the floor, she heard a tap on her door. Before she could answer, her father stuck his head in.

"How are you feeling?"

Seeing him, remembering how he'd reacted to her coming home, made her wish that she'd slipped back under the covers, pretending to be asleep. But there was nothing she could do now. She clicked on the lamp on the nightstand. "I'm okay, I guess."

He nodded his head and took a cautious step into her room. "You know I just want what's best for you."

"I know."

"Come on out here." He motioned with his head toward the door. "We all need to talk."

"We?" Joyce's eyes narrowed. "Who . . . is . . . we?"

"Me, you, Vernon, and your mama."

"He's here?" She glanced at the clock once again. "It's too late to do any talking," she said wearily. "And anyway, I don't want to talk to him."

Her father's look was as firm as his tone. It was the expression that he used to give her when she was a child. And now, like then, she felt like she was in trouble. "Look, you made the decision to drop out of school for this man. You made your bed and now it's time to lie in it."

"So, you think it's okay that he hurt me?"

"Did he hit you?"

Why was he asking that question? "No, of course not."

"Then anything other than that, you can work through it. Now, come on," her father said.

Joyce couldn't believe it. Even though she hadn't told her father what had happened, he had to know. He had to know that Vernon was a cheater. Did he want that for his daughter?

But before she could explain more, he'd marched out of the bedroom. So she did the only thing she could—she got up and reluctantly followed him through the hallway and finally into the dining room.

Vernon was sitting at the table, his eyes drooping and bloodshot, like he'd been beat up by someone. Her mother sat stone-faced across from him. Her father took a seat at the head of the table, then motioned for Joyce to sit next to Vernon. She sat two seats over, grateful that their dining room table sat eight.

Her father assessed the two of them, glancing back and forth. "Does someone want to tell me the problem?" he asked in his supervisor's voice.

When neither of them responded, her father bellowed, "Hello, am I speaking a foreign language?"

Still, silence.

Her father released a frustrated sigh. "When you stood before that minister and said until death do you part, those were not words to be taken lightly."

Vernon finally spoke. "Sir, this is all my fault." He took a deep breath to stall. Then, with more courage than Joyce thought he had, Vernon said, "I have been unfaithful to your daughter."

Joyce's mouth opened wide, but then her father shocked her as much as Vernon just had.

"Did you love the woman?"

Why was he asking Vernon that? Joyce wondered. *Why was he asking anything?* Joyce had expected her father to snatch Vernon by the collar and throw him out of the house.

But when he didn't do that, she answered before Vernon could. "He's a liar," Joyce said. "He told me he'd fire her and he just kept screwing her." Facing her husband, she added, "Vernon is a liar and a cheat!"

Her father ignored her. Instead, he stared at Vernon until he finally replied, "Absolutely not, sir. I love no one but your daughter." He turned his body totally toward Joyce. He spoke to her father, but his eyes were on his wife. "I love her with everything inside of me. I don't want to lose my family."

"You should've thought about that before you cheated on me."

"You're right," Vernon said in a voice so low it could hardly be called a whisper.

A heavy silence hung in the air before Joyce's father said, "Son, is my daughter not enough for you?"

Vernon shook his head. "On the contrary. She is everything I want and more."

"Then, why?" Joyce's mother spoke for the first time. With a glare she said, "If you love her so much, why would you cheat?" Then, with a move that Joyce did not miss, her mother slowly turned her gaze to her husband. "I don't understand how you could say you love her and then cheat on her like that."

While her mother kept her gaze on her husband, he kept his eyes pinned on Vernon. He was avoiding his wife's silent condemnation, and Joyce had a terrible suspicion that she knew why. Her father? And mother?

"I don't know why." Vernon lowered his head. "I don't have an answer. I could try to make up some excuses, but they'd be just that, excuses. I just want her to give me another chance."

"I gave you another chance."

"He's said that he loves you," Joyce's father said to Joyce. "This affair, it doesn't mean anything to him."

Joyce's eyes widened. There were so many things she

wanted to say to her father—like tell him that he should be coming to her defense, not Vernon's.

"His affair had to mean something since he was willing to hurt me over it. Or are you saying that it's okay to break my heart?"

"The bottom line," her father said, leaning forward on the table, "is you two have a commitment to one another. You have a son. You made vows. For better or for worse. This is the worse. But you can get through this."

Joyce shook her head in disbelief.

He continued: "Joyce, you know you are my everything, but I cannot in good conscience contribute to the breakdown of your family."

"What does that mean?" she asked sharply.

"That means, go in there and get your things, and go home with your husband."

"Charles!" her mother said.

"No, it's settled." He sat back, but he didn't give Vernon a total pass. "You need to get it together, son. What you're not going to do is continue to hurt my daughter."

Joyce felt a little relief. There was the man she'd expected to stand up for her. But still, he was sending her home and that brought tears to her eyes.

"She's given up everything for you," her father continued. "Her education, her career. My grandson needs his father. So go home and work this out."

The tears thickened in Joyce's eyes, but Vernon wore a smile that was big enough for both of them.

"Thank you so much, Mr. Thornton. I promise, I'm going to spend my life making your daughter happy."

"Good," was all that her father said.

Joyce sat in a state of shock. This man had told her father that he cheated, and her father had basically said that she needed to get over it. That was not the way for a father to protect his daughter, so Joyce turned to her mother. But her mother lowered her head as if they'd both gone down in defeat.

It was obvious to Joyce that her mother didn't agree with her father's decision, but she wasn't going to challenge him. She never challenged him on anything.

"Go on," Joyce's father said. "Go on and get your bag. Your mother will get Julian."

"Come on, baby," Vernon said, taking her arm, helping her up. "Let's go home."

Joyce's eyes popped open, snapping her away from that memory. Maybe that's why Vernon kept cheating, because he'd got her back so easily the first time. She set the standard for her marriage that day. A man would only do what you allowed him to do. And she'd allowed the women, and so the women kept coming.

Sitting up, Joyce reached for the receipt again. What she needed to do was file this away with her important papers. She might need it in divorce court because right now, that looked like where she and her husband were headed.

seven

Lauren loved these days at church. Sunday morning was the only time when Lauren was hopeful that her family would stay together.

Outside of church, her family was falling apart. Her mother and father yelled and fought so much, she was sure one of these days her father would just pack his bags and walk out.

She couldn't quite determine why her parents were fighting so much. They always stopped fighting when she walked into the room. But she figured it had to stem from all the lady friends that her father had.

Even though she'd kept her father's secret, her mother had to know. So many nights her father had come home late. Or at least that's what her mother yelled about during their arguments, and Lauren had been awake a few times herself when he'd come home after midnight and she'd started yelling.

Even so, Lauren wasn't prepared for what happened on the steps of their church, right after Sunday service. Lauren clearly read the look of horror on her mother's face when a woman stomped toward them in a too-tight zebra print dress that was completely inappropriate for church. Her long auburn hair bounced like she was doing a shampoo commercial.

Lauren's mother stood poised to perfection, the consummate southern belle ready to fend off a rival.

The woman didn't give Joyce a second look, though. "Well, look at the happy family," she sneered. All of the people gathered in front of the church could tell that she was about to go off. Lauren could tell by the way they were trying to pretend they weren't watching. But Vernon kept a smile on his face as he leaned toward the angry woman and whispered, just loud enough that Lauren overheard, "Cecile, have you lost your mind coming here? Don't *ever* disrespect my family like this again."

Lauren wasn't able to make out what he said after that. But whatever his magic words were, they were enough for Cecile to force a grin as she took a step back. "Mr. Robinson, I'm sorry for any misunderstanding," she said. "I just came over because they're trying to take my mama's house away, and I really need you to finish my paperwork."

Lauren knew that even though her father was a big-time attorney, he did a lot of work for free. Correction, a lot of work *for women* for free. But even Lauren knew that nobody was buying Cecile's fake-sounding explanation.

"Well, Sundays are my family time," Vernon casually replied. "Call my office in the morning and we can take it from there." He raised his voice an octave to ensure all the nosy folks heard. He didn't say another word as he took his wife's hand, motioned for Lauren and Julian, and walked down the steps with the coolness of the October breeze that swept over the lawn of New Hope Baptist Church. Still, Lauren was mighty glad when they reached their black Cadillac.

Tension filled the car, but no one said a word until they were three blocks from the church.

"You must think I'm stupid," her mother said from the front seat.

"Not now, Joyce," Vernon said, not taking his eyes off the road.

"When then?"

"When we're not in front of the children," he said through gritted teeth.

Lauren and Julian were sitting in the backseat. Julian was playing on a handheld game, blocking out their impending fight. Lauren never knew if her brother did that on purpose or if that was his escape mechanism, but she always watched her parents with bated breath.

"I can't believe you can't keep your hoes in check," her mother snapped.

"I don't have any hoes," Vernon replied, his grip tightening on the steering wheel. "And we're not going to talk about this now."

"Who is she, Vernon?"

"She's a client," he replied.

"You think I'm stupid. That's what it is. You think I'm a fool. But you know, I'd think I was a fool, too, since my fool behind keeps taking your cheating ass back."

"Would you. Just. Shut. Up?"

Her mother reached over and smacked him on the side of his head nearest her. It caused him to swerve and Lauren froze in terror, wondering if her father was going to turn around and slap her back. But instead he navigated the car off to the side of the road. He got out, walked over to the passenger side, and pulled her out of the car.

"Have you lost your damn mind?" he screamed, slamming the car door. "Don't you ever put your hands on me."

They continued to fight, argue, and scream. And Julian continued to play his game.

Tears ran down Lauren's cheeks at the way her parents were going at it. Finally, her father threw up his hands and came back around the back of the car. When he opened his door, and Lauren saw her mother still standing outside, her heart dropped. That made Julian look up, too.

"Put your seat belts on!" her dad snapped to them as he started the car. That was strange because no one had been worried about a seat belt when they pulled away from the church.

Julian looked out the window at their mother screaming and crying and finally spoke up. "Dad, we're not leaving Mom here, are we?"

"Your mother is having a meltdown and I'm not about to deal with that mess." He started to pull out.

"We can't leave Mom!" Julian cried.

"You that worried about her, get out and walk home with her," her father snapped, slamming on the brakes.

Julian glared at the back of her father's head. It's like the older Julian got, the more he couldn't stand their father. The two of them argued all of the time. This time, though, Julian didn't say a word as he slowly opened the door and got out of the car. Meanwhile, Lauren sat in silence.

"You going, too?" Vernon yelled. He took a deep breath and said, "Or are you still Daddy's girl and rolling with me?"

Lauren looked through the rear window at her crying mother. Julian was hugging her, trying to comfort her. It was a sad sight. But Lauren didn't want her father to be alone. That's what she was always afraid of, him going off alone and leaving them. "I'm going with you, Daddy."

eight

Forsaking all others.

Joyce wasn't sure why that portion of her marriage vows flashed through her mind at this very moment. No, she knew exactly why. She needed the reminder as she stared at the six-foot-three, two-hundred-pound man who looked like Denzel Washington's little brother and was standing at her door.

"Hello, Mrs. Robinson," he said. When she didn't respond he said, "It's me, Norman Martin."

Norman was the man who had sold them their life insurance policy. But he'd been an overweight nerd with dreadlocks.

"Wow. Norman?" she said, still dumbfounded at what was nothing short of a total transformation.

"I know, quite different, right?" He flashed a smile. "It's amazing how death can make you reevaluate life."

"That's right. You had . . ."

"A kidney transplant." He patted the right side of his abdomen. "But now I'm like new and figured since I had a new lease on life, I needed to make the best of it. So, I got on a plan, lost the weight, cut the hair, and here I am back to work."

"Wow, you look . . . you look . . ."

"I hope the word you're looking for is *good*."

"Yes, yes." She nodded. "*Good* is definitely the word."

They stood in awkward silence for a minute, before he finally raised his briefcase.

"Your husband said it would be okay to stop by and go over the policy updates. Now that Julian is about to graduate, he wanted to boost your coverage."

Joyce was lost in his beauty. She always thought Norman was cute, and he'd flirted with her from the first day she'd met him. But she'd never paid him any attention because she'd never been able to see past the weight. But now . . .

"Ah, yeah, he mentioned that," she said, finally stepping to the side. "Please, come in."

"Well, would you like to go in the dining room?" he said.

The bedroom would be better. She almost gasped at the wicked thought that had raced through her mind.

Joyce had never so much as given another man a second look. But after that woman showed up at church last week, maybe Joyce needed to give Vernon a taste of his own medicine.

No!

She shook away the thought. She wasn't about to bed some other man to get back at her husband.

"Yes, we can go over everything in here," she said, pointing toward the dining room.

Long after the paperwork was signed and put away, Joyce and Norman were still talking. She admired his new outlook. She'd heard about his kidney issues but had no idea that he'd gotten the transplant.

"Well, it's been so great catching up with you," he said, glancing at his watch. "But I guess I'd better get going. Your husband probably won't think too kindly of me having spent all this time here with his beautiful wife."

Joyce didn't want him to go. She didn't realize how starved for companionship she was. Oh, Vernon showed her attention, but the baggage that came with him outweighed a lot of his affectionate acts.

"No, my husband won't be in until late," she found herself saying. "And the kids are at my sister-in-law's."

"Yeah, I heard your husband works long hours," Norman said. "He does a lot of pro bono stuff, right?"

His tone told Joyce that even he knew better. She shuddered at the thought of what people around town must be saying.

"Yeah, he does stay quite busy."

"So, where does that leave you?" Norman asked pointedly. He had leaned in closer and it should've made Joyce uneasy, but a surge of excitement actually shot through her body.

"Well, it does get kind of lonely. I mean, I have the kids, but Lauren is always off with her dad and Julian is always with friends," she said.

"What about you? You don't have friends?"

"I have a couple that I talk to occasionally. But"—she motioned around the house—"this is my life."

"That's not good," he said. "A fine woman like you, you should get out, dance, have a good time."

"The only new people I meet show up at my door."

That brought a smile to his face.

"Your husband has no idea the jewel he's neglecting."

She wanted to ask him how he knew she was being neglected. But maybe it was the way she was breathing so heavily, dang near panting as he scooted closer.

"I'm going to say something and if you want to slap me after I say it, I'll understand."

She didn't say a word, fearful that if she opened her mouth, the wrong thing would come out.

"I have always admired you. Wanted you." His voice was husky. His cologne penetrated her nostrils. His closeness sent her heart racing. "I would never disrespect you. But if you ever decide that what's good for the goose . . ." He slipped his card in her hand, letting his fingers linger inside hers. His lips moved close to her ear, as he whispered, "I would love to take you to ecstasy and beyond." He leaned back, licked his lips, then stood. "I'd treat you like the queen that you are."

He said that matter-of-factly. Like he knew all of Vernon's dirty little secrets.

"I will get these papers processed and everything should be good to go in three days. I will see myself out."

Joyce still didn't say a word as he put a hand on her shoulder and gently squeezed. "I really do hope to hear from you soon."

She couldn't move. She couldn't remember the last time a man had excited her so, and she didn't know if it was because she genuinely was attracted to Norman, or if she believed being with him would be the perfect revenge against Vernon.

"Why are you sitting in here in the dining room?"

Joyce hadn't even heard Vernon come in, but when she glanced at her watch, she realized that she'd been sitting for over an hour.

She stood. "Just sitting here, thinking."

He sighed, like he knew what she was thinking about. "Look, Joyce. I told you, Cecile is just a—"

"Yeah, I know," she said, cutting him off. "A client. They all are."

She eased the business card into her pocket as she walked past her husband. No, cheating wasn't her nature. But if she wasn't going to leave just yet, she needed to find a way to cope, and maybe Norman would be that way.

nine

The little piece of paper in her hand should've made her happy. Should have.

But the way things had been going between her and Vernon, a baby was the last thing they needed. Julian had just graduated. Lauren was going into high school. Why in the world would she want to start over with a baby?

And then there was Norman.

After months of back-and-forth flirting, and more lies from Vernon, Joyce had made the decision to take him up on his ecstasy offer. Now she just needed to lose his number.

The baby changed everything.

Joyce tossed the beat-up piece of tissue she'd had crumpled in her hand, along with the piece of paper confirming that she was eight weeks pregnant, on the passenger seat and started her car. She'd been sitting forlornly in the parking lot of the doctor's office for the last hour, shedding tears at the news that she was about to be a mother again.

Joyce cried because at one time she'd wanted a houseful of kids. Five, to be exact. But if two made it hard to leave him, five would've made it impossible. So Joyce had religiously taken her birth control pills for years.

"Nothing is foolproof."

The doctor had uttered those words with a smile. Probably because she thought the news she was giving Joyce was good. But it had taken everything in Joyce's power to not burst into tears right there in the doctor's office.

Joyce glanced over at the dashboard and saw it was two o'clock. Her mother should just be wrapping up her soaps and her father wouldn't yet be at home. She needed to talk to her mother.

Joyce made a U-turn and headed toward her parents' house.

Thirty minutes later, she was sitting in the living room of her childhood home with a cup of hot tea set in front of her.

"Okay, start talking," her mother said, sliding into the seat across from her.

"How long before Daddy gets home?"

"He'll be here in about an hour," she said. "I'll be glad when he retires at the end of this school year. Because he's getting more and more sickly. He doesn't need to be working so."

Joyce often checked on her father, who seemed like he kept a case of bronchitis. But in typical male fashion, he refused to see a doctor or get treated.

"I know you didn't come over here to get an update on your father, so what's going on?"

"I just left the doctor."

Her mother's hand went to her chest. "Is everything okay?"

"No," Joyce said, burying her face in her hands. "It's not."

"Oh my God." Her mother jumped up, raced to her side, and immediately put her arms around Joyce. "What's wrong?"

"Mama, I'm pregnant," Joyce whispered, barely looking up.

Her mother stiffened and took a step back. "What?"

"I'm pregnant," Joyce cried.

Her mother smiled. "Chile, I thought something was really wrong."

Joyce frowned. Of course her mother would react this way. "Are you serious? Something *is* wrong. I have two children almost out of the house and a husband that has given me grief since the day I said 'I do' and now I'm about to start all over? What could possibly be right about that?"

A clouded expression filled her mother's face. "Well, you've always wanted a big family."

"I gave that dream up a long time ago."

"There is nothing wrong with you having another baby."

"Mama, I was just waiting on Lauren to leave so I could leave."

Her mother sighed. "And do what, Joyce? You've been a housewife for seventeen years. How much of a nest egg do you have stored away?"

"Nothing," Joyce said resentfully.

"Exactly. So you're gonna leave and do what?"

She had thought about that at least. "Vernon would have to pay alimony."

"And a judge will say what's wrong with you, why can't you go to work?" Her tone softened. "All I'm saying is, you said yourself that Vernon had been acting better."

Joyce lowered her head in shame. Her mother didn't know half the drama Joyce had endured.

"We don't need a baby," Joyce said with finality.

"Maybe this is what you need to fix your marriage."

"A baby is not the answer," she repeated.

Her mother shot her a stern look. "Is Vernon a good father?"

Joyce thought about that. His relationship with Julian had been strained the older their son got. But Joyce knew that was because her son was resentful of the way Vernon treated her. And there was no denying his love for Lauren.

"Yes, he's a good father," she admitted.

"Then everything else is fixable." Her mother sat back down, crossed her arms, and continued. "Honey, let me tell you, you get rid of this one and get you another one, and he's going to cheat on you as well. You might as well stay with the devil you know."

Joyce tilted her head, her mind racing back to the conversation the night Vernon showed up at their house to get her to come back home. Had that been what her mother was doing? Staying with the devil she knew? Joyce shook her head. "There's something wrong with that, Mother."

"Ninety-two percent of men cheat on their wives."

She knew her mother had just snatched that statistic from the atmosphere. But Joyce found the strength to say, "Is Dad in that ninety-two percent?"

Her mother at first avoided the question. She walked over to the stove, picked up the teapot, and refilled Joyce's cup.

"Your father loves me," she said. "I don't have to condone or agree with some of the things he's done, but at the end of the day, he comes home. And I know his love for me is one hundred percent real."

How could her mother find peace with that?

"Don't look at me that way," her mother said. "You've dealt with it for this long."

"Yeah, and I was looking forward to leaving with Lauren."

Her mother waggled a finger at her, as though she knew better. "And now you look forward to my new grandbaby." She clapped her hands. "I can't wait to tell your father. He's going to be so excited."

Joyce couldn't take any more of this. She stood and grabbed her purse so she could leave before her father got home. If her mother was thrilled about this news, her father would be overjoyed, and right about now, she didn't know how she'd muster up any enthusiasm about the child growing inside her.

ten

Lauren watched her brother throw his belongings in a duffel bag. She wanted to ask if he was going to bother folding anything up. But the way he was ramming everything into the bag, she knew that she had to choose her words carefully.

"Are you okay?" she asked, her voice soft.

"I will be when I get out of this place," he growled.

"Is it really that bad?"

He spun around on her. "Pregnant?" he snapped. "She's pregnant. Yeah, I'd say it's pretty bad."

Lauren was trying to see the bright side of that. "It might be cool to have a little brother or sister."

Julian looked at her like that was the dumbest thing she'd ever said. "Whatever. She can stay here and be tied to him the rest of her life. Let him keep dogging her out."

"Daddy loves Mama," Lauren said defensively.

"Yeah, if that's what love is, they can keep it." He zipped the bag up.

She hated that his last day in town before he left for the army was ending up like this. They were supposed to be happy, celebrating. In fact, that's what they had been doing before this day took a turn for the worse.

Her mother had cooked a big farewell dinner for Julian,

who was leaving in the morning. They were enjoying a rare family dinner when her parents broke the news.

"We have some news," her father said.

Lauren couldn't help but notice the uneasy expression on her mother's face. Lauren's first thought was that they were about to announce they were divorcing, but the giant smile on her father's face quickly caused her to dismiss that idea.

"You two are going to have a little brother or sister," her father proudly announced.

The news wiped the smile right off Julian's face and left Lauren stunned.

A baby?

If she were younger, Lauren might have been upset because she never wanted to share her status as Daddy's girl, but the more she thought it about, having a little sibling around might be cool. Julian, on the other hand, had stood up and stormed out.

"Why are you so mad about it?" she asked. While her father had told her to give Julian time to process the news, Lauren had followed him into his room. "It's not like you're going to even be here."

"Do you see what he does to her?" Julian's rage was evident. Lauren knew he didn't really cut for their father, but right now he was acting like he couldn't stand him. "No, you know the answer. You see it," he said, narrowing his glare at her, "and you cosign it."

Lauren was speechless. How did he know her secret?

"I-I don't cosign anything," she replied.

"Whatever, Lauren. Mama may be stupid, but I'm not."

"Don't call her that," Lauren said.

Julian waved her off. He grabbed another bag and snatched

his top dresser drawer open. "All Dad has to do is buy you a little gift and you're just fine with what he does," Julian said, pulling out underwear, then stuffing it into his bag. "Who cares if it hurts Mama?"

Those words hurt Lauren. What was she supposed to do? She wanted to ask her brother that, but when she opened her mouth nothing came out.

"Y'all can have this life," he mumbled.

"I hate that you're leaving upset."

He took a deep breath before turning to face her. "Look, Sis. It is what is. I've been begging Mama to leave for years and she won't. If she doesn't care about what he does to her, I can't make her. I just know if I ever get married, and I doubt I will, given the sterling example that has been set for me, you won't have to worry about me treating my wife the way Dad treats Mom. His cheating makes me sick to my stomach."

Lauren wanted to come to her father's defense, but she simply reiterated, "He loves her, though."

Julian rolled his eyes at her naïveté. "Whatever."

"I'm gonna miss you," Lauren said.

His stance softened. "I'm gonna miss you, too. I really am. And I don't mean to be snapping at you." He shook his head. "But I'm telling you, you'd better find you a college far, far away because, a baby and fighting parents? That does not make for a happy home."

For a minute, she thought her brother might be right. But then she had a flash—what if the baby was just what her father needed to let his outside girlfriends go? Yeah, that would be great. Lauren decided she would say a special prayer that her little brother or sister would change her father, and hence, change all of their lives.

eleven

There was no love like the loving Vernon Robinson gave. Once again, her husband had loved her to oblivion and beyond.

"You want some water or a beer?" Joyce said as she climbed out of bed. The moon's rays beamed into the bedroom as if they were putting an exclamation point on their lovemaking. They had weathered some serious storms, but these last few months had made Joyce optimistic that they were back on the right track. The only thing Joyce hated was that Julian had yet to come around. He was off in basic training and had only called once in the month since he'd been gone. Joyce remained hopeful that he'd accept the baby. And she couldn't wait to tell him how loving and attentive Vernon had been. Maybe her mother was right. Maybe this baby would save their marriage.

Vernon smacked her bare behind as she reached down to grab her robe. "Just some water, babe, because I need to stay hydrated for round two."

Joyce slipped her robe on, then leaned down, planted another kiss on her husband's lips, and made her way into the kitchen. Lauren was fast asleep on the sofa in the living room, her lean teenage body covered from head to toe by the down blanket. A videotape was still playing in the recorder. Joyce pushed the off button on the remote, cutting off both the TV and the VCR.

Joyce had just grabbed a bottle of water from the refrigerator when the house phone rang. She wondered who would be calling so late. But she picked up the phone and said, "Hello?"

No one answered.

"Hello," Joyce repeated.

Finally, a female voice said, "Is Vernon there?"

Joyce's breath caught in her throat. "Umm, may I ask who's calling?"

"I need to speak with Vernon," she said, this time with much more attitude.

"Excuse me," Joyce said, "may I ask who's calling?" Her whole body had grown tense by now.

"I need to speak with Vernon." The caller now enunciated each word.

Joyce enunciated right back. "And I need to know who the hell wants to speak with my husband."

She huffed, like Joyce was the one calling her house at two in the morning. "It is very important that I speak with him."

"If you can't tell me who you are, or what you want, you won't be speaking to anyone on this line."

"Put him on the phone!" she screamed.

"Bitch, please." Joyce slammed the phone on the cradle. "Tell it to the dial tone."

Of course, it rang right back. Joyce contemplated ignoring it, but curiosity got the better of her and she snatched the phone back up. "What?"

"Put Vernon on the phone," the woman repeated, though her voice was a lot calmer.

"Look, I don't know who the hell you are, but you will not call here demanding to talk with my husband."

"I just need Vernon." Her voice quavered now. It sounded like she was crying.

She could dissolve in a giant puddle of tears, but she was not about to talk to Vernon. "I don't know what you need with my husband, but it ain't happening."

"You know what?" she said, her voice a mixture of sadness and anger. "Tell your husband to meet me at the hospital because I'm about to give birth to our child. I'm at Duke Memorial." And then it was her turn to slam the phone down.

Joyce stood in the kitchen, absolutely mortified. She didn't notice that Vernon had appeared in the doorway.

"Who is that on the phone, and what's wrong with you?" he said.

Joyce looked at her husband, searching for traces of deception. There were none. This had to be some horrible, horrible prank. Maybe the woman had the wrong number. But then Joyce quickly remembered that she'd asked for her husband by name.

"Who was that, Joyce?" Vernon repeated.

"It was . . . it was for you," she mumbled, trying to keep her rage at bay. There had to be an explanation. Vernon had promised her that he would do right from now on, so there had to be an explanation to this call.

"Okay, if it was for me, why didn't you give me the phone?"

"She hung up."

"She?" His tone betrayed the fact that he knew that this wasn't going to be good.

"Yeah," Joyce continued, walking close enough to him to

feel his hot breath on her face. "It was someone who said you need to meet her at the hospital because she's about to have your child." Her eyes bore into her husband. She wanted him to look as mortified as she. No, she wanted him to laugh and say that somebody was playing a stupid joke. But his silence said everything.

"Who is she?" Joyce asked.

"I-I-I don't know," he stammered. "You answered the phone."

"Which of your women is pregnant?" Joyce said, pulling her robe tighter, suddenly feeling self-conscious of being nude.

"I don't have any women," he responded with more certainty. "And I don't know why some woman would call you with that mess."

"Who is it? Don't lie to me!" Joyce shouted, slamming her palm down on the counter.

"Stop before you wake up Lauren," he whispered.

"Who is she?" Joyce repeated without lowering her voice.

He released a defeated sigh. "It may be Cecile. She's been talking crazy about being pregnant."

"Pregnant?" Joyce asked in disbelief.

"Babe, let me explain."

"Is it yours?" Joyce demanded to know. As if sensing her impending rage, she felt the baby fluttering in her stomach. Joyce's hand went to her belly and she finally lowered her voice. Stress wasn't good for an unborn child. "Is one of your women pregnant at the same time I am?"

"It's not my baby. I promise you it's not my baby. She's just trying to pin this on me because she knows I have money." He raised his arms to embrace her. "Sweetheart, you've got to believe me. I have been faithful since I promised you I would do right. I swear."

Joyce stepped out of his grasp. "But if she's trying to pin this on you, that means it could be your baby?" Her voice cracked. He wasn't talking like a man who hadn't done anything with this Cecile woman. He was talking like a man who wanted desperately to believe that he would pass a paternity test.

"Please," she softly cried. "Please stop with the lies. Did you sleep with her? Could it be your baby?"

He let out a heavy sigh again. "It was just one time. But it was before you and I recommitted."

Hearing these awful words, Joyce let out a wail that came from deep down in her soul. Just one time? She was supposed to believe that? The tears immediately began streaming down her face as she fell back against the kitchen wall and slid to the floor. As she continued to scream, an excruciating pain shot through her stomach. Her screams became of mixture of hurt, anger, and fear.

"Oh my God," Vernon said, coming to her side. "You're bleeding!"

She glanced down and saw the blood trickling down her legs. "The baby," she cried. As another severe pain shot through her body, Joyce knew. The baby that she thought would save her marriage, the baby she didn't want but had come to love, her baby, was gone. The stress of her marriage to Vernon had had the ultimate effect.

twelve

This past year had been a year of losses.

Not only had Lauren lost her baby sister, but her grandfather had died three months ago. The double loss had overwhelmed her mother, and now Lauren had lost her as well. Oh, physically she was still here. But emotionally, she was gone.

For the past year her mother had walked around in a fog—when she bothered to get out of bed.

As if it were possible, her parents' relationship had gone from bad to worse. Her dad had lost his smile—probably because of the constant state of depression her mother stayed in. It was like a dark cloud had parked over their house and refused to leave.

She hated the fighting. With every fiber of her being, Lauren hated the fighting. But it seemed that was all her parents knew how to do these days. And when they fought, Lauren was often caught in the crossfire. Like last week: Lauren had won a city-wide fashion competition for an original dress she designed. Two hours before the awards ceremony, her mother wouldn't get out of bed.

"Mom, please. This is important to me," Lauren had begged her.

"I don't feel well," her mother had snapped for the tenth time. "Call your father."

Lauren had wanted to cry. Her father was out of town on business and had tried to get back for her ceremony, but his plane had been delayed. At least he was devastated. Her mother couldn't have cared less.

After trying to no avail to catch up with her aunt Velma, Lauren did something she had been trying desperately not to do. She called Miss Callie.

"Sure, sugar. You know I'd love to take you," Miss Callie had said without hesitation after Lauren had explained everything.

From that day on, her bond with Miss Callie had been cemented.

Lauren had gotten to the point where she enjoyed being with her father and Callie more than being at home, because they were always happy. In fact, that was the only time her father was happy. Her father really didn't want to take Lauren around Miss Callie, but after the first two times, Lauren had begged him to let her come, which in turn made Lauren's life happy. They did fun things. They laughed. None of the things that she did with her mother. In fact, Lauren couldn't remember the last time their family had laughed together, let alone went out and enjoyed quality time. Her mother stayed in a constant state of depression and it only depressed everyone around her. And while she didn't like seeing her mother hurt, she understood why her father didn't want to be at home, because honestly, neither did Lauren.

The few arguments that Lauren had witnessed between her father and Miss Callie were because Miss Callie wanted more. She wanted them to be together for good. She wanted him to leave her mother. Miss Callie had asked Lauren as much one day when she was taking her to get her nails done.

"So, baby. Wouldn't you like me to be your mother?" she asked her as she paid for Lauren to get extra rhinestones on her pinky finger.

Lauren wanted to tell her that she had a mother and didn't need a replacement. But she just smiled.

"Yeah, we would do so many great things," Miss Callie continued. "I'd make your dad really happy."

Lauren didn't know what to say. She wasn't going to become part of Miss Callie's campaign to break up the family. Later, when Miss Callie had brought that up, things got heated.

"How long do you think I'm going to hang around and just be your side piece?" Miss Callie had said to Vernon.

"Baby, you knew that I was married when you met me."

"I know, but you said . . ."

"Come on, Callie. You know how I feel: the best mistress is a quiet mistress."

And just like that, Miss Callie had sat back in her seat and shut up.

Instead, Miss Callie focused on making Lauren and her father happy. Like today. They were out shopping for a dress for Lauren to wear to the homecoming dance. Miss Callie had been all too happy to step up when Lauren mentioned that her mother wasn't feeling up to shopping.

Lauren felt a twinge of guilt when she shared these special moments with Miss Callie. She knew her mother was just in a bad space, but what was Lauren supposed to do? Wait and hope that her mother returned to normal? At this point Lauren felt like this deranged, depressed attitude was the new normal. And if that was the case, where in the world did that leave her?

thirteen

For the past year, depression had consumed Joyce. The pain of losing her baby had torn apart her soul. Making matters worse, a DNA test revealed that Cecile's baby wasn't Vernon's. He wasn't lying—at least about her trying to pin the paternity on him.

But the fact that they even had to have a test meant nothing had changed. *He* hadn't changed. And she'd lost her own child over Cecile's lie.

Then her father's death had sent her spiraling into oblivion. Outside of his support of Vernon, she had adored everything about her father. He had been strict growing up, but he'd never hesitated to show her how much she was loved. The sudden stroke that took his life had been devastating.

Julian was gone. He rarely even called home. Joyce knew Lauren needed her, but she seemed to have lost all motivation. She had to make a monumental effort even to get out of bed on a daily basis.

Vernon had tried to get her to see a doctor, but unless they had a prescription for a broken heart, no one could help her.

But the call Joyce had just received was enough motivation to get moving.

"Your mother is in bad shape."

The call had come from her mother's longtime friend. Esther had moved in to help care for Joyce's mother after her father died last year. She'd called twenty minutes ago to tell Joyce that her mother had been rushed to the hospital.

Of course, no one was at home with Joyce. No one was ever at home. Both Vernon and Lauren stayed gone, no doubt trying to escape the gloom that pervaded their home. Joyce thought she heard Lauren say she was spending the night at a friend's, but honestly, she wasn't sure.

Joyce fought back tears as she navigated her car into the Duke Memorial parking lot. She hadn't driven in six months, but when she got the call that her mother needed her, Joyce put anything she was feeling to the side.

"Oh, Joyce," Esther said, jumping up from her seat once Joyce arrived at her mother's hospital room. "I'm so glad you made it."

Joyce couldn't bother with formalities. "What happened?" she said. Her mother was lying in the hospital bed, her eyes closed. "Is she . . ."

"She's resting," Esther said. "She passed out and we had to rush her here."

"Passed out? Why? Was she dehydrated?"

Esther shifted uneasily.

"Esther, what's going on with my mother?"

She looked over at her friend, released a sigh of regret, then said, "Your mother has brain cancer."

The words made Joyce fall back against a chair. She had to grab one of the arms to steady herself.

"What?"

Esther nodded. "Yes. Advanced. She didn't want to tell

you, because, well, she found out around the same time you lost the baby, and you've been going through so much. And she knew you'd just lost your daddy."

Joyce had to take slow, deep breaths to keep a panic attack at bay. She was going to lose her child, her father, and her mother in the same year? What kind of cruel God would do that?

"So, she's known and she didn't tell me?" Joyce managed to say.

Esther just shook her head. Joyce couldn't believe that her mother had been dealing with this while she wallowed in self-pity.

Before Joyce could ask any more questions, her mother's eyes fluttered open. "Joyce, baby, is that you?" Her voice was weak. Her light skin was pale and splotchy. Seeing her so fragile made Joyce's heart feel like it was enduring major surgery with no medication.

"Yes, Mama, I'm here." Joyce raced to her side and took her hand.

"I'm sorry you had to find out like this."

"I can't believe you didn't tell me," Joyce said, swallowing the lump in her throat.

"Y-You've just been going through so much." Her mother was wheezing, as if it hurt to talk.

"Okay, shhh," Joyce said. "Just rest."

Her mother shook her head. "I want you to know I love you, and I need you to be strong. Y-You're dying, baby. You have to live. Vernon loves you. Those other women don't mean anything."

"Mama, hush," Joyce said.

"You just tell my grandchildren that I love them something fierce."

"You can tell them when you get out of here."

She coughed, caught her breath. "You know I'm not getting out of here," she said wearily.

A doctor stepped in, interrupting them. "Hi, I'm Dr. Owen. Are you her daughter?"

Joyce nodded. "I am."

"Can I talk to you a minute?"

Joyce looked back at her mother. She'd already closed her eyes, like she needed to rest.

"I'll stay with her while you talk to the doctor," Esther said.

Joyce followed the doctor out into the hallway, her heart pounding.

"Is there someone you can call to be here with you?" the doctor asked.

The fact that that was his first question meant the news he was about to relay was not good.

"Can you just tell me what's going on with my mother?"

He slipped into a doctor's clinical monotone as he said, "Your mother's cancer has spread. It has covered about eighty percent of her brain and is causing her internal organs to shut down."

Joyce could feel the floor dropping away. "Well, can you do something about it?" she said weakly.

Before the doctor could respond, Esther came running to the door.

"I think she's having a seizure!" she cried.

Joyce raced back into the room with the doctor to find her mother's body convulsing like she was going into cardiac arrest.

"Code Blue!" a nurse shouted as she ran into the room. In

the middle of the chaos the machine her mother was hooked up to emitted a long beep. Several other hospital staff rushed in, their faces filled with alarm.

"Ladies, can the two of you please step outside?" one of the nurses asked Esther and Joyce.

Joyce considered demanding that she be allowed to stay, but she knew that their attention needed to be focused on her mother. Esther took her hand and led her out of the room, both of them trying desperately to keep their panic at bay. Joyce's entire body shook with fear as she peered through the small windows as the doctors and nurses worked madly around her mother. They had to save her. They had to. Her mother was always so good to everyone . . .

Joyce watched until the doctor's posture changed. He stood up, removed the mask from around his face, and shook his head.

Joyce fainted where she stood.

fourteen

Vernon didn't come home until four in the morning. He staggered into the living room to find Joyce sitting in the dark on the sofa. She'd been trying to go to sleep, but it refused to pay her a visit.

"Hey, why are you sitting in the dark?" Vernon said, flipping the light on. He seemed shocked that she was out of the bed.

Joyce just glared at him. She was all cried out and anger had shoved aside her tears. Both she and Esther had tried calling Vernon at the office, and even had his answering service page him, but they couldn't get him. Esther had ended up bringing Joyce home and sat with her until the hour had grown embarrassingly late, then left.

"What is wrong with you?" he asked, loosening his tie.

She answered his question with a piercing stare.

"Okay, let me guess, you're mad about me coming in so late. But I've been working and I figured you'd still be in bed—"

Joyce stopped him before he got too far into his lie. "I called your office."

"I wasn't working in the office."

She gave him the meanest look she could muster.

"Why are you tripping?" he asked. "All you want to do is stay up in this house and be depressed. You know that's not me, so I was in no hurry to come home."

"I needed you," was all she said.

"Needed me for what?" He tossed his keys onto the bar and came closer to her. He finally noticed the puffiness around her eyes and said, "What's wrong?"

"They had to rush Mama to the hospital."

His mouth fell open. "Oh my God. How is she?"

All this sympathy was coming far too late. "She's dead, Vernon." Then she got up, walked to the bedroom, and locked the door behind her.

She ignored his banging on the door as she crawled into bed and cried herself to sleep.

fifteen

I know she lives around here somewhere," Joyce said as she gripped the steering wheel and peered through the car's windows into the dark streets.

Lauren released a long sigh of exhaustion. Why did her mother feel compelled to drag her along on this Vernon-hunting expedition? Julian was off at Fort Benning, and right about now, Lauren wished that she was alongside her brother, serving on a secret mission or something. Anything would be better than this mission her mother had her on.

I'm never going to do this, Lauren vowed as her mother drove at least ten miles an hour below the speed limit, studying the front of every single house. *I'm never going to let a man make me so crazy that I'm acting like this.*

It had been months of this madness. Her mother alternated between being so depressed that she couldn't get out of bed, and getting out of bed and doing this craziness. Right now was the *ultimate* in craziness.

Her mother dropped one hand from the steering wheel and glared down at a handheld contraption that looked like a compass. "The tracking device says he's here." She peered out of the window at the row of apartments. "But I don't know which one."

Lauren did everything that she could to keep her lips pressed together rather than letting her mouth open wide. Tracking device? Had her mother really resorted to using a tracking device?

"There is his car!" her mother exclaimed as if she'd just discovered the cure for cancer. She tossed the device onto the console and pointed toward Vernon's Cadillac.

Her mother pulled into the space behind her father's car and threw her vehicle into park. Before Lauren could even get herself together, Joyce swung open the door, jumped out, and stomped up the sidewalk with the energy of that Energizer Bunny on TV.

"I'm going in here and beat this trick down," Joyce grumbled.

Trick? Beat down? Who was this woman and what had happened to the real Joyce Robinson?

There was just one problem; Lauren watched her mother stomp toward the wrong apartment. The way her father's car was parked, Lauren knew why her mother was marching to the apartment on the left. The only thing — Miss Callie's apartment was the one on the right.

"Mama, don't," Lauren called out after her after she finally scooted from the car. "Let's just go home, please?"

"No, I'm sick and tired of this!" her mother cried. "He has stripped me of everything and he's still cheating!"

Even as Lauren tried to catch up to her mother, she was torn. Should she just let her mother go to the wrong house? With the way her mother was behaving — talking about beating down tricks — she was sure that her mother would be banging and screaming on that door in just a few seconds would happen then? Just last week, there was a story on the news about a woman being shot dead in a scenario just like this. The woman had confronted the wrong person and ended up with a bullet right between her eyes. What if that happened to her mother?

The memory of the news report made Lauren shout, "Mama, no!"

"Get back in the car." Her mother's volume matched Lauren's.

When her mother was less than three feet from the door, Lauren pressed her lips together and then spit out the words, "That's not her house."

Joyce's hand was already in the air, ready to bang on the door, when she spun around, her head turning like she was that girl in *The Exorcist*.

"How do you know that?"

Even from where she stood, she could see that her mother's lips hardly moved. Lauren stood frozen, the moonlight casting a hollow glow on her mother's face. Now she really did look like she was in the middle of some horror movie, and Lauren felt like she was in one, too.

Her mother turned all the way around and took several slow steps toward her. "How do you know that?" she repeated, her voice rising about four octaves.

Lauren's trembling was her only reply.

"Have you been here before?" her mother said.

"I-I . . ." Lauren couldn't help it. The tears began to fall.

Joyce was right in her face when she shouted, "Answer me!"

"Y-Yes," she mumbled, not being able to look into her mother's eyes. "I—" Before she could finish, her mother reached back and slapped her. "You've come over here with him and you don't tell me? My own child? You betray me like this?"

Lauren sobbed. The tears wouldn't stop. And the rage from her mother would only get worse. Lauren just knew her mother was about to haul off and hit her again when she heard her father's voice.

"Joyce. What in the hell are you doing?"

Joyce spun around to see her father standing there in a T-shirt and lounging pants. The sight of him wearing the lounging clothes he normally wore at home must've infuriated her because she momentarily forgot about Lauren.

"What am I doing?" she screamed. "You're the one laid up here with some tramp."

The person in the apartment next to Miss Callie's opened her door and peeped out. A neighbor on the other side stared from her patio. Miss Callie stood on her front porch, her arms folded across her chest in a defiant pose.

Lauren knew her father was humiliated. "Go home, Joyce."

She looked up the walkway at Callie. "Is that her?" Joyce didn't give anyone time to answer as she started stomping up the walkway. Miss Callie turned and bolted inside, slamming the door behind her. "Oh, no!" Joyce screamed. "Don't run, tramp!" she shouted toward the door. "You're woman enough to be sleeping with my husband, come out here and face me!"

Forget her father being humiliated. This deranged madwoman acting like someone from one of those hood movies made Lauren sick to her stomach.

"Joyce, stop it. You're making a fool of yourself." Her father struggled to grab Joyce from the back. Of course she went ballistic at his mere touch.

"It can't be any worse than the fool you've made of me." She clawed at his face.

"Just stop it," he said, grabbing her arms and trying to pin them down.

As Joyce screamed, the elderly woman in the apartment across from them said, "I called the police."

"Ma'am, we have it under control," her father replied.

"Don't look like you got it under control," the woman called out. "The police are on their way."

Vernon released Joyce and she slumped to the ground. "Did you hear that?" he said. "Police. I'm not doing this." He reached in his pocket, grabbed his car keys, and headed toward the car. Joyce managed to pull herself up and follow him.

"Get back here. We're not done!" she yelled.

"I'm not doing this with you, Joyce," he said, speed-walking to his car.

Lauren held on to the edge of the porch, weeping as she watched the scene unfold. Her father got in the car and screeched out of the driveway without ever even acknowledging Lauren.

Joyce sat on the ground sobbing and moaning uncontrollably. More people had come outside and were staring. Lauren couldn't take it anymore.

"Come on, Mama," Lauren said, trying to help her mother off the ground. Her mother cried, but allowed Lauren to guide her back to the car. As Lauren put her in the driver's seat and closed the door, she looked over her shoulder and saw Miss Callie peering out of the living room window.

As a siren wailed in the background, Lauren scurried to the passenger's side. She never wanted to choose sides, but Miss Callie would have to understand that if she was forced to, no matter what they'd been through, Lauren would always choose her mother.

Lauren sat on her bed, feeling nearly catatonic. She knew she shouldn't have allowed Miss Callie to do all those things for her. The last four hours had been brutal. Her parents had fought every moment since they returned home. Now her mother had left—to clear her head.

"You okay, baby girl?" her father said, entering her room.

"Yeah," she replied to her father, even though she wasn't.

"I'm sorry you have to deal with such adult stuff."

There were so many things that Lauren could say in this moment, but there was just one question she had. She'd been trying to muster up the nerve for weeks to ask her father this and now, finally, she found the nerve because she just had to know. "Daddy, why don't you just leave?"

His eyes filled with sadness. "I've asked myself that many times, sweetie." He shook his head. "I don't want to hurt your mother. No matter what you or anyone thinks, I love her very much. But your mother has some ways. And one of those ways is she hangs on to stuff. She's vindictive, and if I leave . . ." He paused as if a million thoughts galloped through his mind in that moment. "The thought of never seeing you again tears me apart."

"My friend Josie's parents are divorced and she sees her father all the time."

"I'm sure Josie's mother wants to maintain that relationship," he pointed out. "Unfortunately, your mother has grown very bitter and I know that she'd do everything she could to keep you from me. I wouldn't be surprised if she moved halfway across the country just so I wouldn't see you."

"What?" Lauren said, the thought horrifying her, just like it had when he'd said these same words all those years ago.

"Your mother and I have our issues, but we're old-school. Couples go through their problems and no matter who else comes in my life, your mother will always be my number one."

That was a hard concept for Lauren to understand. And now that she was sixteen, she understood a lot. One thing she knew was that she would never be someone's number one. She would only be his only one.

"Well, I'll be going away to college soon. So, are you gonna leave her then?"

He gave her one of those inscrutable parent looks. "Your mother is sick right now. The doctors said she's suffering from postpartum depression because of the baby."

Lauren side-eyed her father. Yeah, she was sure her mother was sad about the baby, but that wasn't the only reason. Didn't her father get that?

Maybe she could explain it a little. Maybe she could help her father to see. "Daddy, I, just, I don't know. Mom is so sad. Maybe you can just be with only her. Maybe that would make her feel better."

His response was instant. "I love only her."

"Not love," Lauren said. "I mean be with. As in let all the other women go. Because if you love only Mom, then . . ."

Lauren didn't know where she found the strength to say these words to her father, but she was just like her mother—tired of the madness.

Vernon gave her a long sigh. "Humans weren't created to be monogamous, sweetie. You'll understand that when you get grown."

"So, you'd be okay if Mommy had boyfriends?"

The look of sheer horror that swept across his face answered her question.

"It's different for men and women, baby," he said, hedging. "That's not your mother's nature. Look, I know you feel bad, and I hate that you're in the middle of this."

Lauren remembered how her mother's head had spun around, then the slap. "I'm sorry I told her about Miss Callie's house. But she was going to the wrong house and I was scared of what might have happened if she started knocking on the wrong door."

He reached out and patted her shoulder. "I understand. Neither one of us should've ever placed you in this position. Just know that I don't blame you for tonight and I love you with everything inside me."

His words made tears sting behind her eyes. "Mom isn't speaking to me."

"She'll come around. She's just upset right now."

Upset was an understatement. Her mother had cried all the way home from Miss Callie's house, wailing so hard that Lauren was sure she'd end up sick. Wailing about how Lauren had betrayed her.

Vernon gave his daughter a hug before he stepped back and said, "Let's both make a pact to make Mommy feel better.

I'll do better, and you say whatever you need to say to make her feel better."

Lauren pulled back, not wanting to wade into any more lies. "What do you mean?"

"Well," her father began slowly, "she's going to have a lot of questions for you. Like she'll ask is Miss Callie the only one? How many times you were over there."

Her father was way too late with this advice. Her mother had already pummeled her with dozens of questions, none of which Lauren answered as she hid behind her own tears. She did get out one promise to her mother, though. She promised not to keep any more secrets from her. But that had seemed to provide little solace to Joyce.

"So you want me to lie to her?"

"No." He shook his head as if he couldn't believe Lauren had said that. "This will be the last secret. And you have to keep this one because you see how much she's hurt now. Telling her anything more will only make it worse for her. And I don't want that for your mother."

Lauren didn't say a word to her father; she just turned around and walked out of the room. How could he ask her to do this after what happened tonight? He had to know just how tired she was of keeping these secrets.

Julian had been right. Now she, too, couldn't wait to get out of this house and away from both of them.

sixteen

Another day, another fight. That's all Joyce and Vernon ever did.

Joyce knew that she should've left him a long time ago. But where was she supposed to go? Especially now that her parents were gone. Yes, they'd had life insurance policies, but those had barely paid for their burials and were certainly not enough for Joyce to live comfortably on.

Besides, Vernon had ruined her life. She wasn't about to leave now and allow him to enjoy a footloose and fancy-free bachelor life; not after everything he'd done to make her suffer.

And then, there was this other thing. A fact that she had a difficult time admitting to herself, but true nonetheless. Joyce still loved Vernon Robinson. More now than she ever did. That thought made her even angrier.

The roller coaster that had become her marriage was literally driving her crazy. Especially since Vernon wasn't even trying very hard to hide his indiscretions now.

Like tonight. Joyce glanced at the clock on the mantel. It was after one in the morning. There was no lie that she would believe, no work dinner that ever lasted this long.

She blew her nose into another tissue, then tossed it into

the pile that was growing on the side table. This was it. She'd cried her last tear. It was as if not even her tears believed her as they continued to fall.

She sat waiting, trying hard to wipe away her tears, but only adding more tissues to the pile. Finally, at about 2 a.m., she heard the key in the door and a second later, Vernon strolled in.

He had just closed the door behind him when he saw her sitting in the dimly lit room. He held up his hand. "Don't start, please."

Joyce shrugged. "There's nothing to say, Vernon. I'm tired of—"

The doorbell rang, stopping her words, freezing them both. They exchanged glances and before Vernon could turn back to the door, Joyce hopped up, scurried across the room, and swung the door open before her husband could take a single step.

"May I help you?" Joyce asked the woman who stood on the step. A *hot mess*—that was the first thought that came to Joyce's mind. That was the only way to describe this woman whose mascara was so smeared her eyes now looked like a raccoon's.

"I'm Callie," she said, with a bit of an attitude, as if Joyce was supposed to know who she was.

Joyce's eyes narrowed and with all the rage that had been building inside her for years, she growled, "What are you doing on my doorstep?"

She'd spoken as if she had courage, but now, with her arms folded across her chest, she shifted from one foot to the other.

"I want to speak with Vernon."

Behind her Joyce heard, "Callie, I know you're not coming to my house." Now he was the one who sounded like he had an attitude.

"I told you if you left I was coming over here."

Vernon tried to step around Joyce, but she turned and pushed him back. "Oh, no!" Joyce said, pushing him back with a pointed elbow. To Callie she said, "Come on in." She made a grand gesture, sweeping her hand through the air. "You want to show up here to talk to my husband, then let's talk."

"Yeah, let's do that," Callie said, pushing past both of them.

As Callie walked into the living room, Vernon hissed, "I cannot believe you brought this to my home."

Callie stopped, spun, and faced him. She stared him down, showing no signs of any kind of fear. "Let you tell it, your home is at my place. And I am sick and tired of playing second fiddle while you continue to lie to me and tell me you're leaving her and the only reason you're here is because she's sick."

Joyce's wide eyes turned to her husband. "Really?" she said, not bothering to hide the shock from her voice. When Joyce turned back to Callie, Callie's eyes were moving up and down, studying Vernon's wife as if Callie were some kind of nurse.

Then Callie said, "She doesn't look sick to me."

"It's because I'm not," Joyce replied. "The only thing that was happening was that I was a bit depressed. My parents died, my baby died." Instinctively, her hand covered her stomach. "I had a right to be sad."

Callie's eyes were on Joyce's hand. Her hand that still rested on her stomach. When she looked up at Joyce, she swallowed, looking as if someone had slammed a sledgehammer into her own stomach. "You were pregnant?" Her words were soft.

"Callie!" he said.

"Vernon!" Callie said.

And then it was bedlam. Three voices. Screaming. Back and forth. Words rising in the air, but not one understood. It kept going and going until . . .

"Daddy, will you guys please stop fighting?" Lauren screamed louder than all of them.

The three adults stopped, turned, and together took in Lauren, who stood in the archway of the living room in flannel pajamas.

They all stared quietly for a few moments, though Joyce's thoughts were anything but quiet. *What kind of example am I setting for my daughter?*

"Hey, baby." Callie spoke first, managing to give Lauren a smile.

Joyce felt as if the ground had been snatched from beneath her feet. "Baby?" Joyce said.

Lauren glanced nervously at her father, and then at Joyce as if she didn't know whether she should speak.

"How much time have you spent with my child?" Joyce asked.

To Callie, Lauren was the trump card. The card that maybe she could play to get Joyce to finally leave. "Sweetie, your child and I have a bond that you'll never have with her. I'm the one she talks to when she's worried about her friends. I'm the one that helped her get ready for her first date; I'm the one who helped her find a dress for the homecoming dance. And oh, I'm the one she talked to about her first sexual encounter."

Lauren's mouth fell open, and now Joyce was sure the ground had evaporated.

"I'm the one that has been a mother to her this past year," Callie said as if she smelled Joyce's blood, "while you wallowed in depression or in whatever was wrong with you."

Joyce looked at her daughter the same way she used to look at her husband when she was begging him to come clean. She needed Lauren to call this woman a liar, to say that what this woman was saying wasn't anywhere near the truth.

But Lauren didn't speak; Lauren couldn't speak.

"Callie, get the hell out of my house!" Vernon said, grabbing her arm.

"No!" She squirmed against his grasp. "You told me we would be together."

But Joyce was no longer concerned about the woman who'd come to ruin her marriage. Her concern was only on the weapon that Callie had used to break her heart.

She stared at her daughter. Lauren had befriended this woman? She'd shared secrets with this woman? Joyce stood there and watched her daughter cry as Vernon and Callie did a wrestling dance toward the front door.

"How could you?" Joyce whispered to her child.

"Mama, I . . ."

"Him, I get. He's been a dog from day one. But you, my own flesh and blood. My child? You wanted to break my heart, too?"

"Mama, please . . ."

Hearing her words, Vernon turned back. Letting go of Callie, he said, "Don't blame her." His eyes pleaded for Joyce to keep her at bay.

"Yeah, don't blame her," Callie sneered, as if she were part of this family.

Vernon turned to her and this time without laying a hand on her, he just growled. "Get the hell out of my house."

It was enough to make her recoil. She took several steps back. But then she stood up straight and squared her shoulders. "Fine. I'm leaving," she said as if leaving were her idea. "But you better believe you haven't seen the end of me. I'll be damned if you toy with my heart and think it's okay."

With a final sneer at Joyce and a good-bye smile to Lauren, Callie stormed out. In the void that her whirlwind left behind, Vernon spoke. "Let me explain."

Before he could finish, Joyce jumped on him and clawed at his face. Lauren screamed. Every ounce worth of rage, all the years of pent-up anger, was unleashed on her husband that night. She didn't want to stop until he was dead. She wouldn't stop until she no longer felt anything inside.

seventeen

Now she was stuck between two women filled with rage.

Lauren was sure of that fact when Miss Callie showed up at their front door. Lauren knew that was a no-no. Miss Callie knew it, too.

Miss Callie was fed up and truly tired of waiting. And now, judging from the fight that Lauren's parents were having, Miss Callie might soon get her wish.

"I want you out!" her mother had screamed after jumping on her father's back. She'd clawed him like an alley cat in the midst of a fight. Vernon had done everything to keep her blows at bay.

He'd wrestled her off and now she was leaning against the wall, crying, her chest heaving. "I'm done. I'm so, so done."

"Fine," he said, heading to grab his keys off the bar. "You want me out, I'm out."

But before he could reach them, Joyce dove and snatched them up.

"You're not going to her!"

He stopped and gritted his teeth, exasperated. "You told me to get out. That's what I'm doing."

"No, we're going to finish this first," she sobbed. "You're

going to admit to all the whores you've been with. Then you can leave for good."

"I'm not admitting to anything," he said defiantly.

"Have you been bringing my daughter around that bitch?"

"I don't want to do this," he replied. "Not in front of Lauren. Give me my keys."

She picked up a vase and hurled it at him. He ducked. It smashed against a cabinet door and shattered into a hundred pieces all over the counter and the tile floor. "See, this is what I'm talking about. I'm not talking to you while you're irrational!" he yelled.

"Answer me!" she screamed.

"And tell you what? That I've been seeing her? Yes, you know the answer to that. Hell, you tracked me down at her place. I'm sorry. It's just that I can't deal with this," he said, motioning around to all of the broken shards of the vase. "I can't deal with you and your craziness. If you're not going crazy, you're depressed. It's just too much."

"So, you admit to it?" A maniacal laugh crossed her face.

He was totally fed up. "We'll have a conversation when you calm down. Give me my keys."

He tried to snatch the keys from her. They struggled as Lauren remained frozen. In the midst of their scuffle, the keys slid across the floor and stopped right in front of Lauren's feet. Instinctively, she reached down and picked up the keys.

Vernon was pushing his wife off him as he said, "Give me the keys, Lauren."

"You better not give those keys to him!" her mother screamed.

"Lauren, you see that your mother is acting a fool." Her

father's voice remained calm. "You see that she is out of control. I just need to leave until she calms down."

Lauren stood shaking, the keys clutched tightly in her hands.

"Do not give him the keys," her mother growled, tears streaming down her face.

Vernon held his hands out. "Baby, give Daddy the keys."

Slowly, Lauren extended her hand. She had expected her mother to slap them out of her hand. But her mother was spent. Her hair all over her face. Her mascara dripping down her cheeks.

"Sorry, Mama, this is best, believe me," Lauren said as she slowly handed her father the keys.

"Thank you, baby." He took the keys, then kissed her on the forehead. "I'll see you later."

As he headed toward the door Lauren had a sinking feeling he would never be back.

eighteen

Lauren wanted to go home. She wanted to go home, bad. Miss Callie had been acting strange all day, alternating between bouts of happiness, anger, and utter despair. She'd heard Miss Callie fighting with her father early that morning. He'd been staying with her for the past three days.

Ever since the big fight, her dad hadn't come home. Her mother cried the whole time, and Lauren felt helpless. Her mother hadn't spoken to her, blaming Lauren for giving her father the keys, for keeping secrets, for everything. She hadn't even come out this morning to wish Lauren a happy birthday. That's why Lauren had been so excited when her father had shown up and told her to ditch school and come hang out with him.

But after an hour at the mall, her dad had seemed tired and upset and told her that he just wanted to go back to Miss Callie's and take a nap, then take her out for ice cream and cake later.

But later never came because midway through his nap, the front door opened and Miss Callie came in. Lauren was in Miss Callie's guest bedroom watching TV, but she could hear everything.

"What are you doing home? I thought you had to work," she heard her father say.

"I couldn't stay at work," Callie said, crying.

Lauren hadn't heard much after that. Just a lot of arguing and fighting. *Not here, too,* Lauren thought.

She figured sooner or later they'd wrap up their argument. And Lauren and her dad could go for ice cream. Twenty minutes later, her father opened the door to the guest room.

"Sweetie, come on, let's go," he said.

"No, you're not leaving yet!" Miss Callie called out.

He sighed as he looked at Lauren. "I'm sorry. Just wait right here for a minute." He closed the bedroom door again.

"I told you I don't want to do this with you," she heard her father say.

Lauren cracked the door so she could peer out to see and hear what they were arguing about.

"You're here with me. You said we were going to be together!" Miss Callie cried.

"I can't do this," Vernon replied. "I miss my wife. I love my wife." He spoke like he was just coming to that realization.

"If you love her so much, what are you doing here with me?"

"Exactly," Vernon said. "I can't keep hurting her like this. She's a good woman. She doesn't deserve this."

"What am I, then?" Callie snapped. "And what do I deserve?"

"You're a good woman, too. You're just not the woman for me."

"So what the hell have you been doing all of this time with me? Stringing me along?"

Her father's back was to her, but Lauren could tell by the

way his shoulders sank that he was tired. "Look, you knew how the game was played. You knew I was married. You knew I was never leaving my wife."

"Yeah, that's what your mouth said. But your body always said something different," she said.

"Okay. I am sorry. I know that it was hard for me to walk away from you. You flash that body and it's like I lose all good sense."

"So that's all I was to you?" Callie said, her voice trembling. "A booty call?"

"Come on, Callie. You know you were more than that to me. But my wife—it's different. I'm not losing my family."

"We can be a family," she pleaded. Lauren had never seen her act so desperate.

"I'm about to gather up my daughter and we're going home. And I'm going to fix things with my wife. With my family. Be the man that they deserve."

So that was what had been wrong with her father all day. He missed her mother.

"No, you're not going anywhere," she said.

Callie grabbed Vernon's hand. He snatched it away. They had a small scuffle and then Callie reached for her purse, lying open on the hall table. She reached inside and pulled out a small handgun.

"You're not leaving me!" she cried angrily. "I told you if I can't have you, nobody can!"

Vernon backed away, putting his hands up. "Callie, what the hell are you doing? Put that down."

"No," she said, her hands shaking.

He shook his head. "I'm going to get my daughter and we're out of here."

Lauren was dumbfounded. Her father was acting like Callie didn't have a gun standing there pointing at his chest.

"Whyyyyy?" she wailed.

Vernon sighed, rubbing his hands over his face. "I told you I need to go make things right with my wife. My wife needs my help, not me to abandon her."

"Your wife is a depressed nutcase."

If Miss Callie didn't have a handgun, Lauren would've stepped out and told her not to talk that way about her mother.

"I'm sorry if this isn't what you want to hear, but it's over. For good. I just pray she'll take me back. I—"

His words were cut short by a firecracker sound. At first Lauren didn't register that Callie had actually pulled the trigger. Lauren screamed as her father toppled against the wall, blood covering his chest.

"Daddy!" Lauren screamed, darting out of the guest room and toward her father. She reached him just as he extended an arm toward her.

"I . . . I'm sorry. I love you," he whispered. "T-Tell your mother I love her with . . ." He struggled to get his words out. ". . . all my soul and I-I'm sorry," he added before closing his eyes for good.

"Daddy, no! Daddy! Daddy!" she cried as she fell across his bloody chest. "What did you do to my daddy?" she said, looking up at Callie, who was standing there, her face streaked with tears as her hands trembled in fear. "You killed my daddy!"

Callie didn't say a word. She gasped at Vernon's slumped corpse in horror and then turned the gun, pointed it at her own head, and pulled the trigger.

nineteen

Her heart was lying in an eighty-four-inch-long titanium box. As many times as she'd wished Vernon Robinson dead, now all Joyce wanted was to climb in that box and forever sleep right next to him.

The organist played a mournful tune as someone stood at the front of the church and said something about her husband.

The past few days had passed in a daze and today was no exception. Joyce was perched in the front pew, knees locked together, trying desperately not to pass out.

Julian sat on one side of her. He looked so regal in his army uniform. But his face could have been carved out of stone. So far he had refused to shed a single tear.

Lauren and Velma sat on the other side of Joyce. As the organ got louder, Lauren reached for Joyce's hand. Instinctively, she shrank away and snuggled closer to Julian.

Joyce knew that she shouldn't act like that toward her daughter, but her heart was cold. She wanted to tell Lauren to go be comforted by Callie's people. She was sure some of them sat among the sea of unrecognizable faces in the sanctuary.

Joyce's rejection made Lauren sob even more, and Velma

pulled her niece to her as she glared at Joyce through tear-soaked eyes.

She'd fix things with Lauren later. Right now Joyce needed to grieve herself. She needed to figure out how to get over the pain of what her husband had done to her and the awful way he died. She needed to figure out why death had become her best friend.

And that wasn't going to be easy because her anger was just as potent as her grief.

She couldn't help it. Joyce looked around the room wondering how many people knew what Vernon had done. As she listened to the minister take the podium and begin eulogizing him, talking about what a good man Vernon was, Joyce almost burst out laughing. If only he knew.

As the ceremony came to a close and the minister asked everyone to rise, Joyce willed her legs not to give out. Lauren was inconsolable. She had Velma, though, so it's not like Joyce had left her to deal with this alone.

After what seemed like an endless line of people offering condolences, it was time for Joyce to stand and take the last look at her husband. She didn't know how she managed to stand over his casket, but she did. She lifted a shaky hand to stroke his cheek. "Why, Vernon, why? I have no one now," Joyce mumbled.

"I'll protect you now, Ma," Julian said as he squeezed her tighter. She squeezed him back as the rage shaded into sorrow.

"I know, baby. I know." Her son was now all she had.

PART II

2016

twenty

The storm cloud burst through the revolving doors of the hotel lobby. Lauren Robinson had seen the look of rage simmering behind a scorned woman's eyes before. She'd seen it so many times in her own mother's eyes. She'd seen it in the eyes of women who had accosted her, and thanks to her father, she knew the perfect way to handle it.

The best mistress is a quiet mistress.

Her father's words rang in her head as clear as the day he'd uttered them. And right now silence would be golden.

The woman approached with steps that threatened to break off her high heels. Lauren turned slightly, pretending not to notice her. "Finally, I've found you at last," the woman announced. "You're the one who's been seducing my husband."

Lauren kept her eyes averted. Maybe the woman's spurt of bravery would fizzle out, being exposed in public. Lauren had no such luck, though.

"So you're just not going to answer me?" the woman standing at Lauren's shoulder snapped.

Lauren sighed, glanced over at her friend, Vivian, who looked worried that something was about to jump off right there in the lobby of the Marriott hotel.

Lauren turned to face the woman dead on. "I don't know where you're getting your facts from, but let me assure you, I don't do married men," she replied. Her voice was calm, unfazed. That was the way to do it. That had been Vernon's rule number one when busted: put the partner at ease.

Lauren and Vivian had been enjoying happy hour drinks. Lauren hadn't even known who the woman in the tight Juicy Couture warm-up, hair up in a ponytail like she was ready to fight, was—until sexy Craig West came fumbling in behind her. The woman held up a cell phone, displaying a photo Lauren had taken last year at the Children's Network gala. This woman must've googled Lauren to get the picture, since Lauren made a point of staying off social media for anything other than her business.

"Is this you?" she asked, thrusting the phone in Lauren's face. "And don't lie because I see the fake ugly beauty mark."

Lauren fingered the tiny mole just above her lip. She'd contemplated having it removed, but men told her it was sexy, so she'd left it alone.

"It's real, first of all," Lauren said, her voice still calm. "Secondly, you are way off base."

"He's not telling me the truth, so you need to tell me," the woman demanded. She looked like she couldn't be any more than twenty-five. Over the years, Lauren had found that young wives gave her the most grief. The older women either learned to accept their husbands' infidelities or chose to ignore them.

"So tell me, are you, or are you not, sleeping with my husband?" Her platinum ponytail bounced with every word. The pain in her eyes contradicted the brave front she was trying to display.

Lauren looked over the woman's shoulder at her Shemar Moore–fine occasional lover. A former running back with the Carolina Panthers, he'd been cut his first year and was now playing semipro ball. Normally, Lauren wouldn't have given someone like him the time of day—but she was blinded by his fineness.

Craig stood behind his wife, terrified at what she would say.

"What's your name?" Lauren asked.

She folded her arms, glared at Lauren, then reluctantly said, "Dana."

Lauren gently put a hand on Dana's arm. "Sister, I've been where you are. I understand the frustration, the not knowing if your man is doing right. But you've got a good one there. Yes, I've met your husband several times, but I am not sleeping with him. He never did anything inappropriate and, in fact, he spent his time raving about you."

That gave Dana pause. She glanced back at her husband, her eyes a mixture of tears and apprehension, like she really wanted to believe Lauren but was unsure. Relief filled Craig's face and he said, "See, babe. I told you. You're up here acting a fool for nothing."

"I get it," Lauren continued as Dana turned back to face her. "I dated a dog. They can make you come out of character in a minute. But Craig isn't a dog. You have a very handsome man, but he's yours, all yours."

Dana was growing confused. "B-But I saw his text about meeting you here tonight. Then I heard him telling a friend about how he dreamed of all the freaky things he was going to do to you."

"I told him all the freaky things I wanted to do to Lauren.

But I was talking about Lauren *London,* the actress!" Craig proclaimed. "I was just messing around. It's not like I even know Lauren London!"

It took everything for Lauren not to burst out laughing. *Really?* Men were so simple when it came to cheating. Why would he be having that conversation with anyone while his wife was in the house? And more important, why would he have her name in his phone? He was supposed to have her listed as Charles, or Mike, or something. That was Player Rule #2.

Dana paused again. Then, suddenly, shame filled her face. "I-I'm sorry. It's just that we've had problems lately and . . ."

"It's okay. I understand." Lauren looked over at Craig. "Did you do the stuff we talked about?" When he also looked confused, she added, "The spa?" Lauren looked back at Dana. "I make custom jewelry and relaxation products. I gave him information on this amazing spa in High Point that carries some of my products. He wanted to do something nice for you because he said you work so hard with the kids."

Craig seemed momentarily flustered, but then he rolled with it. "Oh, yeah. I did. But she was trippin' so hard, I didn't give it to her." He had the nerve to act irritated.

Dana's mouth dropped open. "Oh. My. God. I've been wanting to go to that place forever. I've heard so many great things about it."

"Well, Craig bought you a weekend getaway," Lauren replied.

"B-But that place is so expensive," Dana stammered.

Craig's eyes bucked. Lauren knew his cheap behind was going to hyperventilate when he saw the prices.

"He said you were worth splurging for," Lauren replied with a smile. "He even had me design a custom bracelet for you." She looked at Craig. "Speaking of which, I'm gonna need that final payment."

Craig kept his face straight, but she could tell he wanted to curse her out. That wasn't going to happen, though. Shoot, he'd better be glad Lauren didn't throw in a necklace and earrings, too.

"You had me a bracelet custom made, too?" Dana asked.

And just like that, the tables had been turned.

An apologetic expression swept over Dana's face. "I'm sorry."

"It's all right, I forgive you." Craig took her into his arms and hugged her tightly. Over his shoulder, he mouthed, "You rock," to Lauren.

He needed to tell her something she didn't know.

"Come on, baby, let's go home," Craig said.

Dana turned back to face Lauren. "I'm s—"

Lauren cut her off. "Don't even worry about it. I told you, I understand."

The two of them walked off hugging like newlyweds.

As soon as they left, Vivian turned to Lauren. "You need an Oscar."

Lauren smiled as she sat back down on the bar stool, then motioned for the bartender to bring her another chocolate martini.

"Hey, just doing my part to keep homes happy."

Vivian stared at her friend. Since she'd been over at Lauren's condo last week when Craig had shown up, Vivian knew that whole scene had just been an act.

"Like seriously, you don't feel the least bit guilty, though?" Vivian asked once they both had new drinks.

"Guilty about what?" Lauren asked.

"Ah . . . you and Craig *are* messing around."

Lauren shrugged as she sipped her drink. "And your point would be?"

"And my point is that you just stood here and convinced his wife that you weren't."

Lauren set her drink down. "Look, I didn't make vows to her. He did. She's young, but they have two kids. She's not going anywhere. So why give her more pain? If anything, I'm doing her a service. I'm sparing her the pain of acting like she's leaving when she knows she's not. I'm letting her live in her idealistic world."

Vivian shook her head. "Okay, but I'm telling you, one of these days you're going to run up on the wrong woman."

Lauren let out a small laugh. "You don't worry about me. If it's one thing my daddy taught me, it was how to be a perfect mistress."

Vivian would never understand. The lessons from Vernon Robinson had led to Lauren's good life. And she had learned to make the best of being second.

"Well, more power to you," Vivian said. "I just want more out of life than to be somebody's mistress."

Lauren didn't know why, but those words cut deeper than she would've ever imagined. She'd been doing this mistress thing since she graduated from college. At one point she thought that it was her destiny, but as she was accosted by more and more Danas, Lauren was really starting to rethink that.

twenty-one

Today had been the day from hell. After she had worked all week to complete a jewelry order, the customer's credit card had been declined and the woman was unable to pay the balance on her custom pieces. Turns out, her baller baby-daddy had cut off her credit card, and Lauren had been stuck with the bill. Granted, Lauren would get to the keep the deposit, but she'd been counting on that money to pay her next month's rent. Now she would have to resort to her backup plan—getting the money from one of her men.

Today Thomas Brooks would get that honor. Lauren knew she should probably feel bad about using these men, but it didn't bother her because she didn't allow herself to care enough for it to have any impact.

Lauren met Thomas the first Saturday of every month for dinner at an exclusive Italian restaurant, so the timing of this month's date was spot-on. She looked forward to those dinners because Thomas was good conversation. She didn't have to pretend like she did with all the others. She really did enjoy talking with him. Plus, Thomas wasn't just after sex. He enjoyed her company as well. He'd married some beauty queen whose only goal in life was to stay beautiful. So while he did love the sex, he really enjoyed the challenge of conversation that Lauren brought to the table.

That was one of the things that she noticed about most of the men she dated. They all came to her for something they were missing at home. She usually felt them out, determined what they were missing, and then made it her business to give that to them. So far she had been pretty good at it: giving one married man after another everything they couldn't get at home, whether it was kinky sex, conversation, or what most of them wanted—their ego stroked. Lauren had made a living at being the perfect mistress. Just like her daddy had taught her.

Lauren arrived at the restaurant ten minutes past seven. She liked to arrive just a tad late to make the anticipation build. She looked around and noticed that Thomas hadn't arrived.

"Would you like to go ahead and be seated?" the maître d' asked.

"Yes. I can have a glass of wine before my date arrives," she replied.

Fifteen minutes later, Lauren was on the brink of irritation when her phone rang.

"Hello?" she said.

"Hey, Lauren." It was Thomas.

"Hi. Are you on your way? I'm at the restaurant."

He paused. "I am so sorry, babe. Major drama at the house. The wife is tripping about me going out. Trying to see why she can't come, and the fact that I was adamant about her not coming only made her want to come that much more."

"I told you about that," Lauren sighed. "You have to play it cool."

That was one of the biggest problems she had with the men she dated. It's like they didn't know the rules of the game. They would send her inappropriate texts and pictures and then want her to send them the same thing in return. That's the one thing that she didn't do because she learned the hard way that men don't like to delete the pictures. And after she had one furious wife call her going off, Lauren let go of the sexting, instead having the men hold on and wait for the real thing. She tried to stay as low-key as possible. The only reason Lauren was even on social media was that she needed it for her business, Avante Designs, and that page was all about her business, not her.

"It's okay, Thomas," Lauren said, making sure to keep her tone cool. The one thing she never did was get upset. It's one of the main reasons they kept coming back. "You need to stay there because the more you push to leave, the harder it's going to be."

He sighed. "Why did I know you would be the voice of reason?"

"Because that's what I do, boo." She released a small laugh. "Look, you handle home. Calm your wife down, put her at ease, and then I'll be waiting for you. You can come see me tomorrow, or the next day, or just wait for our regular time next month." She didn't bother telling him that tomorrow she had another date, and on the next day she would be resting.

"You are unbelievable," he said.

"Thank you. I probably wouldn't be good company anyway. One of my clients wrote me a bad check and now I'm not going to be able to pay my rent." She let just the right amount of quavering into her voice.

"What?" he replied. "I told you to stop taking checks from folks."

"I know, baby. You were so right. I should've listened. But I'll figure something out."

He blew a frustrated breath, but then quickly said, "Well, you know I got you."

"Thomas, I don't . . ."

"You're not going to fight me on this. That's what I'm here for—to take care of my woman."

She smirked at that. His woman was his wife, but whatever he needed to tell himself . . .

"How much is it?"

"Five thousand."

"What?"

"I owe for last month, too. But if you just cover one month, I'll be eternally grateful."

"I'll transfer six thousand dollars to your account tonight, all right?"

"Thomas, I don't know what I would do without you."

She permitted herself a small smile. Her rent was only $2,500, so she'd pay next month, too, and have a little extra to shop with.

"Well, hopefully, you never have to find out. I gotta go."

"All right, babe. See you soon. I have some tricks I want to show you."

She could hear the huskiness in his voice as he replied, "Damn. Okay. Talk to you later."

Lauren hung up the phone and prepared to enjoy her romantic Italian meal—all alone. It was one of the drawbacks to the life she lived—but since she would soon be six thousand dollars richer and didn't even have to sit through dinner to get it, Lauren guessed she couldn't complain.

Lauren thought back to her father's women. She wondered how much money he spent on them over the years. He didn't have crazy money like Thomas, but the way those women went crazy, he had to be sliding them a little something.

"Are you ready to order?"

The sound of the waiter's voice snapped Lauren out of her thoughts.

"I'm sorry," she said. "Yes. I'll take the lobster linguini."

The waiter motioned toward the seat across from her. "Will your guest still be joining you?"

Lauren smiled. "No, it looks like I'll be dining alone."

Suddenly a strong, commanding voice said, "Now, that's a shame a beautiful woman like you would be dining alone."

Lauren turned and prepared herself for the brush-off that she usually gave men with these lame lines, but when she saw who it was, her eyes lit up.

"Matthew King!" she said, jumping from her seat. "Oh my God, it's been forever!" She threw her arms around his neck. His touch was still invigorating. His cologne still gave her goose bumps.

"Look at you," he said, pulling back and examining her.

She swirled to give him a full body view. Her white Valentino sheer blouse hugged in all the right places. It dipped in the front, showing just enough cleavage to be sexy, but not too much to be trashy. Her sleek black trousers accented her Pilates-toned behind.

"Dang, just as fine as always," Matthew said, nodding his approval.

"You, too. Wow, it's been what? Fifteen years?"

"Yeah, something like that." He reached in and hugged her tightly.

The waiter stood like he was trying to figure out what to do. "Should I take the other place setting?"

"As a matter of fact, I just wrapped up drinks with a colleague and I am quite hungry. Do you mind if I join you?" Matthew asked.

And just as quickly as her excitement came, it was gone as she remembered why they went their separate ways.

"Umm, hello," Matthew said when she didn't answer. "Can I join you?"

"Ah, yeah," she said, forcing a smile. "I mean, sure I guess."

Matthew seemed confused by her reaction. She had been excited to see him, but dinner meant talking, talking led to feelings, feelings led to lies, and before Lauren knew it, she would be caught up with him again.

Lauren returned to her seat, trying to process the conflicting feelings racing through her body.

Matthew was an ex-boyfriend she'd first met her sophomore year at Carolina State University and was the first real love of her life. But he had been focused completely on school, and then going on to pursue his PhD. He'd left college when Lauren was a sophomore, and had moved across the country to UCLA to get his master's and doctorate. They tried to make it work, but he was always so preoccupied with school, and then there were the excuses.

"I didn't get your message."

"I've been working late."

"I fell asleep over at a friend's."

All the same excuses her father used to give. Once those started, Lauren knew it was time for her to bail.

"I'll get you a menu," the waiter said, not wanting to be privy to their reunion.

"No need. I'm going to have the lobster and scalloped potatoes." Matthew slid into the seat across from Lauren.

He flashed a smile, but Lauren couldn't make herself return it. It was obvious she still cared about him, based on her initial reaction of seeing him after all this time. But she hadn't forgotten about how much he'd hurt her, moving on without a second thought. She'd done everything she could to erase him from her mind. And she never again let herself get in a position where she loved someone more than they loved her. So far she'd done a good job.

"So, what's going on?" Matthew asked. "How have you been?"

Lauren made herself relax. "Just doing what I do." She filled him in on her jewelry business and some surface things going on in her life. Talking to him did relax her, and just as the waiter brought their meals, she skillfully deflected attention away from herself. "So, tell me about yourself." As long as the conversation stayed cheerful and harmless, Lauren figured she would be okay. "What's been going on? How's life? I didn't know you were back in Raleigh."

"Yeah." He nodded. "I've been back about a year. I'm the vice president at Carolina State University. Keeping my fingers crossed because I'm up for the main job—president."

"What?" she said. "Are you kidding me?"

"Nope." He smiled proudly.

Lauren felt a bit strange over the fact that he'd been here

but hadn't bothered to reach out to her. If the situation were reversed, there's no way she would have been in town this long and not made contact. But then, that was indicative of what went wrong in their relationship. She loved him more than he'd loved her, and that was a definite no-no. "Wow on the fact that you've been here for a year and the fact that your career is soaring like that."

She didn't know if her face gave her away or what, but he quickly put in, "I tried to find you on Facebook . . ." He shrugged. "But I know we didn't end well, and since I had a hard time finding you, I left it alone."

Didn't end well? That was the understatement of the century. She'd cussed him out when she'd called and a female voice answered his phone. He tried to tell her it was just a friend, but as far as Lauren was concerned, friends don't let friends answer their phones. Matthew had already been pulling away, giving her all of those Vernon-type excuses, and that was just the final nail.

"It's cool," she said, even though it wasn't. She hated that he was just able to walk away, and she'd cursed herself for opening up her heart to him to be hurt.

He chuckled. "Figured it was. Everything was always 'cool' with you."

Lauren didn't know what that was supposed to mean, but she wasn't going to give Matthew the satisfaction of letting him know if anything he said bothered her.

"Well, congrats on the job," Lauren said with a genuine smile.

"I don't have it—yet. The current president is retiring and they're expected to name a successor in the next six months."

Lauren had no doubt he'd get the job. His ambition was one of their issues back in school. He had tunnel vision and was so focused on his education that she often felt like extra baggage. "I'm glad to see you doing so well, although it's not surprising. I knew you were going to make it big," Lauren said.

"Thank you. You know I've always wanted to work in higher education, and you know our alma mater has risen to be the number-two HBCU in the country, so this truly would be a dream come true."

That impressed her as well. She could only imagine the pride of coming back to head the school he'd graduated from. "So, how do the wife and kids feel about your success?"

"I'll let you know when I get them," he replied.

She hated that that made her insides smile. No family? Maybe . . . *No,* she told herself. She refused to go down that road again.

Luckily, Matthew launched into a full-scale update on his life, then began asking her more questions.

Before Lauren knew it, the waiters were giving her the evil eye because she and Matthew were the last ones in the restaurant.

"Oh my goodness. I didn't realize we've been here all this time," Lauren said.

"That's because we just fell back in a natural groove." He seemed pleased that a few hours had flown by without them noticing it. "You remember how time used to just pass by and we didn't even realize it?"

Oh, boy, did she remember. It was one of his biggest gripes about their relationship. He had started limiting their time together because he claimed he wasn't productive when they were seeing each other. She'd even tried to get them to study together, but they would always end up distracted. After he got a C in a class, he quickly put an end to that.

"We need to do this again." Matthew nodded matter-of-factly. "Real soon. I've enjoyed this, Lauren. And if I'm being honest, I'd love to do this again."

Lauren smiled but made no promises. No thanks; it had taken years to get over this man.

He stood awkwardly before finally saying, "Well?"

"Well, what?"

"Your number? How are we supposed to do this again if I don't have a way to get in contact with you?"

He had an expression across his face like he'd expected her to jump at the opportunity.

"Umm . . ." she said, weighing whether she wanted to travel back down the path of the past.

"It's only for hanging out, Lauren," he said when he noticed her reluctance. But then a wide smile crossed his face. "Don't worry. I'll wait until date number three before I start talking marriage."

That made her relax some. Matthew might be ready to settle down, but she wasn't. Nor would she ever be the marrying kind, and she didn't see what Matthew could ever say to change that.

"What's your number?" she said, pulling out her cell phone. "I'll call and you can lock me in."

His smile was his stamp of approval.

twenty-two

"Come on, Mrs. Joyce. When are you going to give an old man a chance? I might not have any get up and go, but my get up can still go."

Joyce Robinson shook her head at the decrepit old man standing in front of her. Ernest Berry had tried everything he could to get a millisecond of her time. Sometimes she humored him, most times she didn't. A man was the last thing on her mind. Especially a seventy-year-old pencil-thin skeleton like Ernest.

"I keep telling you, Ernest," she said, "I'm not messing with you."

"Why not?" he replied, pulling up a chair next to hers like he had a personal invitation. They were all seated in the recreation area of the Evergreen Center, the treatment facility Joyce had called home for the past six months.

Joyce hated it here. But she'd fallen victim to the disease that had claimed her mother, and Joyce's children thought the nationally known Evergreen Center would help her beat brain cancer.

Joyce wasn't optimistic. After her mother died, Joyce had learned that a genetic strain had led to her mother's brain cancer, and she had waited for it to claim her, too. But after years with no issues, she thought she'd be fine. Until a year ago, when excruciating migraines had revealed that she, too, had the deadly disease.

Joyce had been ready to just let the cancer claim her. After all, she hadn't really lived since her husband had died; she'd become a recluse. But Lauren and Julian wouldn't have it. They insisted that she come to this facility, where they were optimistic that she could beat cancer.

"Pretty lady like you shouldn't always walk around with a snarl on your face," Ernest said, flashing a wide, toothless grin. "Why won't you give me a chance? I bet I could keep a smile on your face."

"I told you, I'm not fooling with you because men ain't sh—"

"Hey, hey." The orderly sitting in the corner of the rec room where they were gathered for socialization hour quickly cut her off. "Mrs. Joyce, I told you about the foul language."

She rolled her eyes at him, too. She was a grown woman. She couldn't stand being told what she could and couldn't say. Just another reason why she hated this place.

"You have never had a man like me," Ernest said, ignoring the orderly.

Ernest always tried too hard. Back in his prime, she imagined Ernest might have been something to look at, but now the few teeth he had left were yellow and decayed. The chemo from his prostate cancer had left him with only splotches of coarse gray hair, reminding her of Grady from *Sanford & Son*, and he slobbered when he ate his Jell-O. There was nothing at all attractive about that. He was in his final stages of cancer. She guessed his family had stuck him there so they wouldn't have to be bothered with him.

"You know she's waiting on Vernon's ghost," her friend Pearl said. And Joyce used the term *friend* lightly.

Pearl was a friend by default. She was the only other person in this place with half a brain. So, she was the only one Joyce gave her time to.

"Pearl, don't start," she said.

"You can deny it all you want." Pearl giggled. "You won't give another man the time of day because no other man is Vernon Robinson."

Joyce suddenly regretted the few times she'd talked about Vernon. Of course, she tried to share the negative stuff, but Pearl had seen right through that and called her on it. She'd said that it wasn't possible to hate someone in the way Joyce claimed to hate Vernon if love wasn't at the root.

She was right about that. Joyce could deny it all she wanted, but she loved Vernon to her core.

"What happened to your husband anyway?" Ernest asked, leaning back and crossing his long, bony legs like she was really about to share her business with him.

"None of your business," Joyce replied.

"Tell us. We want to hear it. You're always so secretive," another woman, named Wanda, said.

"That's 'cause I don't like folks all in my business." She motioned toward the card table. "Now, are you going to play your card or what?"

They had been playing bid whist. Something old folks did, so she wasn't really enjoying it, but it beat being holed up in her room, which is where she spent the bulk of her time when she wasn't in treatment.

"I'm just saying, you know all about me and my Walter," Wanda said.

"Everybody knows about you and Walter because you tell everyone from the janitor to the owner of the facility," Joyce snapped.

Pearl cackled. Wanda looked offended, but Joyce didn't really care.

"Well, I want everyone to know what kind of low-down, dirty dog he is," Wanda said.

"Wanda will never get over that man leaving her for a younger woman," Pearl said.

"She ain't that much younger. What he gonna do with a fifty-year-old alley cat anyway?" Wanda mumbled.

"Obviously, what he ain't doing with you," Ernest laughed.

"Oh, shut up, you old snaggle-tooth bird," Wanda snapped.

"Will somebody just play?" Joyce said, cutting them off.

This place made her feel so old, and at sixty-three, she didn't consider herself elderly. Half the time, if folks weren't wandering around like they were waiting on death to come take them off the rolls, they were sickly and depressing. She just wanted to get better, beat this stupid cancer, so she could go live with Julian. As soon as she was better, she fully intended to convince her son how good she would be for his family. She could be a built-in babysitter for the twins.

"On a serious note, though, Mrs. Joyce," Wanda asked as she put her card on the table, "is your husband still living?"

That was a subject Joyce never wanted to broach and she definitely wasn't about to do it now with gossiping Wanda Ransom.

"Rumor has it he was a good-looking man," Wanda continued.

Joyce didn't know where Wanda was getting her rumors from, but she was right on the money about that. Those good looks had become Joyce's blessing and her curse.

Vernon Robinson might have been good-looking, but he dang sure wasn't good. Two weeks after her wedding—that was how long it took her to come to that realization.

Joyce's mind traveled back to when she caught Vernon with Alicia, the intern.

"It's your play, woman!"

Joyce snapped out of her thoughts as Ernest tapped her arm. The whole table was watching her, as if they had been waiting on her to play for a while.

"Oh, sorry," she said, laying her card on the table. Thoughts of Vernon had a way of taking her away.

The chatter resumed and her mind went back to that day in his office with Alicia. Vernon had used his kisses to weasel his way out of many situations. She didn't know if she had spent all those years after that being oblivious because she *wanted* to believe his words, or because she knew that no matter what, he loved her in spite of all the hurt he'd caused her.

Joyce had never gotten the answer to that. And at this point, it seemed like she never would.

twenty-three

The sounds of Mary Mary filled the convertible BMW. Lauren had the music on full blast as she zipped down Interstate 40 heading toward Cary.

Today was one of those beautiful North Carolina days that made her love living in Raleigh. She'd thought about moving to Atlanta or, like her brother, across the country, but her mother was born and raised in the tri-state area, and despite how Joyce treated her, Lauren hadn't been able to leave her behind. She especially couldn't leave her now that her mother was battling brain cancer.

"*I luh God,*" Mary Mary sang.

Lauren didn't usually listen to gospel music, but anytime she had a visit with her mother, she needed all the help she could to summon up her strength. Her mother despised this "secular gospel," as she called it, so even though Lauren was thirty-four years old, listening to this music was her piece of quiet rebellion.

As much as she would like to stop visiting her mother, Lauren was all her mother had.

"You'd never know it, though," she muttered, not the way Joyce raved about her prince, Julian.

As if she'd summoned him up, Lauren's cell phone rang, and her brother's number popped up on the screen.

She reluctantly answered. "Hello?"

"Lauren? What's all that noise?" her brother yelled.

"Hold on." She turned the music down, then pushed her Bluetooth headset closer to her ear. "Yeah, what's going on?"

"I can't hear you. Do you have the top down?"

"Yes," she replied.

"How do you expect somebody to talk to you with all that wind?" he huffed.

"Ugh," she said. She slowed down in order to pull over to the side of the freeway. She wasn't supposed to talk while she was driving, anyway, she thought. Just to make Julian wait a little longer, she raised the top on her convertible. It yawned over her head with satisfying slowness. "There. Is that better?" she said once the top was up.

"Much," he said. "Where are you?"

"Where I am every Saturday?" she replied.

"Well, you're late. Mom has already called me, going off because you're not there."

Lauren took a deep breath and turned the gospel music back up a tad. "I'm not there because I'm on my way."

"I don't understand why you do this every week. You know how she gets about you being late. Is it so difficult for you to leave earlier?"

Lauren inhaled, summoning up her inner strength. Even though her mother was in a special-treatment facility, caring for her had been brutal. They'd discovered the tumor nine months ago after her mother passed out while at dinner with friends. She'd been rushed to the emergency room, where doctors found a grapefruit-size tumor. They all had been devastated to find out it was cancerous. Doctors were able to remove most of the tumor, but the cancer had spread, and now her mother endured chemo twice a week in an effort to beat the disease before it beat her.

Unfortunately, with Julian living so far away, Lauren had by herself carried the burden of her mother's hospitalization, subsequent recovery, and now treatment. But that didn't stop Julian from calling every single week to give his three cents.

"Julian, do not start with me, please," Lauren said. "At least I'm going."

"Well, if I lived there, I would go."

"But you don't live here."

"What?"

"You don't live here," she repeated. "And you refuse to bring Mama out there with you, although you know that's where she'd rather be."

Julian was currently serving in the army, stationed in Killeen, Texas, going on his twelfth year. At this point he was in it because he wanted to be. He could easily get out, get a normal job, and let their mother come live with him and his family.

"I've told you a hundred times. Rebecca does not have the patience to deal with Mom and the twins."

"Of course she doesn't. Your precious Rebecca can't be bothered with a decrepit old lady." Lauren rolled her eyes. Her twin nephews were three years old. If Rebecca didn't have motherhood down by now, she wasn't going to get it.

"Don't go there. You know I'm liable to get papers to go anywhere at any time. Plus, Mom's doctors are there. Her treatment is there. What kind of doctors do you think they have here?"

"Army doctors! Aren't they supposed to be the best?"

"You're being ridiculous, Lauren."

They were rehashing the same old recriminations. "Whatever, Julian. You just use that as an excuse to put the burden of caring for Mom on me."

"I'm not going to have this argument with you. I'm the one paying for her care. The least you can do is visit her."

Forget subjecting herself to her mother; Lauren didn't understand why she kept putting up with her self-righteous, do-nothing-but-send-a-check brother. Oh, and call her to make sure she showed up.

"What did you say?" Lauren asked, deciding she'd had enough. "I can't hear you."

"What do you mean, you can't hear me? You sound fine."

"Are you talking? Are you still there?" she said. "I'm losing you. I'm losing youuuuu . . ." Lauren picked up her phone, pressed the disconnect button, and tossed her phone back on the seat.

Her brother drove her almost as insane as her mother did. He was always trying to dictate things from eight hundred miles away. He was happily living his perfect little life, with his perfect little wife in Killeen. All she got from him these days was grief. Just like her mother.

Lauren pulled into the parking lot at the Evergreen Center. Lauren knew that her mother hated it here. But the facility where she received chemo was right next door, and Evergreen had a full-time staff to care for Joyce.

Lauren parked her car, took a deep breath, then mumbled, "Time to go face the devil," before getting out and heading inside to continue her penance.

twenty-four

Everyone thought Joyce was crazy, and sometimes she did a little dance with crazy, but she was very much in her right mind. Well, except for when she forgot things, which she seemed to be doing a lot of lately, thanks to the damn chemo. That's why she had balled up the letter she'd just received from the resident psychiatrist, urging her to set up an appointment to talk. Joyce had spent sixty-three years *not* talking about her business, and she wasn't about to start now.

As a little girl she had dreams of being the perfect wife. The perfect mother. And she thought she had her perfect life the day she said "I do." She just had no idea that perfect man would be at the center of all of her pain. Standing right next to him in the middle of that pain-filled circle was the woman strutting across the parking lot, heading in Joyce's direction.

She watched Lauren from the window of her room. Her daughter was the spitting image of her. From her chestnut brown, naturally curly hair, to her high cheekbones and caramel-hued skin. Even her toned body and curves were a direct replica of Joyce thirty years ago. Lauren was so much like her in some ways and so unlike her in others.

For starters, Joyce would have never betrayed her mother.

She'd fought hard to find her way back to a happy place, or at least a place of forgiveness. Some days were better than others. Every day was hard. And so far she hadn't been able to get in the same neighborhood as happy, let alone the same address. Even after more than fifteen years she hadn't been able to forgive her child for helping her husband break her heart.

She continued watching as Lauren opened the front door to the facility. She darted across the room and plopped back down into her chair, acting like she had been engrossed in a Lifetime movie about a cheating husband.

"Hello, Mother," Lauren said, walking into the room.

"Hi." She kept watching the TV.

Lauren set her purse down on the bed—some expensive, overpriced number Joyce was sure she had screwed some man to get.

"I hope we're going to have a good day," Lauren said.

Joyce finally turned to look at her. She gave that smile that said, "I'm here even though I don't want to be." On one hand, Joyce felt like telling her to stop visiting, since neither of them wanted her here. But on the other hand, Joyce wanted her daughter to suffer. Suffer like she had suffered. And if Joyce was completely honest with herself, sometimes she enjoyed having Lauren here. Sometimes she forgot about what her daughter did and relished her company. Sometimes, though the times were few and far between, Joyce had glimpses of when she used to truly love her child.

After graduating from college, Lauren had moved to Florida to work for a small marketing firm. She'd used the distance as an excuse for the distance between them. When she'd moved back to Raleigh eight years ago, Joyce thought maybe their relationship would get better. But if anything, seeing her made the bitterness grow.

Joyce felt a twinge of discomfort. She didn't have any other real visitors. Her sister-in-law, Velma, visited occasionally. Her son, her baby, her pride and joy, Julian, came when he could, but he was very busy with his job and his family. He was big-time in the military. Not to mention the fact that he lived hundreds of miles away. And since Joyce had never gotten around to having those five children she'd wanted, she had to settle for just her one girl as a visitor to this dump.

"What are you watching?" Lauren said.

Joyce shrugged. "Some movie on Lifetime."

"I don't know why you watch that depressing station," she said, sitting down.

"What else am I going to do in this godforsaken place?" Joyce cut eyes at her and she could feel Lauren take a short breath.

"Well, I was thinking today that I could take you out. Maybe we could go get some tea. I saw a nice little coffee shop on the way in. I think the name was the Coffee Grind."

"The health department said they had rat droppings."

"Okay," Lauren said, wincing as though from a blow. "Maybe we can find some other place."

For the first time Joyce fully noticed what she was wearing. "Why are you all dressed up?" she asked, taking in her sleek black pants and sheer blouse, which looked like they cost way more than she could afford on a jewelry designer's salary. "I know you didn't do all that for me."

She flashed a brittle smile. "Actually, I have a date when I leave here."

"Hmph. A date? With whom?"

"You don't know him, Mother."

Lauren didn't share much of her personal life. Never had. "So, any future with this one? I would like some grandkids before I die."

"You have grandkids," Lauren said wearily.

"I'd like some from you." Joyce had issues with her daughter, but she would've gladly taken her kids.

"Okay, can we not have this discussion?"

"It's the least you can do since you destroyed my life."

She huffed like she knew that was coming. "You know what," she stood, "I didn't come here to be berated by you."

"How is that berating you? Asking for grandkids?"

Lauren looked like she was fed up. That happened awfully fast. She usually lasted ten minutes before she got that way. "Mama, I don't understand why we can't have one good visit without you coming down on me, saying something smart, or sarcastic, or ugly."

Joyce shrugged nonchalantly. "I'm still trying to figure out how me asking for grandkids translates to all of this." Then Joyce did what she did best: put on her victim face. "I know we have our issues, but it's like everything I say, you just take offense and get all irritated with me."

Lauren's shoulders drooped, and an apologetic expression filled her face. "Okay, I'm sorry," she said. "Can we just start over?"

Joyce took a long look at her daughter. Start over? After the hell they'd been through, she didn't know how that would ever be possible. But she didn't feel like fighting, so she simply stood and said, "Fine, let's go get tea like a perfect mother and daughter."

twenty-five

Just once Lauren wanted to leave a visit with her mother not feeling stressed. Vivian said Lauren was a glutton for punishment for continuing these visits, and Lauren was starting to think that her friend was right.

"There's no way I could let that woman torture me like she does you," Vivian had told her just last night.

But as much as Lauren wanted to turn her back, she simply couldn't. The woman had loved her, taken care of her. Lauren hadn't taken sides with her father, not really, despite what her mother said.

When she'd moved home after working in Miami—a place she didn't really care for because it was too fast for her taste—Lauren had hoped that she and her mother could rebuild their relationship. Save the occasional "how's school?" phone calls, they had been estranged for years.

Lauren's father had left her some money, which she'd gotten on her twenty-eighth birthday, and her mother had even resented that. Lauren had resolved that her mother was just happy wallowing in bitterness.

Lauren decided to push aside thoughts of her mother as she continued to navigate the hilly terrain leading back into Raleigh. Her favorite Jill Scott anthem came on and she pumped up the volume. She was completely into the lyrics when the music was interrupted by the navigation system on her car alerting her to an incoming call. Lauren smiled when she saw Lewis's number.

Lewis Cole was an investment banker who loved flying her to places like Rome, Paris, or Fiji—when he could pull himself away from his overbearing wife.

She pushed the ACCEPT button. "Hello?" she sang.

"Hey, sexy." His bass-filled voice boomed through the car's intercom system. "How are you today?"

"Fabulous as always. Better now that I'm hearing from you, Daddy," Lauren purred. That was one of the tricks she learned from the women who stroked her father's ego. For some reason, that got men going. So she made it her mission to always stroke their ego. "But I would be doing a lot better if you were driving me down this hillside."

Lewis was a powerful man who enjoyed being in a position to do things for her. So she made him feel like she was a lot more helpless than she really was.

"Whoo. I wish I was there, too, honey. And later, I want to hear all the things you would do for me if I were. But I'm running into this meeting. I saw that you called me earlier, and since you don't normally call, I was just checking to see what's up."

She envisioned him multitasking as he talked to her.

"Yes, I called." Lauren's voice was dripping with sweetness. "I just wanted to remind you what today is."

He paused, like he was thinking. "Am I supposed to be doing something for you?"

"No, babe. Umm, it's your anniversary."

"Doggone it," he huffed. "I told Emily to remind me of that."

Lauren knew that his incompetent secretary would forget,

which is why she made it her business to remember. That just made him more indebted to her. "Saks just got a new line of Christian Louboutin nude shoes in. You should get her that."

"Great, I'll call right now."

Lauren was confident that when Lewis called Saks to order the shoes for his wife, he'd place an extra order for her, too.

"You know, you are something else," Lewis said, sounding relieved. "I tell you. Not many women would keep track of another woman's anniversary like that."

"I just want you to have a happy home so that when you come to see me, you have no worries," she cooed.

"And that's why I'm going to keep coming to see you. Hold on a second." He bellowed for Emily.

"You're an important man who is stressed enough as it is," Lauren said once he came back on the line. "You don't need extra stress at home."

"I don't know what I would do without you," he said. She could hear the adoration in his voice.

Oh, her gift was as good as on its way.

"Okay. I gotta go. I'll talk to you soon," Lewis said.

"Bye, sweetie. See you soon."

Lauren hung up the phone. She smiled, but noticed that she wasn't as satisfied as she normally was when she got something from a man. She couldn't find the word to describe what she was feeling inside.

As she drove a little more, the word came to her. *Unfulfilled.* She felt unfulfilled. Suddenly, she felt an overwhelming desire to call Matthew.

"That's not good," she mumbled to herself—even as she picked up the phone to dial his number.

twenty-six

I want to see you."

Those were the first words Matthew uttered after "Hello."

They made Lauren both smile and frown at the same time. She both loved and hated that she was drawn back to Matthew so.

Yet when he asked her to meet him on campus, she hadn't hesitated. Sybrina Fulton, the mother of Trayvon Martin—a black teenager killed by a man who thought he looked suspicious—was speaking on campus, and Matthew thought she'd enjoy the lecture. Lauren wasn't into socially conscious issues like she should be, but that case had fascinated her—especially after the man who killed Trayvon was found not guilty—so she thought it would be interesting to hear his mother speak.

Matthew directed her to meet him in his office in the administration building. He arranged for her to park right in front, and as she stepped out of her car, a wide smile spread across her face.

Coming here brought back so many memories. The statue of Harriet Tubman rose in the middle of the campus across from the admin building. Her heart warmed as she remembered meeting Matthew at that very spot. That was where he'd dried her tears after she'd been crying because Jerome Wilson had broken up with her.

"It's not you. It's me," Jerome had said that gloomy October day.

Lauren had fought back tears, not wanting the students who passed by to see her crying. Jerome had been her first, and she'd hoped they would be together forever. But after a couple of rolls in the sack, he was ready to move on.

"I don't believe you're doing this to me," Lauren told him.

"Dang, stop acting like a little girl," Jerome snapped.

Just then Matthew moved in. Lauren didn't know him. She'd seen him a couple of times around campus, knew he was an upperclassman, but they'd never met because she had devoted all of her time to school—and Jerome.

"Hey, Lauren, what's up?" Matthew had said, planting himself in the middle of their conversation.

Lauren looked confused. Matthew continued playing it cool, ignoring Jerome's scowl as he kept his eyes fixed on Lauren.

"So, I hear you're single now," he said with a sexy smile. "You know, I've been trying to get with you since you got on campus."

Lauren didn't know what to say, but Jerome didn't give her a chance. "Yo, dude, for real?"

Matthew towered over Jerome—both in height by four inches, and weight by forty pounds—so Lauren didn't think Jerome would try to jump bad.

"So, are you free now?" Matthew had said, continuing to ignore him. "We can go grab something to eat, then go see the new John Singleton movie."

"Man, you're trying to get jacked up," Jerome said, taking a step toward him.

Finally, Matthew turned around, looked past him like he was looking for someone, then said, "By who?"

Lauren figured now would be a good time to say something, since Matthew's height and weight didn't seem to be intimidating Jerome.

"Um, I'm okay," she said, putting a hand between the guys.

Matthew turned back to her. "Not yet. But you will be. Dude tryin' to dump you right out here in public, in front of everyone." He motioned around to the people standing around staring.

"This ain't got nothin' to do with you," Jerome said.

Matthew waved him off. "Come on, let's go. You don't need this. Or him."

Before Lauren could protest, Matthew had taken her hand and pulled her away, leaving Jerome standing next to Harriet Tubman, embarrassed and humiliated.

"Sorry about that," Matthew said once they were on the other side of campus. "I can't stand to see a guy treat a girl like that."

"Thank you," Lauren managed to say. "Thanks a lot, umm . . ."

"Matthew. Matthew King."

She and Matthew had become the best of friends after that.

The memory warmed her heart as she made her way into the administration building. Matthew had texted her that he was still in a meeting and to come on up. His secretary was waiting and led her back to his office. "He'll be with you in just a few minutes," the classy gray-haired lady said.

"Thank you." Lauren took a seat on the sofa in his office. While she waited, she took in the surroundings. The wall was covered with his degrees, awards, and framed photos of him with notables like President Barack Obama, Spike Lee, and Maya Angelou. Lauren was definitely impressed. She didn't want to appear too nosy, but she leaned over to check out the photos on his desk. She had to make sure he didn't have any pretty young women on display.

There were none, but Lauren couldn't help thinking, as she gazed at a picture of Matthew accepting a medal at what looked like a marathon, that there had to be pretty young women in Matthew's life. He was too fine for there not to be.

"Who is she?"

Lauren's thoughts drifted back to one of her last conversations with Matthew before they broke up.

"For the one hundredth time, she's just a friend," he claimed.

"You must think I'm stupid," she had said, realizing she was echoing her mother's words. "That's it. You think I'm stupid."

"I think you're overreacting," Matthew snapped. "I'm up here, trying to get my master's, minding my business."

"Letting tricks answer your phone," she added.

Matthew sighed. "She's not a trick. She's a friend. And I didn't *let* her answer. She thought she was doing me a favor by answering because I was outside taking the garbage out."

"Which was it, taking the garbage out or talking to a neighbor, because the first time you said you were talking to a neighbor!"

"I was talking to a neighbor while I was taking the garbage out!" he yelled.

Lauren had rolled her eyes. He sounded so like her father, couldn't even keep track of his lies.

"I'm not doing this with you," Matthew said. "This is ridiculous."

"I'll call her myself and ask her are y'all messing around."

"You do that," Matthew said, then rattled off her number. "And when you get done talking to her, don't bother calling me back."

He'd slammed the phone down, and when she'd tried to call him back, she got a busy signal all evening.

Lauren had never called the girl. After she simmered down, she told herself that was something her mother would've done—accosted the other woman. And not only was she not about to become that chick, but this conversation told her she needed to change her approach to men altogether.

"Hello," Matthew said, snapping her out of her thoughts. "What are you thinking about that put such a scowl on your face?"

Lauren had to push back the anger she hadn't realized was still simmering after all those years.

"Hey," she said, standing and giving him a halfhearted hug. He was being so friendly, just as he had been so friendly all those years ago—to her and everybody else.

"Are you okay?" he asked.

"Yeah, but umm, I just, umm, I just realized I have an order that needs to be completed by tomorrow. So I'm not going to be able to go to the lecture."

He looked surprised. "Oh, wow. You can't spare a couple of hours?"

"Not really," she said, heading to the door. "I just wanted to tell you that. Maybe we can hook up another time. Thanks for the invite."

Lauren hurried out the door, leaving Matthew bewildered.

twenty-seven

When it came to creating, Lauren put her full heart into it. Whether she was creating the perfect cover-up story, creating the perfect atmosphere to make a man happy, or in this case— creating the perfect piece of jewelry.

"That is so nice," Vivian said, running her fingers along the oversize marble pieces.

"You like it?" Lauren held the intricate necklace up to her neck. Pink and green alternated, with a splash of marigold.

"Yeah, it's gorgeous," Vivian replied. "You don't see those colors together a lot."

Lauren laid the necklace back down on her kitchen table, where she did most of her custom jewelry designing. Her eye for a beautiful stone had led to her custom pieces and a comfortable career.

"You must not have had sororities on your college campus," Lauren said.

A forlorn expression swept over Vivian's face. "No, I didn't go to college. I got married right out of high school. After I spent the first five years trying to get pregnant, I spent the rest of the time trying to be the best mother and wife possible."

Lauren didn't know how to respond to that. She never understood women who devoted their lives to a man. When that man left them, they often ended up right where Vivian was—alone, unskilled, and working for pennies in retail.

"Well, this piece is exclusively for one of my clients," Lauren said, not feeding into Vivian's suddenly somber mood. "She's presenting it to her mother to celebrate fifty years in her sorority."

"Were you in a sorority?" Vivian asked.

Lauren gently packed the necklace into a suede-lined box. "Naw. That wasn't my thing. I'm a loner, I'm afraid. I don't play well with others."

"Was that because you were always stealing their men?" Vivian tried to laugh like she was making a joke. Lauren gave her the side eye because she didn't see anything funny.

"Girl, I'm just playing," Vivian said once she noticed Lauren's sour face. "I didn't mean anything by it."

Lauren let the issue drop. She wasn't going to let Vivian spoil her mood. Matthew had called and all but demanded that she meet him for breakfast this morning. She had expected him to be a little salty about her bailing on the lecture yesterday, but he didn't even bring it up. He'd cracked jokes, made her laugh, and put her at ease. He always made her laugh. By the time breakfast was over, Lauren found herself promising to stop focusing on the negativity from the past and remember only the good times they'd had.

"But seriously," Vivian continued, like she was trying to clean the situation up, "you just like keeping to yourself?"

"I prefer to keep my circle tight, let's put it that way," Lauren replied.

"Then I guess I should be honored."

"You should." Lauren flashed a smile in her direction to let her know that all was well.

They were interrupted when Lauren's cell phone rang.

"Oh, I have to take this," Lauren said when she noticed her mother's doctor's office number appear on the caller ID.

"I'm gonna run use your bathroom," Vivian whispered as she stood and motioned toward Lauren's bedroom. Lauren started to tell her to use the guest bathroom, since she didn't like people in her personal space. Instead, she just nodded and answered the phone.

"Hello, this is Lauren."

"Hi, Lauren, this is Sonya with Dr. Rodriguez's office. I have him on the line."

"Okay," Lauren said, easing down into a chair. She dreaded the doctor's calls because he never called with good news.

After a few seconds he came on the line. "Hi, Lauren."

"Hi, Doc."

Dr. Rodriguez was very thorough, but he was straightforward, so she knew he was going to skip all the formalities. "I just got your mother's test results back. Unfortunately, the cancer has returned."

Lauren let out a deep, wounded sigh. They'd been hoping that between the surgeries and radiation, their mother would go into remission.

"So, we're going to have to get more aggressive with her treatment."

"That radiation drains her," Lauren protested. She hated seeing her mother's vibrancy sucked away by the chemo treatments. She rubbed her temples, trying to process the bad news. How could the cancer come back? "Will this really help, Doc? It's like we keep doing this stuff and nothing works."

"All we can do is try. And if you're a praying family, pray."

Ha. That was a joke. The Robinson family hadn't seen any parts of prayer in a long time. They used to go to church all the time, but the women had driven her mother away from church . . . and the Lord. Lauren occasionally watched Joel Osteen on television, but that was the extent of her religious participation. Shoot, God would probably laugh at her and tune her out if she went to Him now.

"Look, I have to run," Dr. Rodriguez continued. "Just get your mother in my office before the end of the week. And, Lauren, I talked with the psychiatrist at the Evergreen Center, and she is very concerned about your mother's mental health."

That elicited another sigh. Her mother had been getting meaner over the years. Lauren chalked it up to old age, but Dr. Rodriguez blamed the tumor. Truthfully, Lauren thought her bad temper was a combination of both.

"Okay, I'll talk with her therapist," Lauren reluctantly said.

"Good. Get with Sonya, set up an appointment, and I'll see you next week." Abruptly she heard a click. That was bedside manner for you.

"Everything okay?" Vivian asked after Lauren hung up.

Lauren opened her mouth to speak, but her words caught in her throat. "Excuse me," she managed to say as she jumped up and ran into the bathroom.

Vivian was her friend, but Lauren wasn't ready for Vivian to see her crying, and right about now she needed a really good cry.

Lauren stood before her sink, staring at her reflection. She dabbed her eyes, trying to pull herself together. Her grandmother had died of cancer, so Lauren should be prepared for the possibilities. But nothing could ever really prepare some-one for a relative living with cancer.

"You okay?" Vivian asked, tapping on the bathroom door.

"Yeah, yeah. I'm fine. Be out in a sec," she called out.

She was grateful when she heard Vivian walk off. Lauren dashed some water on her face. She didn't know how in the world she was supposed to be strong when it seemed like her mother's death was inevitable.

Lauren was about to head back out into the living room when the phone rang again. Julian's number flashed across the screen, and she contemplated not answering. Finally, she pressed the ACCEPT button.

"Hello?"

"Hey, did the doctor call you?"

She was grateful that her brother's tone was soft because she couldn't take anything other than a sympathetic ear right now.

"Yeah."

"So what now?"

She leaned against the sink. "I don't know. All that treat-ment and we're back to square one."

"We just have to remain optimistic. Thankfully, she's al-ready in the facility and they can just boost up her treatment." This must've really been taking a toll on Julian because he sounded more exasperated than she'd heard him sound in years.

"When are you going to go tell her?"

That made her close her eyes and inhale. She was about to ask, why didn't he fly out here and tell her himself, when she heard yelling in the background.

"Who is that, Julian?" the voice screamed.

"Hold on, Lauren," he snapped. His tone caught her off guard because he'd gone from demanding to angry. "It's my sister, Rebecca. Can I talk to my sister about my sick mother, please?"

An exchange of heated words passed that Lauren couldn't make out. She was surprised, because the few times she'd met her sister-in-law, Rebecca had seemed meek and timid.

"Sorry," Julian said, coming back to the phone. "Rebecca is having a hard time with the twins and stressing out . . . But anyway."

Lauren wanted to ask her brother if he wanted to talk about the problem since she'd never heard Rebecca go off like that, but given the way he quickly changed the subject—and the fact that he never talked about his personal life—Lauren knew such an effort would be futile.

"Just tell Mom we're going to continue trying to get her the best treatment. The therapist there also thinks she should get into some psychological treatments, so if you can mention we want her to do that as well."

Lauren sighed as her brother continued rattling off his to-do list.

As he talked, she couldn't help but wish that she had heeded his warning when he left for the army: *If I were you, I'd finish school, move far, far away, and put North Carolina in my rearview mirror.*

Unfortunately, it was too late now.

twenty-eight

Lauren had had a sleepless night. Today she had to go break the news to her mother that the cancer was back. On the list of things she wanted to do, this fell right below a root canal.

She was irritated with her brother's call. Julian could direct her on what to do but didn't have to help his mother's sadness. Thankfully, Matthew knew that she was having a hard time and so he met her for lunch.

"What can I do to make you smile?" he said.

"You're doing it, just by having me here." That was the truth. In fact, she had smiled more in these last two weeks than she had in months.

"I find it hard to believe that nothing has gotten better between you and your mother since college."

Lauren shook her head. "I've tried. Lord knows I've tried, but you can't make someone love you."

"I'm sure your mother loves you."

Lauren had never shared the real reason she and her mother were so at odds. She'd never shared it because it sounded so foolish that a mother would harbor any animosity because of her father's infidelities.

"Everyone wasn't meant to have a loving family like yours, I guess."

"What kind of mother would you like to be?"

She laughed. "A godmother."

That made him laugh as well. "So, you still don't want children?"

She shook her head.

"I think if you meet the right man—or realize that you've met the right man," he corrected with a smile, "you'll change your mind. There's a nurturing part of you that I think will enjoy motherhood."

Lauren didn't answer. She would hold out for some guarantees that she wouldn't have a dysfunctional relationship.

Lauren was about to comment when she looked up to see Craig and his wife walking toward her. Her eyes met Craig's and he immediately tried to beeline. But it was too late. His wife had spotted them.

"Hello. Lauren, isn't it?" she said, approaching their table.

Lauren nodded.

"I'm Dana, Craig's wife. You do remember Craig, right? You helped him get the spa deal and bracelet that I've yet to get."

Lauren couldn't tell where she was going, but she did know she wanted it to end, tout de suite. "Hello to both of you. This is my friend Matthew, and we were in the middle of something, so it was good seeing you."

"Hey, all right, it was good seeing you, too," Craig quickly interjected, trying to pull Dana away.

"Naw, I wanna ask her a few questions," Dana said, her voice filled with attitude.

"Would you come on?" Craig said, dragging her off.

"What was that about?" Matthew asked.

Lauren sighed. "He was one of my clients. He bought some jewelry from me and his crazy wife thinks something is going on."

"Ha, as if you'd mess with someone's husband," Matthew said. "Miss Goody Two-Shoes."

Lauren shifted uncomfortably. "Well, I need to get going and go have this conversation with my mother."

"Are you sure you don't want me to come with you?" Matthew had offered on the phone and when they'd first sat down for lunch. What she wouldn't give to have him join her. But she hadn't let him meet her mother in all the time they were dating. She wasn't about to start now.

"Nah, I'm good. I'll call you later."

She stood and before she could give him a friendly hug, their lips met, right in the middle of the restaurant.

"Oh, wow," she said.

"I've been waiting to do that."

She smiled, then surprised herself when she said, "I'm glad you did."

"Call me when you leave. No, come by when you leave."

Lauren pushed back the feeling that had been having her flip-flopping since she'd reconnected with Matthew. Why was she fighting anyway? "I think I'll take you up on that offer. Just have me a good stiff drink ready. I'll need it."

As Lauren approached her mother, she was greeted by an incongruous sight. She was sitting with some old man. It was funny because someone passing by might think they were an old married couple. Of course, as far as Lauren knew, her mother hadn't given a man the time of day since her father died. So that picturesque view of the two of them talking and laughing was purely a mirage.

"Hey, pretty lady," the old man said, noticing her first.

"Hi. Ernie, right?"

"Ernest." He stood and shook Lauren's hand. "Just trying to keep your mother entertained."

"You're not entertaining me."

"She tries to play hard, but I know she's feeling me."

That made Lauren laugh. "She's feeling you?"

"Yep, the race is not won by the swift but the steady. Or something like that." He flashed a cheesy grin. His demeanor immediately put Lauren at ease. Maybe Ernest's companionship was good for her mother.

"What is that supposed to mean?" Joyce asked. "What race?"

Ernest just blew her a theatrical kiss as he walked away.

"So, what's going on with that?" Lauren asked once he was gone.

"Absolutely nothing," her mother said, shutting down. "And what are you doing here on a Friday?"

"I can't come see you at random times?"

"You don't."

"I wonder why," Lauren mumbled. She contemplated working into the subject she'd come about, but then decided the sooner she got the news out, the sooner she could leave. "Look. I came because I talked with Dr. Rodriguez."

"And let me guess, he gave me a clean bill of health and I can go home today?"

"Not quite, Mama."

Their eyes locked in a glare. "Then, anything else, I don't want to hear," Joyce said.

Lauren sat down across from her mother. The pain behind her mother's eyes was heartbreaking, and despite everything Lauren understood her unhappiness. How much could one woman be forced to endure?

Lauren began relaying the devastating news.

twenty-nine

Joyce really didn't know why she needed to be here. She hated these silly sessions. Her mother had always told her, "Keep your business to yourself. You don't tell anybody but God."

That's the motto she'd lived by all of her life. Her husband's sister, Velma, was the only one who knew the true hell she'd been through. And she only knew because she was a witness to most of it.

Nope, Joyce didn't believe in sharing her dirt. So, why her children thought she needed to come talk to some quack about her problems now was beyond her.

The cancer was back. With a vengeance. She was going to die. Nothing else mattered. If they couldn't heal her body, what was the point of healing her mind?

"So, Mrs. Robinson, how are you feeling today?" the therapist asked, greeting Joyce inside the doorway to her office. She was petite, with cat-eye glasses and a mushroom haircut that didn't fit her tiny face. Her plant-looking hair appeared to be sitting on her head, trying to swallow it up. So it aggravated Joyce not only that she had to sit here and pretend to open up, but that she had to do so looking at this woman, who was looking a hot mess.

"I'm doing the same way I was doing two days ago," she snapped.

"Did you do any of the exercises I gave you?" She motioned for Joyce to take a seat. On their first meeting, she'd given her homework like she was an eighth grader.

"Umm, nope. So sorry. I've just been so busy. You know I keep a full calendar around here." Joyce didn't bother hiding her sarcasm as she plopped down on the chaise. She was too old for this therapist mess. Even if she was one of those Chatty Pattys who told people all her business, how would it have any impact?

The therapist—Joyce didn't remember her name—didn't seem fazed by her sarcasm. She sat down across from Joyce, crossing her legs primly as she opened up her notepad.

"So, as I told you last week, today I really want to talk to you about your family, your husband, your children," she began. Joyce didn't know if she was used to reluctant patients or what, but she showed no reaction to the way Joyce was acting.

"I don't understand why we have to keep rehashing this," Joyce said wearily, although she did stretch her legs out on the chaise. If she had to be here, she might as well get comfortable. Maybe she could even nod off.

"We're all concerned about your state of mind."

"My husband cheated on me from the day he said 'I do.' My daughter betrayed me by keeping his secret, to the point of killing him. And my son is too busy to be bothered with me. That's my story. The end. Can I go now? The Home Shopping Network is having a sale. Oh, wait. I can't do that either because I'm broke. Just give me some morphine and take me out," Joyce quipped.

Again, the good doctor didn't react to the rant. She simply said, "You seem to focus a lot on the bad stuff."

Joyce shrugged. "That's all there is."

"I doubt that," she said soothingly. "How long were you married?"

"Twenty-four years."

"Well, those years couldn't have been all bad."

Joyce weighed that statement. She was right. They weren't all bad, just mostly. But Joyce had stayed because she thought he would change.

"You didn't fall in love with a bad man, did you?"

That made Joyce smile against her will. She was right about that. She had a flashback to some of their happier times.

"Do you mind sharing what you're thinking about?" the therapist asked.

Joyce turned her attention back to her mousy inquisitor. "Sorry, I was thinking about that awesome applesauce they have lined up for dinner today."

The therapist let out a disgusted sigh, which Joyce was sure had to be against the shrink code of ethics.

"Let's get started," she said, returning to her usual chirpy brightness. "So, the last time we were here, you ran off the list of women that your husband had cheated with, or with whom you at least thought something inappropriate was going on." She flipped the page on her legal notepad. "I think you said you have seventeen on your list."

"Those are just the ones I know about. I'm sure it was triple that, given all of those I don't know."

The therapist went back to her original page. "So then the question begs to be asked, why did you stay?"

Joyce didn't answer.

"Joyce, I don't know why you keep tuning me out, but we're not going to make progress if you don't open up," the therapist said. "You have to talk about Vernon."

"I don't want to talk about him," she finally said, shaking away her memories.

The therapist let out a sigh, then said, "Okay, let's talk about Lauren."

"I don't want to talk about her, either."

"Joyce, you're not well. And we believe in healing the whole person. The mind and body go hand in hand. I'm very concerned about your psyche."

"My psyche is just fine. I'm bitter and I have every right to be."

There, she couldn't be more plain about how she felt.

"Fine. What do you want to talk about then?" the therapist asked.

"Since you want to talk about my family, let's talk about Julian." Just saying her son's name made her smile. Yes, it hurt that he didn't want to be bothered with her, but in a way, she understood. He had an important job and a family.

"Your relationship with Julian is fine," she said. "It's your relationship with your daughter that I'm concerned about. You have some issues that you really need to address to help you both heal. We have to do this before . . ."

Before I die? Joyce wanted to snap. The therapist let her words trail off, but Joyce knew that that was why she was here. This was supposed to be a state-of-the-art facility, but she'd seen too many people die. It's like they sent anyone over sixty and battling a disease here to wait on death.

"I'm trying to help you," she said, her tone even as if she was trying to put Joyce at ease.

"You tell me how I'm supposed to get over betrayal from a child I brought into this world?" She sat up. "You know what?

Don't tell me because there is nothing that you can say to me. The only reason I tolerate her now is so that she can constantly be reminded of the pain she put me through."

"You don't mean that."

"Don't tell me what I mean." She folded her arms across her chest and glared.

"You don't," the therapist said. The calmness of her voice was pissing Joyce off.

"You may not be ready yet," the therapist continued, "but we have to address it. You may not know this, but I'm honest with my patients. You're on a downward spiral. Cancer is . . ."

Joyce covered her ears like a two-year-old. She hated when they brought up the C-word. If cancer was gonna take her, she just wished it would show up in the middle of the night and do it, the end.

"I'm stressed, I've had a hard life, now my body is all jacked up on the inside, and I'm pissed. That's what's wrong with me," Joyce retorted.

"Just because you don't face unpleasant truths doesn't mean they go away," the therapist said as she closed her notebook. "I think you know that. But I'll let you go for today. I need you to understand, though, I'm not releasing you from the sessions until I see a breakthrough."

Joyce swung her legs off the chaise and onto the floor, then stood up. She guessed they would be doing these sessions until the day she died because when it came to her daughter, there would never be a breakthrough.

"I'll see you next week," the therapist said as Joyce walked to the door.

Joyce silently cursed all the way back to her room.

thirty

Lauren had known Vivian Harold less than a year, since they met in a hot yoga class. But the two had instantly connected and had become extremely close — closer than Lauren had been to any woman since high school. That's why Lauren looked forward to their twice-a-month happy-hour outings.

Vivian was divorced. She didn't like to talk about her ex much, but she didn't seem bitter, which was surprising since she'd lost custody of her son in the divorce. Vivian said that losing her son had torn out her soul and sent her into a deep depression for over a year. But she said she was doing better and now trying to focus on the positive: her ex was a lousy husband but a great dad.

Vivian had now embraced her single life. She did get to see her son every other weekend, so that gave her some joy. Lauren had never met him because Vivian was adamant that their time together was sacred.

"Sorry, girl," Vivian said as she returned to the table. "These margaritas are going straight through me."

They'd been sitting in the bar area at Saltgrass Steak House for the past hour. Vivian was on her third margarita.

"Pick up any new men while I was gone?" Vivian asked, sliding back into her seat.

"Ha-ha," Lauren replied. "No, I don't need any new men."

"Oh, that's right. Your roster is full." Vivian shook her head. "I don't know how you do it. So what's up for the weekend? Which one of your guys is up?"

"Believe it or not, I'm free. And the only one I want to spend time with is heading out of town."

"Oh yeah, Prince Matthew."

As Lauren laughed, her phone started vibrating. She picked it up, then smiled and turned the phone to show Vivian who was calling.

"We talked him up," Lauren said. She pushed the ACCEPT button. "Hello?"

"Hello, beautiful."

Matthew's voice had a way of warming her insides.

"What are you doing?" Matthew asked.

"Having drinks with my friend Vivian."

"I can't wait to meet her. The fact that a female managed to get close to you is mind-boggling," he replied.

"I know, right?" Lauren laughed and smiled in Vivian's direction. "She's cool. I like her a lot. You'll get to meet her at some point. What are you doing?"

"Leaving a meeting. Trying to see what your plans are for this evening. My flight was pushed back till tomorrow, so I won't be going out of town tonight. I was seeing if you wanted to go catch the old-school hip-hop concert with me."

"The one with LL Cool J and Doug E. Fresh at the PNC Center?" she said eagerly.

"Yep. That one. Front row, baby."

Lauren hadn't done anything like that in years. Despite her initial reaction, though, she started feeling a fluttering in her stomach. That sensation was growing every moment she spent with Matthew. He was so easy to love, and that, Lauren didn't want, especially because it had taken her so long to stop loving him.

"Ah, you know, I'd love to, but I have a full calendar this weekend. How about I give you a call later?"

His voice was filled with disappointment. "Oh, okay," he said. "You do that. Call me if anything changes."

Lauren ended the call and looked across the table at a shocked Vivian.

"I thought you said you didn't have anything to do this weekend."

"I don't."

Vivian looked confused. "I thought you said you liked him."

"I do." Lauren shook her head. "But he's single."

Vivian rolled her eyes. "That's the person you should be going out with."

Vivian didn't understand how complicated it was. "He's single and I have feelings for him. Shoot, I used to be madly in love with him. Maybe I *still* love him. Nope, not a good combo. I'm not about to get my heart broken."

Vivian swirled her finger around the rim of her glass. "Maybe that's what you need. A man of your own."

Lauren wasn't that crazy about all the free advice. "Well, my, aren't we the judgmental one?"

"I'm not trying to be judgmental. It's just that I watch you with all of these guys and you try to pretend that you're happy, but you're really not. And here's this guy that you already know, that you have feelings for, that has a good job with benefits, that is really feeling you. You want to push him away because he's not wearing a wedding ring. Do you hear how ridiculous that sounds?"

Lauren couldn't deny that to most people it did sound strange. "Sure, but . . ."

Vivian seized upon her hesitation. "I'm just saying, you should give Matthew a real shot. You and these married men, all you're doing is helping with the destruction of the black family."

"I date white and Latino guys, too," Lauren said, laughing.

Vivian didn't laugh with her. "It's not funny."

Lauren lost her smile, getting irritated with the remarks from someone who couldn't possibly know where she was coming from. The reason she and Vivian had gotten along was that Vivian didn't judge her. If that was about to change . . .

"Wow, who pissed on your parade?"

Vivian's look of anger quickly disappeared. "I just want you to get your own slice of happiness. That's all."

Lauren took out her credit card to pay for their drinks. Vivian had pissed her off and she was ready to wrap up this unhappy hour outing. "Well, don't worry about me. I'm good."

"Are you really?" Vivian asked. "Everyone gets tired of playing the field. I know you say you don't want to ever get married, but do you really want a lifetime of being second?"

Lauren didn't reply. She didn't want Vivian to know how much those words were cutting her.

thirty-one

Today was one of those rare days when Lauren got to lounge around the house and relax. She had broken down and called Matthew back to take him up on his offer to go to the concert. They'd ended up having the best time they'd had in years.

The two had been talking almost daily over the last three weeks. They'd fallen right back into their natural groove, and she loved that not once had he talked to her about sex. They'd had amazing sex in college, but she was so much more experienced now. She'd love the opportunity to show him that. At some point.

Everything inside her had wanted to invite Matthew back up to her place after the concert last night, but she knew that would be opening Pandora's box. She'd bowed out of a nightcap with the excuse that she had to finish a jewelry order for the Houston Women's League for seventy-five custom necklaces as gifts for their Mother's Day luncheon—an order that was actually finished two weeks ago.

That Women's League order should allow her to sit pretty for a while, since her pieces cost so much. So today she would be doing nothing but relaxing and getting caught up on her marathon of *Scandal*.

She'd already turned on "do not disturb" on her phone. The only numbers allowed to come through were from her favorites. She added Matthew to that list of two, which included Vivian and her mother's rehab, which technically wasn't a favorite but was a necessity.

The credits were rolling on the first episode of *Scandal* when her phone rang, which surprised her because she knew Matthew was on his flight to Hong Kong and Vivian had her weekend with her son. Her heart dropped when she saw the number for the Evergreen Center.

"Hello?"

"Yes, is this Ms. Robinson?" the woman said.

"It is."

"This is Sophia at the Evergreen Center."

"Yes," Lauren said with trepidation.

"We, umm . . . have a situation here. Your mother, well, she took a pretty bad fall."

"A fall?" Lauren's heart started racing. "What?"

"She's okay, but they are transporting her as a safety precaution."

"Okay. Transporting her where?" Of course her mother would find a way to mess up her serene day. Lauren shook off that thought. Her mother didn't know she had a day off, let alone conspired to destroy it.

"Well, where is she?" Lauren repeated.

"I just wanted to let you know that, again, she is okay, but that did spark cause for concern. She's at Duke Regional."

"Okay," Lauren said, throwing back the afghan and getting up. "I'll be there in about thirty minutes."

Exactly thirty-three minutes later, Lauren pulled into the

hospital, then whipped into a handicap parking space. She'd come move her car later, she thought, as she grabbed her purse and raced inside.

"Yes, I'm here to see Joyce Robinson," she said once she reached the nurse's station.

The woman tapped some keys on her keyboard. "Yes, she was just admitted. And you are?"

"I'm her daughter, Lauren. Is she okay?"

"Oh, yes." The nurse was one of the cold, efficient sorts. "Your mother is fine but you'll have to talk to the doctor about specifics. She's in Room 236."

Lauren raced down the hall to find her mother sitting up on the edge of the bed, arguing with the nurse who was trying to get her to lie down.

"Get your hands off of me, lady!" her mother cried.

"Mrs. Robinson, please. Calm down," the nurse said.

"Mom," Lauren said, poking her head in the door. Their eyes met and briefly they connected. But, just as quickly all recognition was gone.

"Mom?" her mother replied, a frown etched across her face. "I don't know you."

Lauren could tell by the expression on the nurse's face that she was confused. "I'm her daughter," Lauren told the nurse as she walked over to her mother. "It's okay, Mom. Just do what the nurse says."

Joyce snatched her arm away. "I don't have any daughters. I just have a son."

Even though she should've been used to the insults by now, it hurt Lauren to hear her mother deny her. Again. And it would be different if she could say for sure if it was the brain tumor.

"Yes, I'm your daughter," Lauren mustered up the strength to say. "Julian, my brother, your son, is out of town. I take care of you." Her words were slow and deliberate, as if speaking them slowly would make a difference.

"I don't need anybody to take care of me," her mother snapped. She turned to the nurse. "Get her out of here."

"Mom . . ."

"Why do you keep calling me that? Who are you? Why are you in here?" Joyce was getting more and more riled up.

The nurse finally stepped forward. "Ma'am, I'm trying to get her settled," she told Lauren. "This may be making it worse."

"I-I'm just trying to help." The realization that her mother wasn't faking tore at her heart.

"Leave me alone. Where's my husband?" Joyce demanded. "Vernon!" she started yelling. "Vernon! Where's Vernon? Tell him I'm in the hospital and to come get me out of here."

"Ma'am, I need you to calm down," the nurse said.

Lauren swallowed the lump in her throat. "Mama, Daddy isn't here."

"He's never here when I need him," she snapped. "Tell him I said get back here. I need him. I need him!" Joyce buried her face in her hands and sobbed.

Lauren wanted to cry, too. If she'd had any doubt about whether her mother was acting, it was gone now. She'd only seen her mother enter that state where she longed for her husband twice before. But each time was more painful than the last. And this time was no exception.

"Mama, you need to lie down and calm down so they can evaluate you, then we can get you out of here. This—"

Before Lauren could finish her sentence, her mother lurched upward and slapped her hard across the face. The blow was stinging and brought even more tears to Lauren's eyes. Her mother hadn't hit her in years, but that blow packed an emotional and physical punch.

"I told you. Stop calling me 'mama'! I would never have a daughter that dresses like a whore." She looked at Lauren's tight jumpsuit in disgust.

The nurse stepped up. Her voice was gentle as she said, "I'm sorry, it might be best if you left."

Lauren glared at her mother as she fought back the tears. *Gladly*, she thought. Sick or not, she was leaving, and the way Lauren was feeling, she doubted she would ever be back.

thirty-two

Years ago, Lauren swore that her mother would no longer make her cry, and for the most part, she had held true to that promise. But on the way home, her emotions were betraying her. She couldn't hold back the river of tears. This visit had drained the life from her.

Lauren had asked the doctor what caused her mother's meltdown, but no one could tell her anything. She hadn't stuck around to find out why her mother had passed out.

Lauren usually bore the brunt of her mother's fiery temper. But today the vitriol was on a whole other level. Despite her love for her mother, Lauren could take only so much.

As she was driving, Lauren could no longer control the waterworks. Then she saw her brother's phone number pop up on her caller ID. She quickly pushed DECLINE. Julian called back two more times and then sent a text:

I know you're sending me to voice mail. Answer the phone.

Although Lauren had no desire to speak to him, she pulled over to the side of the road so that she wasn't driving down the freeway screaming at her brother. And she had no doubt that this conversation would end in a screaming match.

"What do you want?" she said when he picked up.

"What the hell did you do?" he yelled at her.

How typical, to blame her. "Look, Julian, don't start with me."

"What happened today? Mama is hysterical. The nurse called me. They can't calm her down. You got her worked up, then didn't bother to stick around."

"You know what?" Lauren yelled right back. "I'm taking a page from your book. Not bothering to stick around."

"Don't go there with me."

"No, you know what, Julian? Let's go there. I'm tired. This woman hates me. She's hated me for years and I have put up with it. I have endured. Meanwhile, you use the distance as an excuse to distance yourself from us."

"What would you suggest I do, Lauren?" Julian huffed.

"Be there for her. Come see her. Hell, move her there with you. She hates me and she doesn't hesitate to let it be known. I'm sick and tired of it!"

"Our mother is sick, Lauren. Cut her some slack."

"You don't think I know that?" Lauren cried, the tears flowing full stream now. "I see the disease literally sucking the life from her. I see the sadness in her eyes. And I put on a brave front even though it's painfully obvious my mother is going to die hating me."

This brought him up short. Several seconds passed before he said, "So, is that what this is all about? You're upset because she's mad at you for betraying her?"

Lauren told herself not to participate in this old game. "I know exactly what I did to her. Neither of you will ever let me forget."

"Look, Lauren, I don't want to fight with you. I'm just really worried about Mama."

"Move. Her. There."

"I've already explained," Julian replied. "You know we can't do that. I have a family."

And I don't and never will, she thought to herself. She knew those were the unspoken words her brother wanted to say. For the longest time, Lauren had never really cared about a family. But the loneliness was setting in. The men in her life were temporary companions. They didn't care about her problems with her mother. They weren't there to comfort her through whatever she might be going through. They wanted a good time, period. Lauren found herself longing for something more. Right now she wanted to talk to Matthew.

"Are you there?" Julian said.

"Julian, I can't do this with you today," Lauren replied. "I'm drained. I'm exhausted and I just want to get home. I'm done."

"No. You're not," he replied. "That is our mother and you will not be done as long as she has breath in her body."

"I can't do it anymore," she cried.

"You owe it to her," he said with conviction.

Lauren leaned her head back on the headrest. She knew those words were coming. He hadn't thrown them in her face in quite some time. But here it was. His rabbit in the hat.

"I think my debt is paid," she replied.

"Your debt will *never* be repaid. Look at your mother. It will never be repaid," he repeated.

Tears slid down Lauren's face. How long did she have to pay? How long *could* she pay? She just wanted to forget. She just wanted to move on, and while she would never utter the words out loud, she was ready for her mother to just die. Then and only then would she finally be free.

"Julian, I have to—"

"Housekeeping!"

Lauren stopped talking at the high-pitched female's voice.

"Uh, are you in a hotel?" she asked.

Julian sounded ruffled for a moment, then quickly answered, "Yeah. I, uh, had to get some classified work done and the twins were driving me crazy, and Rebecca's sister is there, so I just came here for a few days."

Lauren didn't really care. She was exhausted and just wanted to get off the phone. "All right, Julian. I really do have to go."

"This conversation isn't over," he said. "We can't add to Mama's stress—"

"Bye, Julian . . ." she said, cutting him off and ending the call.

We weren't doing anything. She was doing it all. And the burden was becoming too much to bear.

thirty-three

A lone leaf fluttered from a large oak tree and settled right outside the window. Joyce couldn't help but notice how it seemed content being alone. The sight took her back to the days when she used to garden and enjoy being outdoors. She further remembered the tree that she and Vernon had planted the day they moved into their house.

"Good morning."

Joyce turned toward the scratchy voice coming from the entrance to her room. Ernest was standing there with his big toothless grin.

"How are you this fine morning?" he asked.

She flicked him off. "What do you want, Ernest?"

"Thanks for asking. I'm doing okay," he replied.

She walked over and blocked his way because he had already taken two steps into the room and Joyce didn't want him to get any ideas. She was not in the mood for company.

He didn't lose his grin. "Well, I just stopped by to see if you want to come play bingo with us. We're about to get a game going in the rec room."

"No," she said.

He shook his head, undeterred. "So, what, you're just going

to stay cooped up in this room? You didn't come to breakfast. You're just going to stay in here and stare out at that old tree?"

"What part of 'I don't want to play bingo, bid whist, shuffleboard, or any other games you old people play' do you not understand?"

His smile finally faded. He reached over to her dresser and picked up Joyce's handheld mirror and thrust it in her direction.

"Why are you giving me this?" she said, taking it.

"Look at it. What do you see?"

"What are you talking about?" she said, her eyes going down to the mirror. "I see me."

He folded his arms. "I see an old person just like the rest of us around here. Only the difference is she's grumpy and mean."

Joyce almost threw the mirror and hit him upside the head. But she held herself back. She merely set it back down on the dresser.

"Bye, Ernest."

He threw his hands up. "You know what? You can sit up here and wallow in whatever misery you choose to put yourself in. Because that's what this is. It's a choice. We can choose to live or we can choose to die."

The look on her face caused him to add, "And we can choose to live even if we're dying. You choose to be miserable and unhappy, and you want everyone around you to be miserable and unhappy, too."

She glared at him, but he wasn't fazed.

"Not only are you mean and bitter," he continued, shaking his head, "but you're negative, too. Instead of having folks

around you—who are going through the same thing as you—
to help you understand and deal with what's happening, you
just push people away. Well, stay on up here in your room. You
don't have to worry about me no more."

This was the first time that she'd seen the perpetually chip-
per Ernest upset.

"Good," she said, even though his vow had touched a
nerve.

He turned around and stomped out of the room. Joyce
stood there, no longer so sure she was right. Then she retrieved
the mirror. She stared at the image and what she saw brought
tears to her eyes. For years she had been wrinkle-free. She had
given new meaning to the phrase "black don't crack." But now
she saw bags developing under her eyes. She peered a little
harder and saw a couple of moles that were sprouting up on
her face as well.

The image made her heart hurt. Joyce was once model
material. In fact, she had once been approached by someone
as she walked down the street, asking if she had ever considered modeling. Her mother had crushed that dream real fast.
But she always felt good to have been approached about it.

Joyce stared harder at her image, wishing that she could
see inside her head. See what was happening to her brain.
Were the parts that were being ravaged by cancer turning a
dark black? She swallowed the lump in her throat and set the
mirror back just as the nurse appeared in her room.

"Good morning."

"Hi," Joyce said.

"So Ernest told me that you won't be joining them today."
Normally, Joyce would have come back with a snarky

reply. But she was feeling some kind of way so she just said, "I'm not up to it."

"That run-in with your daughter got you down, huh?"

Her eyebrows furrowed as Joyce exclaimed, confused, "What?"

The nurse stopped what she was doing and turned to Joyce. "The run-in with your daughter yesterday. When you slapped her."

"What?" Joyce repeated.

Concern spread across her face. "Oh. You don't remember?"

"No," Joyce said, racking her brain to form an image of what the nurse was talking about. "I . . . I know that Lauren usually comes and visits me on Saturdays, but I don't remember her coming. I remember feeling out of it, then woozy." She continued trying to recall yesterday, but it was all a blur.

"Oh, she was here," the nurse replied. "She was here and she left after you hit her and told her that she wasn't your daughter."

Joyce's hand went to her mouth in shock.

The nurse looked sympathetic as she stepped toward Joyce, "If I'm being honest with you . . ." She waited until Joyce nodded for her to go on. "Frankly, I'm surprised that she still comes because you treat her real bad."

A part of her agreed. But then that other part, the part that felt like Lauren deserved it, caused Joyce to shake away any sympathy. "Well, I'll just talk to her next time."

The nurse shook her head. "If there is a next time." She set down the medicine that she had brought in Joyce's room. "Ms. Joyce, I suggest you deal with whatever is ailing you before you are left all alone. I see it too much around here, and that's where you're headed."

"That's why I'm here," she replied. "So you all can try and help me deal with this stupid disease that is destroying my brain."

"I'm not talking about the cancer." She walked over and touched her heart. "I'm talking about what's ailing you here. You better fix that before you run off the only person that seems to care about you. I've seen a lot of misery here, and the last thing you want to do is go through this alone."

She gave Joyce one last pitying glance before walking out of the room.

thirty-four

Lauren hadn't been able to get that painful scene with her mother out of her head. It hurt her more than anything had in a very long time. She didn't know if it was the slap, or the fact that in the midst of her madness, her mother had managed to forget her own daughter.

"How did we get here, Mama?" Lauren mumbled as she laid an outfit across the bed. But even as she muttered the question, she knew the answer. The betrayal cut deep. So deep that Lauren didn't know if they would ever heal.

She shook away thoughts of her mother and returned to the task at hand: getting ready for her date with Matthew. Lauren couldn't believe how much she was looking forward to tonight.

She stared at her reflection in the mirror. She was excited about the upcoming date. Too excited. A different kind of excitement. When she went out with one of her stable of men, she was doing what she needed to do. She considered it business. But being with Matthew felt more personal, more pleasurable. The fickle feeling inside her stomach both excited and terrified her.

They had reconnected only five weeks ago, but they had

spent every day talking for hours on end. If she didn't know any better, she'd think he didn't work, with the amount of time they spent on the phone. It felt like old times, and that's why she was once again anxiously waiting for him to come pick her up. She had made sure that her house was immaculate. She had just lit a candle to send a sweet fragrance throughout the room when her doorbell rang. She opened it to find Matthew standing there with a bottle of chardonnay, her favorite.

"My two favorite things, you and the wine," she said, lightly kissing him on the lips and then taking the bottle of wine from him. "That's how you greet a woman."

He laughed and then followed her inside. "How was your day?" he asked.

"Stressful," she replied. She usually didn't get into her personal life with the men she dated, but she needed to vent with someone about what happened. She wanted to be comforted by Matthew. "I went to see my mom today." She set the wine down on the bar.

"How was she?"

"Today was not a good day." Lauren motioned for him to take a seat, which he did. "It didn't end well. Actually, no, that probably would be an understatement. It was a disaster. She slapped me."

"What?" he said, his hand immediately going to check on her cheek.

"No, I'm okay." She was moved that his first concern would be for her.

"What happened?"

"I don't know. My mom was having some kind of spell. She got mad and the next thing I knew, she slapped me."

Lauren's shoulders sank with the weight of retelling the story. Then she voiced an opinion that had been forming all afternoon: "I'm done."

Matthew looked shocked. "What do you mean, you're done?"

"I can't take any more of her abuse."

"But didn't you say she's sick?"

"Yeah, but does that mean I'm supposed to take all that she dishes out? We have some major issues that I had hoped to work out, but that's not going to happen. I give up."

He took her hand. "I know it's hard, Lauren, but if ever there was a time when your mother needed you, this is it."

She unhooked her arm from his grasp. The last thing she wanted to hear was words of support for her mother.

"Please don't be mad, but you know I'm going to be honest."

"I'm never going to see her again," she said with finality.

Matthew shot her a disappointed look. "Did you do anything bad when you were younger or a teenager that drove your mother crazy? That made her want to drop you off at the nearest orphanage?"

That made her chuckle. Oh, she had been a fireball in her preteen years, so she could only imagine the gray hairs she had given her mother.

"Yes, but what does that have to do with anything?"

"Well, it's her turn to drive you crazy," he pointed out. "You'll get a chance to have your kids do that later."

She narrowed her eyes at him. If only he knew that she had no desire to ever bring a child into this world.

"But my point is, she didn't give up on you then, so you can't give up on her now," Matthew continued.

"So, I'm supposed to just take it?" She shook her head. "You sound like my brother."

"Well, from what I remember of your brother, he was pretty intelligent."

"Whatever," Lauren said, nettled that he was still pursuing this line of argument.

"No, no one is saying that you have to take abuse. You can leave at that moment, but you can't give up. Your mother is going through a storm, and sometimes that means you're going to get wet in trying to save her. You just can't give up."

Lauren didn't want to admit it, but what Matthew said was making sense. Her mother was dying. And dying with a broken heart. That had to be a hard pill to swallow. Lauren just hoped she'd be able to go see her mother and pretend that nothing was wrong.

"You know what? Let's forget about all that," Matthew said, standing. "Tonight is all about making you feel better. So get ready. I'm about to take you out for a night on the town. You're going to enjoy yourself. But"—he eyed her feet—"those three-inch heels need to turn into some tennis shoes."

That caught her by surprise. "What? Tennis shoes? What kind of date is that?"

"I got a night planned that you won't forget."

She smiled and bounced into the bedroom to change.

An unforgettable night. With Matthew. Yep, that was exactly what Lauren needed.

thirty-five

Lauren found solace in only a few places: her home, the beach, and here, at her aunt Velma's house. A robust woman with a smile that lit up the room, Velma Robinson had never been married, never had children, and she seemed just fine with that. A humorous woman with a big personality, Aunt Velma was always the life of the party.

For the longest time, Lauren had believed that she would end up just like her father's sister—only now Matthew had her rethinking her plans. Their date had been amazing. He'd taken her to play paintball. And while she'd vehemently protested at first, she'd given in and ended up having a lot of fun. Afterward, he'd taken her out to Jordan Lake for a midnight picnic.

That's where he'd told her how he was falling in love with her again.

Love.

That word scared the mess out of her, so she didn't reciprocate his declaration. He said he was okay with that, but she could tell he was disappointed. That's why she was spending a rare Sunday dinner with her aunt, who she hoped would give her some insight on what to do about Matthew.

"You know, everybody at church was raving about that necklace you made me," Velma said, pushing a bowl of her famous gumbo in front of Lauren.

"I'm glad you liked it, Aunt Velma."

"I appreciate you getting me that for Mother's Day." She paused, then gently said, "Did you get your mother something?"

Lauren turned her lips up. "You know I got her something, even though I don't know why I bother."

"Did you get her something as nice as my necklace?" Velma asked bluntly.

Lauren didn't want to answer because she hadn't. Why bother? Her mother not only wouldn't appreciate it, she wouldn't take care of it. Since nothing Lauren could've done would've made her mother happy, she had delivered a bouquet of her mother's favorite flowers and chocolate-covered strawberries, which was her mother's guilty pleasure.

Velma took Lauren's silence as her answer. She slid across the seat from Lauren. "You know that I'm honored that you treat me like I'm your mother, and you will always be like a daughter to me, but you have a mother, and one day you're going to have to face the past so the two of you can heal y'all's relationship."

"It's not me, Aunt Velma," Lauren protested. "Mama is the one that doesn't want to have anything to do with me. I'm the one there taking care of her, going to visit her. And she treats me like crap. It's brutal."

Aunt Velma nodded in understanding. "Still, she's your mother and the Bible says—"

"Unh-unh." Lauren cut her aunt off. "Can we talk about

something else?" Aunt Velma wasn't one of those super-religious types, but she didn't hesitate to pull out a scripture to support her argument. "What's that?" Lauren said, quickly changing the subject as she pointed to a big shoe box placed on the end of the table.

Velma smiled. "Oh, I had taken these out because I was putting some stuff in storage and I came across this big box of family photos." She got up and picked up the box. She slid it toward Lauren. "You'll find some wonderful pictures in there. You really should take a look."

Lauren saw the pictures were all of her family. Those pictures lied: her family seemed happy in the pictures. None of the photos from her childhood reflected the true turmoil that the Robinson family had endured. Her only happy moments came when she was gallivanting around town with her dad. Julian always had done his own thing, so he seemed oblivious to the things that were going on.

"Look at this one. You ever seen this?" Velma said, pulling a five-by-seven photo out of the box. The black-and-white photo made Lauren smile. Her father, in an army uniform, looked incredibly handsome.

Lauren could understand why women were drawn to him. He had light hazel eyes, curly sandy hair, and smooth brown skin. She slowly fingered the picture.

"You remember this one?" Velma asked, setting another picture in front of her.

Lauren picked it up and her lips curled. That was Easter Sunday when she was about nine years old. They had been standing in front of the church. This is what she meant by the pictures not capturing the true stories. They'd taken this like they were one big happy family, when the truth was, that day was very far from happy. That picture was taken just moments before Cecile Santiago sashayed onto the church grounds.

"I think you should take these and show them to your mama," Aunt Velma said. "You know how she loves family photos. Maybe you could even get some of your own copies printed. You can just take the whole box."

She was talking fast, like she didn't want to give Lauren room to protest.

"You know I don't normally loan out my pictures because folks don't take care of stuff that's important to me, but I think sometimes we need to let the good times overpower the bad. Maybe these pictures can bring a slew of good memories back."

Lauren seriously doubted that. Still, she took the bag her aunt handed her and began filling it with the family photos. She'd take them, but she doubted she'd ever show them to her mother.

thirty-six

Over the last year, physically Joyce had had some good days and a lot of bad days. She denied it to everyone, but she knew something was wrong long before anyone else. After all, cancer had claimed her mother. Why would it not be passed down in the family?

Joyce considered the fact that she was in denial about the possibility that it would take her prisoner, too. But it had and now she was spiraling into an abyss that she had no control over, and she absolutely hated it.

Today, thank God, was one of the good days.

She had had a dream last night about the day she met Vernon. And the day he proposed was the most special time ever. That's what she had dreamed about.

But now that she was awake, reality was setting in. For every good memory Joyce had with Vernon Robinson, there were three bad ones to go along with it.

Joyce didn't realize that she was crying until Pearl stuck her head in the door. Joyce hated that these rooms didn't have locks.

"You coming to dinner?" she asked.

"You ever heard of knocking?" Joyce snapped, dabbing her eyes.

"Sorry." She eased the door back closed.

Joyce tried to pull herself together. Pearl was the only somewhat friend she had here. She didn't mean to be so mean, but she couldn't control the bitterness that burned inside her. Maybe if she had some closure before Vernon died . . . Maybe if she could find forgiveness before she died.

Joyce didn't know. What she did know was that she was tired of hurting. And if her heart couldn't be healed, maybe death wouldn't be such a bad thing, after all.

Joyce took a deep breath. Her mind was getting all jumbled. This man had been dead for years. Why in the world did he still get to her so?

"Knock, knock," Ernest said, knocking on her door and walking in at the same time. Normally Joyce would've gone off on him, but for once she welcomed his company.

"Hey," she said softly.

He did a double take at her response. "I-I was just checking on you," he said. "I heard about what happened with your daughter, you know, you slapping her."

Hitting Lauren made Joyce wonder if she had pushed her away for good—and that thought scared Joyce to death.

thirty-seven

"Yeah, baby. Just like that. Oh, yeah. You're making me so hot," Lauren moaned as she shifted the phone from her right to her left ear.

"You want it, don't you?" he moaned, his voice husky and passionate.

"I do, Daddy. I do," she said as she opened the washer and took the load of clothes out. She loaded the clothes into the dryer as Thomas continued to moan. Lauren had no idea why men got off on phone sex. It did absolutely nothing for her. But because it made her men happy, she did what she had to do.

Lauren rolled her eyes as Thomas reached his climax. She glanced at the time on her phone. This time it had taken him a whole four minutes.

"Girl, you sure know how to make a man feel good," he said, breathless.

"Only for you, love. Only for you," she replied as she moved the next load of clothes into the washing machine.

"All right, let me get back to work," he said, his voice filled with satisfaction. "I'll call you later."

"Okay, baby," she replied. Not that she was participating, but Thomas hadn't been the least bit concerned about her enjoyment. Typical. *Maybe it's time to change my number*, she thought. With the way things were going with Matthew, she didn't know why she was still fooling with Thomas anyway. Maybe because letting him go would mean she was committing totally to Matthew, and Lauren wasn't sure she was ready to do that.

Lauren had just hung up the phone when her doorbell rang. She started the dryer, walked over, and looked through the peephole. Her brow narrowed in confusion when she saw Matthew on the other side.

"Matthew, hey," she said as she swung the door open.

"Hey, beautiful," he replied with a big grin.

"So, you just drop by without calling?" She wasn't used to pop-up calls from men. She didn't pop up at anyone's house, and she didn't like anyone popping up at hers.

Matthew lost his smile. "Wow, that was not the reaction I was expecting."

Despite the popcorn visit, a part of her was excited to see Matthew. He wasn't supposed to be back in town until tomorrow.

Lauren regathered herself, now that the surprise factor had worn off. "No, I'm sorry. I'm a little irritated doing some stuff for work. Come on in."

"Well, I would have called, but my phone died." He held up his phone. "Can I use your charger?"

"Yeah, it's over there on the bar," she said, pointing toward the kitchen area.

He walked over, plugged his phone in, and then came back until he was right up close. "Can I have a kiss? I missed you."

That brought a smile to her face. He was so handsome. With smooth chocolate skin and deep dimples, he needed to be starring in someone's soap opera.

"Yes, I'm sorry. I was just doing some chores."

"You want to come to my place next?"

"Yeah, I'm barely getting them done over here."

They laughed as she motioned toward the kitchen table.

"Come on in the kitchen and I'll fix you something to eat."

"I love the domestic side of you," he said, following her into the kitchen.

She glanced back over her shoulder as she opened the refrigerator and pulled out leftover chicken salad. "Don't get too used to that. I'm anything but domesticated."

She made them both chicken-salad sandwiches, and they sat and talked for over an hour. She absolutely loved the interest he showed in what was happening with her. She hadn't had that since the last time they were together.

After they had finished eating, Matthew brought up a new subject. "You know, my niece's graduation is this weekend."

"Tati?" Lauren said. "Tati is graduating?"

"Yep."

"Wow. I haven't seen her since she was like five."

"I know, and she would love to see you."

"She wouldn't remember me."

"But I know she'll love you."

She had a feeling this was leading in some specific direction. "Maybe one day I'll get a chance to see her," she remarked.

He flashed a sly smile. "Well, I told my parents that we were back together."

That wasn't a direction she wanted. They'd never discussed being "back together."

"Umm, did I miss something?" she asked.

"I mean, I'm not trying to be forward," Matthew said. "But you know, I was just hoping that we could be together. Like exclusively."

"The minute you give him your heart, he'll start giving you grief."

"One day you'll fall in love so hard, and he'll cheat on you and break your heart. Then maybe you'll understand my pain."

Lauren's mother's words rang in her head. She didn't want to know her mother's pain. She'd rather stay single than end up miserable and bitter like her.

She didn't know how to react. As much as she was feeling Matthew, as much as she enjoyed him, this exclusive thing wouldn't work. She had committed to a lifetime of being loved, yet not loving in return.

"Wow, Matthew. Umm, this is a bit too much," she said.

He pulled her down onto his lap. "No, it's not. I've missed you so much," he said, kissing her ferociously.

Her mind told her to pull away. Her body told her mind to shut up.

"You know, I haven't been able to stop thinking about you," Matthew replied, nuzzling her neck. "I'm not letting you get away this time."

She finally broke free, stood up, and walked away to give herself some distance. "Matthew, I thought we were just chilling."

He looked at her in confusion. "I'm too old to chill."

Images of her father's infidelity flashed through her mind.

No, she wasn't about to be anybody's wife. And that's where serious relationships ended up.

"Okay," she said, pacing across the kitchen. "I think I might have given you the wrong impression."

"What?"

She spun to face him. "I've enjoyed reconnecting with you. But exclusively? That's not what I'm looking for."

He continued to be mystified. "So what are you looking for? What are we doing?"

"We're kickin' it." She tried to force a smile.

He stared at her like he had to process whether he'd heard her correctly. "I don't need to *kick* it," he said. "I'm too old to kick it."

Lauren kept her smile, hoping it would diffuse the impending negative reaction.

"Matthew, I don't want a relationship," she said. This was so hard because she really liked him.

He stood up and walked around the open area, thinking. "Wow. I thought we had really reconnected and this was going somewhere."

"I care about you a lot. I love being with you," Lauren said.

"Then what's the problem?"

"I'm just not getting involved like that. With anyone."

His face took on a guarded look. "Okay. Message received loud and clear. Obviously, I read you wrong." He headed toward the living room. "Sorry for dropping by unexpectedly. I'm going to let you get back to what you were doing."

"Come on, Matthew," she said, following after him. "Don't be like that. We can just chill and watch a movie or something."

He grabbed his keys off the coffee table. "Nah, I'm good. It's like you said, this is not what you want and I don't want to waste your time or mine."

She huffed as her hands went to her hips. "Really, Matthew?"

He stopped right before he reached the door. "Yes, really." His shoulders drooped as he turned to face her. "I'm falling back in love with you, Lauren. Hard. Truthfully, I never stopped. I begged you to love me once. I swore I'd never do that again."

He was right about that. In college, he used to joke that he'd never worked so hard for something in his life. He'd pleaded with her to take a chance on loving him. The problem was, she had done so and had only ended up heartbroken.

"I did love you, and you left me," she said.

That put his back up right away. "I left to get an education," he clarified. "So I could build us a better life. And you did what you do best—you ran. First chance you got, you ran."

"I . . . I just, I called and that girl answered."

"And I told you she was a friend. That's it. We were studying and nothing more." He released a frustrated sigh. "For whatever reason, you think all of us will be like your father."

Lauren's mouth dropped open in shock. "I can't believe you went there."

"It's the truth. It was the truth then and it's the truth now." He pulled the front door open. "Lauren, I'm looking for a wife. I have been single a whole lot longer than I wanted to. I could never really connect with anyone. When you came back into my life, I was sure it was because God had been saving me for you. But I get that that's not what you want.

And since I do know that, it would be crazy for me to stick around."

Lauren still was mad that he would take her issues with her father—something that she'd told him in confidence—and throw it in her face. He must've known that he'd pissed her off because he said, "I'm sorry about what I said about your dad, but the truth is the truth, and until you face it, you're never going to be happy."

She wanted to go off, tell him that she *was* happy—but when she opened her mouth, nothing came out. And he simply shook his head and walked out the door—and as it felt, out of her life.

"Men weren't meant to be monogamous."

As her father's words rang in her head, Lauren pushed away all desire to go after Matthew. She told herself it was for the best.

thirty-eight

All of her life Lauren had been a loner. She had a few male friends throughout high school, but the guys usually only wanted to date her and the girls despised her. Nor did she make much effort to get close to anyone. That's why she was surprised at how quickly she and Vivian had bonded.

"Here you go," Vivian said, handing her a glass of Moscato.

"Just what I need," Lauren said, taking the oversize wineglass.

"Now, give me the whole scoop," Vivian said, sitting down next to her.

Lauren had come over directly after Matthew stormed out. For the first time in her life, she wanted to cry over a guy, and that wasn't cool. That's why she had to leave and come hang out with Vivian. Of course, Vivian wanted all the details.

"So, what happened?"

Lauren let out a long sigh, then told her about their argument.

"Wow," Vivian said when she was done. "Matthew really went there."

"I know, right. I mean, usually it's the guy who doesn't want to get serious." Lauren sipped her wine. "He just got really upset and said he didn't want to waste his time. He wants more than I'm ready to give. He said he's ready for marriage."

Vivian shook her head. "And let me guess, you're not?"

Lauren shrugged. The pain she felt inside was exactly why she didn't want to be in love.

"Lauren, you're thirty-four years old. At what point will you be ready for marriage?"

"I just see too many marriages falling apart."

Vivian tsked. "That's because outside forces are always trying to make these men think there is something better out there."

Lauren didn't know if that was a dig at her or what. She knew Vivian didn't approve of her seeing married men, but outside of a few snide remarks, her friend had never stood in real judgment of her.

"Whatever. Did you know only fifty percent of marriages make it?" Lauren said. She'd heard that statistic wasn't exactly true, but it's the one that had been stuck in her mind for years. "That's pretty sad."

"That's because people don't know what 'for better or for worse' means. You're supposed to work through the bad stuff." Vivian's voice turned nostalgic, as if she were remembering her own failed marriage.

"I'm just saying. Marriage isn't for me."

"Are you going to spend the rest of your life alone?" Vivian asked.

Lauren downed the rest of her wine, then said, "I'm alone, but not lonely."

Vivian took issue with that idea right away. "Whether you

want to admit it or not, you're lonely. You go from man to man and get all this stuff, but what you're really craving is real love."

"Okay, Dr. Phil Vanzant." Lauren rolled her eyes. If anything, Vivian and her failed marriage should make her understand why Lauren didn't want to go down that road.

"Call me what you want. It can't be fulfilling to know that you're second in someone's heart."

So much for being nonjudgmental. "Wow! Way to make me feel good, Vivian. Remind me to come over here every time I need cheering up," Lauren said, her voice full of sarcasm.

"I'm just keeping it real with you," Vivian said. "And one day you're going to run up on the wrong woman and you're not going to be able to talk your way out of a situation. You need to give Matthew a chance."

Lauren ran her finger over the rim of her glass. Her friend was right. Her lifestyle was getting old. And that maternal bug, which she never dreamed that she would have, seemed to be sneaking up on her. Lauren was about to say something when suddenly they were interrupted by a banging on Vivian's front door.

"What the . . . ?" Vivian said, jumping up.

"Girl, who is that?" Lauren sat on the edge of her seat. The way the person was banging, Lauren thought it might be the police.

Vivian went to the door and peeked out the peephole. "Oh my God," Vivian said. "It's my ex."

Lauren relaxed a bit. "Okay, and? You never said he was dangerous. Why are you acting like that?"

Vivian was nervously shaking her hands like she was trying to calm herself down.

"I'm not in the mood to deal with him now," Vivian said.

"So, you're just going to leave him out there?"

"Vivian, what's going on?" he shouted. "Open the door. I see your eyeball."

Lauren stood. "I can leave if you need to see him."

"No!" she said a little too quickly.

This was definitely strange, because while Vivian couldn't stand her husband, she'd never acted fearful of him.

"Do you want me to answer and tell him that you're not here? I can play it off," Lauren asked.

"No," she said, still looking agonized.

"Vivian, what's going on?" Lauren frowned because the whole scenario wasn't making sense. "Are you scared of him?"

Vivian ignored her and shouted toward the door. "Go away. I have company."

"And?" he replied. "I don't care. I need to talk to you. I need these papers signed now."

She walked over and eased the door open, then stepped outside. Their voices were muffled, but it sounded like they were arguing.

After a few minutes, Vivian walked back inside, a troubled look across her face. Lauren asked, "What was that about?"

"Long story," she said. "My ex is moving and has to have my permission to move my son and I won't give it to him. But he's gotten a judge to order me to sign."

"Wow." Lauren wanted to note how that exchange just proved her point about marriage, but she didn't want Vivian to get any more upset.

"I just can't let him take my son away." She slumped down on the sofa. "I hate him. I swear to God, I hate him."

"How did your relationship with him get so bad?" Lauren asked after they'd sat in silence for a few minutes.

Vivian sighed as she picked up the bottle of pinot grigio and refilled her glass to the top. She drank the entire glass nonstop. When she was done, she closed her eyes. "Maybe one day I'll tell you all about it." She refilled her glass again. "But today isn't that day."

thirty-nine

Staring out the window at the old oak tree just outside her room had become a daily ritual. And Joyce was getting tired of it. That's why when she saw Pearl in her doorway, tapping on the door, Joyce motioned for her to come in.

"Hey, Pearl," Joyce said.

She seemed surprised at Joyce's pleasant attitude. "Good morning. Just wanted to tell you you have a visitor. And it's not your daughter."

Joyce's heart jumped. Had Julian come to see her?

"Who is it?" Joyce asked in anticipation.

"Don't know. Some older woman," Pearl said.

Now she was confused. She didn't have a lot of friends. Her two closest had died several years ago.

"Do you mind telling her I'm on my way?"

Pearl nodded and walked out.

Joyce checked her appearance and made her way up to the front lobby. She stopped in her tracks at the sight of her sister-in-law, Velma.

"Surprise!" Velma said.

She was right about that. Joyce hadn't seen Velma in almost a year, though she'd talked to her on the phone. Velma claimed that her diabetes prevented her from getting out much. It didn't prevent her from going up to Atlantic City for the casinos, but Joyce didn't bother pointing that out. Truthfully, they hadn't been as close since Vernon died. Velma had adored her baby brother, and Joyce believed that she reminded her sister-in-law of him too much.

"To what do I owe this pleasure?" Joyce asked, hugging her.

"I just wanted to check on my sister-in-law."

"I'm still alive, so I guess that's something."

"I'm sorry I haven't been by here to see you before."

Joyce wondered when the excuses were going to start. She motioned for her to take a seat in the lobby, which she did.

"I told Lauren, soon as I was feeling better, I was gonna get over here."

Velma shifted like she was trying to get comfortable, squeezing her robust frame into a chair that looked like it was being swallowed up by her behind.

"You know Carl had the cancer and it just broke my heart to watch him disintegrate," she said, referring to her on-again, off-again boyfriend of nineteen years. They'd never married because she had no interest in marrying.

"Well, I'm not that bad. Yet. Truth be told, I think my kids stuck me in here so they wouldn't have to be bothered with me."

Velma narrowed her eyes. "Now, you know better than that. From what Lauren has been telling me, it's been kind of rough." Velma reached over and patted her hand. "Now, stop trying to be hard. How are you really doing?"

"It hasn't been easy . . ." Joyce admitted, her voice trailing off. "Most days I feel like my regular self. But some days . . ."

If she could be honest with any person in this world, it was her sister-in-law. They might not have been close lately, but at one time, they truly were. And since Velma had lived through having a loved one fight cancer, Joyce wanted to open up. "What was it like with Carl?"

A hint of compassion glossed over her eyes.

"It was one of the most difficult things I ever had to go through," she confessed. "You know Carl was full of life and spunk and well, that disease just came on so fast."

She took a tissue out of her purse and sniffled into it. When she looked up again, she said, "I'm worried about you and Lauren. She came by to see me. She told me things aren't getting any better with you two."

Joyce didn't know what to say about that. She knew that Velma adored Lauren and would never see Joyce's side in anything, so trying to explain her feelings would be useless.

"It is what it is."

"Why can't you shake this bitterness toward her?" Velma asked.

She didn't respond. Velma knew the history.

"You know I love you like you're my own blood sister, so I'm going to shoot straight with you. You're wrong. Just plain wrong."

"I don't need a lecture, Velma."

Of course that wasn't going to stop her.

"You know Vernon was my heart," she continued. "I loved him to my core. But he wasn't no good. He was a great brother. A great father. A great man, and a lousy husband. You knew that before you married him, and you knew that after you married him. But you stayed. You chose to stay."

"No, I didn't—"

"Un-unh, don't even fix your lips to lie to me. I can't count the number of houses we rolled up on, the number of women I talked you out of calling."

"I'm just saying—"

"I understand what you're just saying, but it's time you start admitting the truth. You *chose* to stay with Vernon. You *chose* to subject yourself to the pain of his infidelity. So that, and all the mess that goes with it, rests solely on your shoulders."

"Okay, so be it. But that doesn't mean my child should've fallen in line with him."

Velma's words were stern. "Your child was a child. Who just wanted her daddy's love."

"I gave her love."

"Okay. And she wanted her daddy's love, too, and there is absolutely nothing wrong with that." Velma leaned back, shaking her head in disgust. "All that anger and bitterness up inside you . . . Chile, you got some healing to do."

Healing. There went that word again.

"Hurt people hurt people," Velma continued. "And until you realize that you and Vernon messed my niece up in the head, everybody is gonna be jacked up."

"Messed up? How do you figure that?"

"The poor child is a lonely woman, but she's too scared to give a good man a chance."

"There's no such thing as a good man."

Velma wagged a finger at her. "See. That's your problem right there. You're projecting your negativity onto your daughter."

Joyce rolled her eyes. "From what I can see, Lauren has never had a shortage of men."

"She's dating, but she won't commit to love."

"Love is overrated anyway."

"Don't deflect your animosity onto your child. We want our children to take the good things about us and not the bad."

Velma was working her nerves. She hadn't seen her in almost a year, and she wanted to roll up in here trying to tell Joyce about how to deal with her kids. "Oh, so now you're an expert on children?"

"You can sass me all you want, but the facts are stubborn."

"Is that what you came here for? To harass me?"

Velma smiled, unfazed by Joyce's attitude. "I came here to see how you were doing, but you know I shoot straight."

"Whatever." Joyce tossed her hand, dismissing Velma, just as Ernest walked up.

"Wow, who is this?" he said, licking his front tooth.

"My sister-in-law, Velma."

"I'm gay," Velma quickly said.

That wiped the smile right off Ernest's face, but then it was quickly replaced with a more wicked expression.

"Well, I don't mind watching."

"Ernest, go somewhere with your old mannish self," Joyce said.

Velma chuckled. "Nah, let him stay. I'm a senior-atrix."

"A what?" Ernest asked.

"Senior-atrix. You know, like dominatrix. Only I get my jollies from sexually torturing old men."

Ernest was reduced to speechlessness. Joyce was struggling to restrain her laughter.

"Joyce, yo' people nasty," he said as he walked away.

"Ooh, chile, you're funny," Joyce said. "You haven't changed at all." Velma used to keep her in stitches, and it felt good to laugh again. In fact, Joyce forgot that just a minute ago, she was mad at her.

They spent another hour, laughing, talking, and catching up.

"Well, I'd better get going," she said. "I promise I'll get back over here to see you soon."

"I won't hold my breath," Joyce said with a giggle, standing with her.

"Ha-ha," Velma said, staring.

"What?"

"I love to see you laugh. You should try it more often. It's so much better than anger."

"Whatever, Velma," Joyce said, still smiling.

She remained serious. "Joyce, I'm praying for you. Before you leave this earth, God's gonna unharden that heart."

"Well, God better get to work because from the looks of things, I got a one-way ticket out of here that I'm about to cash out."

"Hmph, God done already worked that out. I'm just waiting for the manifestation."

Joyce pushed her toward the exit. "Bye, Reverend Velma."

She hugged Joyce. "Talk to you soon." She motioned toward a gift bag that Joyce hadn't seen, leaning against the side of the sofa. "Brought you something. Use it. The fact that you hadn't been using it has probably been the source of all your problems."

She winked, then wobbled away.

Joyce picked up the silver-and-pink gift bag. What kind of gift had her sister-in-law left? She dug in the bag and pulled out a burgundy Bible. A yellow Post-it note on the front read:

Try me.
You might like me.

Joyce smiled. She hadn't cracked open a Bible in years. Maybe she would try it. At this point, she had nothing else to lose.

forty

As hard as it had been, Lauren had not called Matthew all week. Well, she had called once, but when he didn't return the call, she took that as her cue and moved on.

So, today was going to be all about Thomas. Lauren pushed away thoughts of Matthew. She'd been waiting for Thomas Brooks to return from his trip overseas for a month. He sent her text messages about all the things he wanted to do with her when he returned. He also promised her that she was going to want to do whatever he suggested once she saw all the amazing stuff he'd bought her in Paris.

Lauren knew that meant he sent his people on a shopping spree. But the logistics of who did what didn't bother her. Thomas might sound like a guy from around the way but, in reality, he was a self-made multimillionaire real-estate tycoon.

Thomas had reserved a penthouse at the Hilton. He had told Lauren to arrive this morning and had given her the full spa package of a masseuse, nail tech, and even threw in a bikini wax. He wanted her rested, relaxed, and dolled up for when he arrived at 8 p.m. Lauren glanced at her watch. Since Thomas was a stickler for punctuality, she knew she only had ten minutes. She raced through her mind and tried to remember his favorite perfume. Between her regular men, she often lost track of who did what or who liked what.

"Kenzo," she said, remembering as she dug through her overnight bag. She pulled out the flower bottle, sprayed both sides of her neck, then dropped the bottle back in the bag.

At eight on the dot, the lock clicked. Lauren went to face the window, her backside toward the door. The lingerie accented her in all the right places. And since her backside was her biggest asset, followed by her breasts and her long, sultry legs, she wanted to make the best first impression.

"Damn!" he said, the door slamming behind him. "You know how to greet a brother."

She smiled as she turned around, letting the lace robe drop open. "I take it that I meet your approval?"

"You know you do." He looked at her hungrily.

She took her time walking over to him because she wanted him to savor every bit of the three-hundred-dollar negligee he'd had delivered and waiting in the room.

"How was your flight?" she said, loosening his tie.

"It was fine," he said, devouring her with his eyes. "My family thinks that I'm not coming back until tomorrow."

"So, does that mean I have you all night?" she purred.

Lauren was having to act more than usual tonight because her mind kept going back to Matthew. In truth, she couldn't manage as much enthusiasm as usual.

"It does." He loosened his top button as she slowly pulled the tie off. "You know I had to finagle some things, but that's all I've been thinking about . . . spending the night with you."

They'd only spent the night together once before, when he had her meet him on a business trip.

"Let me take a shower and"—his eyes roamed up and down her body again—"you just wait right here for me."

"I'll be here sipping this wine, waiting on you," she said, falling back across the bed and crossing her legs.

He licked his lips, hunger dancing in his eyes, and then he darted into the bathroom.

"Hey, order us some room service," he called out as the shower started. "I'm famished. I'd like the filet mignon."

"Got it," she said.

She placed the order and then went back to waiting across the bed. She set her iPhone to the Slow Jams music channel. She wanted the mood to be just right.

Thirty minutes later, they'd gone through round one, which she told him was the appetizer. He'd get the full-course meal after he ate. She enjoyed the look on his face, like he'd just gone to Heaven. Too bad it didn't give her heart joy.

The doorbell to the suite rang. "Room service."

Thomas walked over, peeked out the peephole, and then opened the door. The waiter smiled as he came in and set up their plates. Lauren had ordered a Caesar salad, which she only planned to nibble on. The one thing she always did was eat lightly around her men.

Thomas signed for the food and then the waiter pushed the cart back out. They had just sat down to eat when someone knocked on the door again. "Room service."

"What are they doing back?" he said.

"I don't know, but I'll get it." She peeked out the peephole, but she couldn't see anything. *Oh well*, she thought as she opened the door. No sooner had she cracked the door than it was kicked open, causing Lauren to stumble as she fell back on her behind. "What the . . . ?"

"You lying bastard!" A woman came storming in. Thomas jumped up from his seat in absolute fear.

"Teresa!" he said.

"You bastard. What are you doing?"

"Baby . . ."

"That's a dumb question," she said, her rage on full blast. "I see what the hell you're doing—laying up screwing this tramp!"

Lauren was completely caught off guard. What was she thinking, opening that door? She knew better than that. She tried to pull herself up off the floor.

"Babe, let me explain," Thomas said.

"I had you followed from the airport when I saw your stupid itinerary that your incompetent secretary sent to me by mistake." She looked around the lavish chamber. "The penthouse suite? You're so damn predictable." The woman spun on Lauren. Her eyes bucked in horror when she spied her robe. "Is that the same negligee set you bought me?"

"I-I didn't know he was married," Lauren said.

This woman was filled with rage, and Lauren would say whatever she needed to calm her down.

"Whatever. I've seen you before. You know he is married. You see the damn ring on his finger."

Lauren cursed herself. She was really slipping. Maybe she was getting too old for this game.

"Teresa, calm down."

Lauren had visions of the woman pulling out a pistol and shooting them all.

Dear Lord, just let me get out of here . . .

Lauren couldn't finish her thought. She hadn't prayed in years. What did she look like now, praying for God to give her grace from screwing another woman's husband?

"You're right," Teresa said, growing eerily calm. "There's no need for me to act like some gutter trash just because my husband climbed in the gutter with some trash."

She glanced at Thomas. "I hope this piece was worth it. Because it's about to cost you—majorly." She gave Lauren a look of disgust. "Both of you."

Lauren didn't know what that meant. She was just grateful when the woman walked out the door. As soon as it closed, Lauren hurriedly slipped a dress on, grabbed her belongings, and headed out.

"Wait, you're leaving?" Thomas asked.

Lauren couldn't believe he planned to go ahead like nothing happened. She decided he wasn't worth the energy of her vocal cords. She was definitely leaving. For good.

forty-one

Good morning, Ernest."

Joyce's toothless friend swung his head around, narrowed his eyes, and peered at her. Then he took his two left fingers and dramatically placed them over his wrist.

"What are you doing?" she asked.

"I'm checking my pulse to see if I'm still alive. Because you walked in here with a smile, which must mean I done died and went to Heaven."

"Oh, stop being so cynical," she said as she slid in the seat across from him at the cafeteria table, where he'd been sitting alone, eating breakfast.

"Well, what has you in such a good mood?" he asked. "'Cause you're the queen of the sourpuss committee."

She opened her yogurt, dipped her spoon in it, then slipped a bite into her mouth.

"My son is coming today," she said with a grin.

"Your son?" Ernest said. "I thought you only had a daughter."

That caused Joyce consternation. "Why would you think that? I told you I had a son."

He shook his head like he was convinced she was trying to trick him. "Naw, you never told me that. Mighta been someone else. But not me. Your daughter is the only one that's ever been here to visit you. I didn't know you had nobody else."

"Well, if you would listen when I talked to you, you'd know," she snapped.

"I listen and if you had told me you had a son, I woulda told you he sorry since he ain't never been here to see you."

Joyce brushed off his comment. "Whatever, Ernest." She refused to let anything mess up her mood today.

"I'm just saying," Ernest continued. "I hope you got a good tongue-lashing waiting on your son when he does get here."

"My son is a very busy man and besides, he lives in Texas."

"Too busy to come see about his mama? You been here six months and I ain't never seen him."

"Hush up," she said. "Don't nobody visit you."

"I ain't got nobody." He threw his hands up. "But I'm just saying."

"Well, he will be here soon and I couldn't be more thrilled."

Several more of her "friends" came over to the table, and they laughed and talked about the weather, the new overnight tech, and a little bit of everything else. Joyce could tell that they were surprised at how pleasant she was.

They had no idea. Julian was her heart. Her precious baby who had always had her back—unlike her backstabbing daughter.

"Well, it's time for me to go," she said, glancing at her watch.

Joyce had dressed in her finest outfit in anticipation of Julian's visit. She had on the pearls and the earrings that he had sent her for Mother's Day.

"She act like she's going to see her man," Wanda mumbled. Joyce ignored her. They were just jealous. She wasn't going to let them steal her joy.

She made her way to the lobby, where she took a seat and anxiously awaited her son's arrival.

"Somebody sure is excited," the morning nurse, a nice woman named Amanda, said. "But then again, I can see why you would be." She motioned toward the young man walking down the corridor with a gigantic bouquet of roses. Just the sight of her son walking toward her, the spitting image of his father, sent Joyce's heart fluttering. He had the same high cheekbones, the same bronze coloring, the same curly hair, and even his deep-set almond-shaped eyes were the exact replica of his father.

She smiled as he approached her. Because as much as he looked like his father, her son was nothing like Vernon Robinson. Julian was a dedicated family man. He was committed to his wife. He told her as much. He promised that he would never hurt a woman the way his father had hurt her. And Joyce respected and loved him so much for that.

"Mama," he said, swooping her up and swinging her around.

She giggled like a schoolgirl. "Boy, put me down." She took the flowers out of his hand, then kissed his cheek. "I am so happy to see you."

"I'm sorry it has taken me so long to visit," he said.

"You hush up with that. You are a busy family man. And you're trying to take care of your family. How are they?"

"They're good. I can't wait to show you pictures of the twins. They're getting so big."

"I sure would like to see them," she said.

She'd gone to visit the twins when Rebecca had given birth. Joyce stayed for two weeks, but Rebecca was one of those free-spirited women that liked to feed babies water before they were three months, and she'd gone ballistic because Joyce had let the babies suck on her finger. So Joyce headed back home, feeling that she had worn out her welcome.

She had to admit that she was a little hurt that she hadn't been invited back since, but Julian assured her it wasn't because of Rebecca, who he swore adored her. A part of Joyce wanted her son to demand that she go back with him. But he'd been adamant that she was in the best place. And that as soon as she got better he'd be more than happy to come and get her.

"So, come, come," he said, taking her arm in his. "Tell me about how life has been treating you. What's been going on?"

Joyce draped her free arm through his. "Well, as you can see, I've been trying to stay busy. The doctors have me on this aggressive treatment that I hate."

"Good. That's all I want to hear," Julian replied. "And the therapist?"

Joyce rolled her eyes.

"Mother . . ."

"I'm going. I ain't gotta like it, but I'm going."

"Good," he said with a smile. "Have you talked to Lauren?"

She shrugged. "She was here last weekend. But today is about us."

"Yes, it is about us. All of us. And that's why I asked Lauren to meet us here."

Joyce lost her smile. The last thing she felt like doing was sharing her son with her daughter.

"Julian!" Joyce said. "I see her all the time. I just want to spend time with you."

"And that would be my cue to exit."

Joyce spun around to see her daughter standing behind her. She hadn't noticed Lauren walk up. Joyce probably should've tried to clean up what she meant, but Lauren had attitude written all over her face, so Joyce didn't think it was worth the try.

However, Joyce could tell by the look on her daughter's face that she didn't want to be there any more than Joyce wanted her there.

Looking at her daughter right now, Joyce truly wondered if the rift between them would ever be healed.

"Come on," Julian said, "it's time to do some talking."

forty-two

Lauren couldn't help but notice the way her mother clung to Julian. The way she touched him. The love that resonated from her body for him. It had been a long time since she'd felt love of any kind from her mother.

A part of Lauren wanted to leave, to pretend she'd never come. But she'd promised Julian that she would show up.

"Hey, lil sis," Julian said, trying to smooth over the uneasiness that was building in the room. Lauren guessed they were just going to ignore what her mother had just said.

Lauren swallowed hard, then forced a smile. "What's up, bro?" she said, approaching the two of them.

"Hi, Mom."

"Hello, Lauren," her mother replied. "I didn't mean . . . I mean, it's just been so long since I saw your brother and—"

Lauren held up a hand to cut off her mother. "Don't worry. I'm used to it."

An awkward silence hung between them until finally Julian said, "So, you're not going to give me a hug?"

She gave her brother a halfhearted hug. She did like to see him, since she really did love her big brother. Six long months had elapsed since she'd seen him—when they admitted their mother to this facility. But the tension that hung in the room was palpable. The no-show was being treated like the savior, and she didn't like it.

"You look great," he said.

"I try," she replied.

"Look at you"—he motioned to her shoes—"rocking Christian Louboutin and everything."

That prompted a smile. "What do you know about red bottoms?" Lauren said, holding out her foot.

"Hmph. What man gave you those?" her mother said, a judgmental scowl across her face.

Lauren bit off the first remark that came to her head. "It's always so good to see you, Mother," she said sarcastically.

Joyce walked over and kissed Lauren on her cheek. Lauren knew that was just for show. It was the first time her lips had been near Lauren in years, and she knew the only reason her mother was doing it now was so that Lauren looked like the bad guy.

"Well, I'm glad we're all here," Julian said, smiling at the exchange. "I really want us to talk. Let's go in here." He pointed to a small conference room off the lobby.

"Why are we going in here?" her mother asked as she followed him in.

Julian pulled out a chair. As they got situated around the table, a petite woman walked in the room.

Julian came over and greeted her. "You must be Dr. Lawson?"

"I am," the woman said, shaking his hand. "It's a pleasure to put a face with the voice."

Joyce was shocked as she looked back and forth between the two of them. "Why are you talking to her?"

Julian sat back down and took both of his mother's hands. "Mom, I'm really concerned about you. I want you to get better, and the therapist said it's crucial that we deal with some deep-seated issues."

Joyce jerked her hands away. "I don't need to deal with anything."

"No, it's crucial that we deal with *that day*."

Lauren's heart dropped into the pit of her stomach. If she had had any inkling that this is what her brother wanted, she would have taken the weekend to go to Tahiti.

"Julian—"

"No, Lauren," he said, cutting her off before she could protest. "We have brushed this under the rug long enough. We tiptoe around it. Mama is getting worse."

"I am not," Joyce said, getting agitated. "I told her all about it. I talked about it." She now sounded on the verge of tears.

"No, you told me what happened. We didn't deal with anything," Dr. Lawson corrected.

Julian turned to Lauren. "We've got to deal with this."

"I just want to enjoy time with my son," Joyce whined. "Is there anything wrong with that?"

"I'm not interested in being here for this," Lauren added as she stood up. The only person liable to get screwed in this heart-to-heart was her.

"Well, as I told your brother on the phone, all three of you need to be here," Dr. Lawson said.

Joyce folded her arms and poked her lips out, upset.

"So if we can get started . . ." Dr. Lawson ignored Joyce's temper tantrum. "Please sit," she told Lauren.

Lauren plopped down in the seat at the end of the table, across from her mother.

"So. Who's going to begin?" Dr. Lawson said, taking out her notepad.

No one said a word. Finally, Julian spoke up. "My mother and my sister need help."

"I don't need help. I'm fine," Lauren said. She didn't understand why her brother had excluded himself from the equation like he was Mr. Perfect.

"Their relationship needs help. The doctors have said Mama's progression is worsening. So, I want this, as you said, addressed before it's too late."

Joyce rolled her eyes.

The doctor nodded. "I agree. I've been trying to get your mother to see that. So we're going to start with you, Joyce. Why are you so mad at your daughter?" she asked point-blank.

A heavy silence filled the air as Joyce glared at Lauren.

"Why don't you ask her why I'm so mad? She didn't just co-sign his cheating. She helped take him away from me for good."

Lauren's hard glare bore into her mother.

This was a conversation that Lauren had been dreading for years. And if there was any way she could have gotten out of it, she would have. But when she saw the disdain pouring from her mother, she knew that it was time. No, it was *past* time.

She turned to the doctor. "You know what? Let's lay it all out, because I'm tired. You want to know the truth? Well, sit back as I tell you how my father died, because you're in for a ride."

Lauren didn't realize that she was crying until Julian handed her a box of tissues.

She looked across the table at her mother, who was trembling. Surprisingly, she'd kept her tears at bay.

This was the first time Lauren had ever recounted the complete story of the night her father died. Naturally, that night Lauren had called 911. She'd been too afraid to call her mother. Of course, the police called her mother, who showed up just as they were loading her father's body into the county medical examiner's hearse. Her mother had been devastated. Lauren had tried to console her, to deliver her father's dying words about apologizing, but that had only sent Joyce into a rage. So, she'd never talked about that night again.

Until now.

Dr. Lawson finally asked, "Joyce, do you have anything to say?"

Lauren braced herself for her mother's scathing remarks, but her mother just shook her head.

Even Julian was shell-shocked. He had never heard all the details, either. No one had. Lauren didn't know what had made her open up today. She thought it would make her feel better. Instead, the sordid tale made her feel worse than ever.

forty-three

Her daughter's tears should have moved her, but they didn't. They only angered Joyce even more. Lauren's retelling of the worst night of Joyce's life reminded her of her daughter's betrayal.

"He was coming home and Callie got mad."

Lauren had told her those words that night, but Joyce had been too distraught to process them. But when the realization set in, she realized that Vernon had chosen her. Her husband was coming home. And that woman had stopped him. And Lauren had helped her.

Yes, Lauren had betrayed her in the worst possible way. She'd betrayed Joyce by giving Vernon those keys. If she hadn't, he would never have left that day and maybe they would've worked through their difficulty like they always did. But she had, and he left and moved in with that scuzzy whore, who ultimately took his life.

Julian instinctively reached to take his mother's hand. Joyce glared at her daughter and didn't realize she was crying until a tear dropped into her lap.

Silence continued to fill the room until the doctor repeated herself: "Joyce, do you want to respond?"

She didn't say a word. She *couldn't* say a word.

"She doesn't need to reply. She has always made her feelings clear," Lauren said.

The indignation in her voice rubbed Joyce the wrong way. "How would you suggest I feel?" she asked her daughter. Julian squeezed her tighter, no doubt trying to keep her from getting upset. But it was too late. In fact, she'd never stopped being upset.

"You don't have any children. But one day you will. One day you will labor, have your body distorted trying to bring a child into this world. You will bend over backward to give her the world, and after loving her from the bottom of your soul, she will turn around and stab you in the back. When that happens to you, then maybe you can tell me how I'm supposed to feel. But until you've experienced your flesh and blood betray you—"

"I was a child!" Lauren screamed, cutting her off. "A damn child! How long are you going to punish me?"

"Okay, let's keep our voices down," the therapist said.

Lauren threw her hands up as she stood. "No, you know what? I'm done. All I wanted was my parents to get along. All I wanted was my daddy's love *and* my mother's love. I didn't want to be in the middle of any marital drama. I didn't want to be there when my daddy died. I just wanted a piece of fictional happiness and not the dysfunctional reality I lived in daily."

"Maybe if you had told him to come home, he would have, since you were his little princess," Joyce said sarcastically. "It was bad enough that you stole his heart from me, but then you turned around and watched him give it to other women."

Lauren stared at her mother like she was crazy. "Are

you freaking for real?" Her voice lowered, her words shook. "Mama, you were absent. You lay in bed all day long. Don't you remember you couldn't ever get out of bed?"

"You replaced me with his whores."

"You wallowed in your place of despair. You left me at the age of fifteen to fend for myself."

They were interrupted when the therapist said, "Joyce, do you think there's some validity to her point?"

Of course she did. To an extent. She knew that in the beginning, her daughter didn't realize what she was doing. But as she got older and decided to keep the secrets, she was just as much to blame as Vernon.

Her silence prompted Dr. Lawson to continue. "That's a lot of weight for a child to carry."

It didn't matter what anyone said, though. Joyce wanted the past to stay in the past. There was no changing it, so no need to revisit it.

"I feel woozy," Joyce told Julian.

Lauren rolled her eyes. "Of course. Anytime she doesn't want to address something, she plays sick."

Joyce kept her focus trained on her son. "I'm sorry, baby." She stood, wobbled, and grabbed his arm. "If you want me to keep trying, I will, but this is too much."

"Oh, give me a break," Lauren huffed.

Julian's face, though, was blanketed with concern. "You know what? Maybe this is all too much. Maybe we should let her rest."

"Fine. I'm out of here." Lauren grabbed her purse and marched toward the door.

"Lauren, wait," Julian called out after her.

Lauren spun around. "No. You got it handled. This is what she wants anyway. Her precious prince is here, and that's all that matters. So, Julian, you stay here and you handle her." She glared at her mother. "Because I'm done. For good."

Then she stormed out of the room. *God forgive me*, Joyce thought, but she finally felt a sense of relief.

forty-four

It was obvious that any love her mother had for her was gone. Lauren needed to face that and stop trying to force a relationship between them.

But even as she vowed to never make this trek up I-40 again, the tears wouldn't stop coming.

The tears blinded Lauren as she sped down the freeway. She'd managed to keep them at bay until she pulled out of the parking lot, but then a wave swept over her. She cried for her father and her relationship with her mother, which today, she finally realized, could never be repaired.

The funny thing is, if Lauren had to do it all over again, she didn't know if she would do anything differently. Because she had been, after all, just a child.

Her ringing phone snapped her out of her thoughts. Vivian's name appeared on her caller ID. She almost didn't answer, but maybe Vivian could take her mind off what had just happened.

"Hey, girl." Vivian's voice chirped through the phone. "What's going on?"

Lauren let out a heavy sigh. "Nothing. Just leaving the rehab facility."

"Are you okay?"

"I'm all right. Just had a horrible visit with my mother. But I don't want to talk about it."

"Oh. I'm sorry to hear that. Well, let's talk about something on a lighter note. Like your date with Thomas the other night," Vivian said.

That caused Lauren to stiffen her grip on the steering wheel. "That would definitely not be a lighter note. His wife showed up."

"What?" Vivian said. "Crazy Teresa and you're still living to talk about it?"

"I know, right?" Lauren replied. "I'm just . . . I'm just tired. I'm tired of all this. I'm tired of my mom. I'm tired of these guys. I just want . . ." Her voice trailed off.

"You want Matthew." Vivian finished for her.

"You know, you're right. What's wrong with me? Why am I thinking about him so much?"

"Because, like I told you," Vivian replied, "all that playing the field gets old. And you need to get out before you run up on the wrong chick. There's nothing like a woman scorned."

"Yeah, I know, although I'm not worried about any of these women. They don't need to be mad at me because I'll do what they won't. Plus, I didn't make vows, their husbands did."

Lauren couldn't be sure, but she thought she heard a sharp inhale.

"How's that working out for you?" Vivian said. "Yeah, you know how to be the perfect mistress to these guys. They love that. But do you love yourself? Because if you do, I can't believe you want this as your future."

Any other time Lauren would've said something, but Vivian was speaking some hard truths. She'd never had an issue with what she did, never even felt the least bit guilty about it. Now, not only was guilt setting in, but so was regret, and a host of other emotions.

But at this point, did it even matter? With all the dirt she had done, could a woman like her ever find redemption? Could she find the happiness that she'd convinced herself she didn't want?

"Yeah, since you got all quiet, I'm gonna let you go," Vivian said. "You don't want to admit it, but if you think about it, you know I'm right. I'll talk to you later."

Vivian hung the phone up without saying good-bye.

Her words were still weighing heavily on Lauren as she exited the freeway. The sound of a honking horn jolted her out of her thoughts.

Lauren looked to her left at a man in a Lamborghini, honking as he tried to get her attention. She noticed the wedding band as he motioned for her to pull over to the side. Any other time, the hot yellow Lambo would have been all she needed. But Lauren was tired. What she needed now . . . what she would love to do now was not meet another rich man—a married man. What she needed was to go home and snuggle in the arms of Matthew King.

The only problem was, she'd pushed him away. So, Lauren thought, with a new determination filling her, she needed to figure out a way to get him back.

forty-five

The Lambo guy was long gone, and Lauren was sitting in the parking lot of Starbucks, trying to figure out her next move.

"... *All that playing the field gets old.*"

Vivian was right. It was played out.

"*You think you're special? You think you'll be that one woman that can get her man to remain faithful?*"

But was her mother right, too?

Lauren thought of all the men she'd been with. She hadn't had to work hard to get a single one of them. Why would she think Matthew would be any different?

"Just call him," she mumbled.

"No," she told herself.

She'd sent him packing, and so calling him was no longer an option. But Lauren didn't want to be alone, either. This visit had taken a serious toll and she needed to be comforted.

Amid her indecision Lauren swiped through her phone until she reached Thomas's name. She really didn't want to talk with him, but at this point he was better than nothing.

"Well, if it isn't my little chocolate drop," he said, answering on the second ring.

"Hi."

"To what do I owe this pleasure, because you don't ever call me?"

"What are you doing?" she said.

"What I'm always doing, working." He paused. "Are you okay?"

"Not really," she admitted.

"Well, Daddy can make you feel better."

Of course, his mind would immediately go to sex. She didn't want sex. She wanted comfort. She wanted Matthew. That was never more clear than now.

"Hey, Thomas, I'm sorry. I have to call you back." Lauren hung up the phone before he could protest. She immediately dialed Matthew's number.

She needed to apologize. She needed to tell him that she realized how much she needed him.

"Hello?" he said.

She breathed a sigh of relief that he picked up. "Matthew . . ." she whispered.

"Is something wrong?" he asked.

That brought a smile to her heart. Unlike Thomas, he immediately knew something was wrong. He knew, and he cared.

"I . . . I need to see you."

He paused, his words unsure. "See me for what?"

"I just need to see you."

"Lauren, I don't think that's a good idea. We —"

"Please, Matthew? Can I come by?"

"I was . . ."

"Please?"

That made him pause again because it wasn't like her to beg for anything.

"Okay, I'm at home," he said.

"I'm on my way."

Twenty minutes later, she was ringing his doorbell. He opened the door looking better than ever in a tweed blazer and jeans. She fell into his embrace. He didn't ask any questions as he held her and guided her inside to his den. His touch comforted her and made the tears reemerge.

"Okay, do you want to tell me what's going on?" he said after she settled down.

She swallowed, overcome with the intensity of the day.

"It's just . . ."

"Is it your mother?" he asked when she couldn't finish her sentence.

Lauren nodded. "I'm sorry. My brother is here and . . . it didn't go well."

"I hate to hear that. Is there anything I can do?"

"Not really. I just needed someone to talk to."

"And you thought of me?" he said, his smile wide.

"Yes, I did."

"Well, I'm listening."

Before he could respond, his cell phone rang. He read the display and the reaction on his face gave her pause. She expected him to ignore it and was taken aback when he said, "Will you excuse me for a moment?"

He stepped into the kitchen. She knew she shouldn't, but she quietly followed him.

"Hey. No, we're still on. Sorry, I'm running a little late. A friend dropped by and she's going through something. I'll be there in about twenty minutes."

That dropped a sickening load into the pit of her stomach. Matthew turned and caught her eavesdropping just as he hung up the phone.

"Really?" he asked.

"Who was that?" She hadn't even realized the words left her mouth, but now that they were out, she wasn't going to take them back. "Am I keeping you from something?"

He sighed. "Actually, I was heading out to meet someone."

"A woman?"

He looked at her strangely, like he couldn't believe that she would ask him that.

"As a matter of fact, yeah."

"So you're seeing someone?"

Matthew asked her bluntly, "What difference does it make, Lauren?"

"I was just asking."

He wasn't letting her off the hook, though. "Why do you care if it is a woman?"

She contemplated telling him that she didn't care. But she did. The reality was the thought of him going out with another woman made her sick. "I was just asking. I mean, just two weeks ago you were acting like you wanted to be with me. Now you're not hesitating to go sniffing behind another woman."

"Wow," he said, his mouth dropping open. "Sniffing? First of all, she's just a friend."

"Oh boy. Here we go again. I've heard that before."

He blinked, shaking his head like he was trying to get this scene to register.

"She is a friend," he reiterated. "Just a friend. Would it become something more? Maybe. At least we're on the same page."

That iron feeling in her stomach intensified.

"But seriously, Lauren, where is this coming from?" he asked.

"Just be honest. You probably were seeing her while you were trying to be exclusive with me."

Matthew huffed his frustration. "Lauren, you said you didn't want to be with me, so I'm not understanding this attitude. You don't want a relationship with me, so you don't get to ask me who I'm seeing."

She couldn't refute his logic. He had said he was in the market for marriage. Why in the world was she about to cry?

"I told you. I'm looking for someone to get serious with," he said, his voice turning gentle.

"So, you're serious with her?"

"No. I just met her." He caught himself, like he couldn't believe he was answering her questions. "Look, I'm sorry about whatever happened with your mother. But I need to get going. I've already kept her waiting."

That hurt Lauren more than she could have ever imagined.

"What?" he said when he noticed the expression on Lauren's face.

"Nothing."

He studied her. It was taking everything in her power to keep the tears from escaping and running a marathon down her face.

"Look, Lauren. Either you want to be with me or you don't," he said. "I can't do this back-and-forth. Make up your mind on what you want to do, then let me know."

He walked over to his front door, then held it open.

Lauren slowly walked toward it. She was just about to step outside when she declared, "I need you."

He remained unconvinced. "Don't do this, Lauren. You're just upset and feeling vulnerable."

Yes, she was upset. And maybe even vulnerable. But she

needed Matthew, and the thought of him going to another woman tore at her inside. Not just because she was jealous, but because at that very moment she realized that she loved him. Really and truly loved him.

She stepped closer to him. "I'm sorry, don't go," she said, her voice soft and low. "Please stay here with me. Let me stay with you. I'm not good at this love thing," she confessed. "But if there is anyone I want to try with, it's you. And this time I want to get it right."

She could tell that he didn't know whether to believe her, so she continued. "Matthew, I'm a little messed up because I didn't have the best example of love in my life, and so I'm scared as hell about getting serious again. But if you'll be patient with me, I promise I'll do everything to not focus on my past, but rather my future."

Her heart raced when he still didn't move. Finally, he reached in his pocket and pulled out his cell phone.

"What are you doing?" she asked.

"Calling Ingrid to tell her I have to cancel."

Lauren had never heard sweeter words.

Yet at the same time she knew full well that her mother had lost herself behind loving Vernon Robinson. Lauren had seen how good her father was at convincing women he was telling the truth. So how in the world could Lauren believe anything any man told her?

How could she know Matthew was any different from her father?

A tear slid down her cheek as she realized that she couldn't. All she could do was trust him—and pray for the best.

forty-six

For someone knocking on death's door, Ernest Berry could be the poster boy for living life to the fullest. He'd had a setback this weekend and had to be rushed to the hospital. But no one would ever know it by looking at him now.

"Good morning," Ernest said, greeting Joyce with a smile.

She wanted to throw her arms around him just because she was happy that he was fine. Instead, she allowed only a smile. "Hey, you. Glad you're feeling better."

"That old cancer can't keep me down," he said.

"What's that in your hand?" Joyce asked.

"Some daisies."

She laughed because the roots and dirt were still clinging to the bottom.

"Did you really pick those from the rotunda? You know Nurse Amanda is going to have a fit."

He shrugged and handed them to Joyce. "Just wanted to put a smile on your face. You walk around mad all the time, and I got to thinking: maybe it's because she hadn't had anyone bring her flowers in a while."

Joyce took the flowers. She really was touched by the gesture because here he was, just out of the hospital and thinking of her. Plus, he was right. She hadn't had anyone bring her flowers in a very long time.

Joyce set the flowers in a vase and returned to her seat by the window. She'd been sitting there, enjoying the beautiful fall day, trying to push aside thoughts of the ugly scene with her daughter. She could have been better than that. Now she had no idea if Lauren was ever coming back.

"How are you today, Ernest?" she asked.

"Better now that I see I caught you on a good day. Mind if I sit?" he asked, for a change.

She motioned to the sofa across her room and he dropped onto it. Apparently he'd come in with an agenda, because he said, "You know, sometimes if you talk to someone who is objective, you can get clarity on things that weigh you down."

She cut her eyes at him. "Umm, I talk to Dr. Lawson."

"I'm not talking about quacks," he said with a chuckle. "I'm just saying, sometimes it's good to open up to a friend. A handsome male friend. About six-one, one hundred and twenty-two pounds. Great personality."

Joyce laughed. "You wouldn't happen to know anyone like that, would you?"

He flashed his toothless grin. Joyce felt grateful for his company.

"I just have a past," she finally admitted.

"We all do."

Joyce didn't think so. "Mine was tumultuous. Let's just say my late husband and my daughter did a number on my heart."

"Hmph," he said. "And it's made you bitter?"

Joyce nodded. "That's an understatement."

"Well, let me just say, you can't allow the negative things

that happened with your husband or your daughter to wipe out in your mind every good thing you've ever believed. Now, I don't know what your husband did, but I'm assuming it involved another woman. If that's true, then yeah, that was really bad, but that doesn't mean everything about him was bad."

"I just can't shake the anger and bitterness," she said.

Ernest shrugged like that was a no-brainer. "You have to make a choice. It's natural to have those feelings, but at some point, you're gonna have to ask yourself, is that where you want to stay?"

Joyce stirred uncomfortably. Her bitterness, she had to admit, led to her daughter storming out of this place. Julian would be visiting only for a little while, and then who would come see her?

"Stress only aggravates your illness," he continued. "We're on a fast track to a date with Jesus. I don't know about you, but I don't want to spend my last days in that place of negativity."

She nodded, actually taking in his words. That did make her think, though, and she said, "Ernest, where's your wife?"

He leaned back in his seat. "Oh, she died years ago. Never been blessed with kids, either. So when I die, my legacy dies with me."

"What kind of legacy do you have?"

"Not much. I don't have much but my name. So if I have any regrets in life, it's the fact that there will be no one to carry my name on. But it just wasn't in the cards. That wasn't the plan God had for my life. He wanted my legacy to end here, I guess."

Joyce thought about what it would be like to die alone. To be like Ernest with no one there in her final days.

"You don't have any other family?" Joyce asked.

"I outlived them all. Got a brother still alive. But dead in the head. Lost him to mental illness. Last I heard, he was homeless in Phoenix somewhere. Got a nephew, he's the one that pays the bill here, but he ain't got time to visit. So it's just me. All alone."

"What a sad life."

He took issue with that. "Who has a sad life? Not me. I live life to the fullest. To the day I take my last breath."

She admired his attitude. She paused, then said, "Can I ask you a question? I mean, you can be honest because we're just friends."

"So we are friends?" he said, grinning.

"You know what I mean. There is no reason for you to lie to me."

"I don't lie. Lies are too hard to remember."

"How long were you married?"

"Thirty-two years, three hundred and sixty-four days. Wife died the day before our thirty-third anniversary."

"Were you faithful to her?"

He cocked his head. "What kind of question is that?"

"I guess that's my answer."

"No, I just wanted to know what kind of question that was," Ernest said. He scooted to the edge of his seat. "Let me tell you something, when I took Lillian Davis as my wife, I forsook all others."

"So, you mean to tell me in thirty-three years, you were never with another woman?" Joyce asked skeptically. "I told you there was no need to lie."

He was offended. "Tell the truth and shame the devil. I

swear on my dilapidated pancreas. Not once did I ever cheat on my wife."

Her skepticism turned to amazement. She didn't think that was possible.

"Oh, I bumped into some pretty women along the way." He stuck his chest out. "And as fine as I was, you know they were always after me." He stroked the stubble on his chin. "But I would always ask myself, *Is she worth it? Is she worth hurting my wife? Is she worth my marriage and losing the love of my life?* The answer was always no. So I never strayed."

"Do you think a lot of men ask that 'is she worth it' question?" Joyce wondered if her husband—and her father—were rare or the norm.

Ernest laughed. "Lots of men don't even think about it. But I can tell you this, it is possible to love somebody and hurt them. Some men—and women, for that matter—just do dumb stuff."

"Repeatedly?" she said.

He nodded. "Repeatedly. Doesn't mean they don't love you. Maybe they don't know how to love. Maybe they just think they won't get caught. Maybe they like the adventure."

"That's a lot of maybes."

"Yep. But I've learned you have to remember the good because the bad will eat you alive. What about you? Were you faithful?"

"I was faithful, stupidly so."

"Nothing stupid about that. You did what was right for you. You can't focus on what someone else is doing. All you have control over is what you're doing."

For the first time, Joyce saw him in a different light. "I didn't know you were so wise."

"That's because you won't take the time to get to know me. Maybe if you did, you'd see. I make a good friend. I make good conversation. I also make good love." He flashed a wicked smile.

"Go on, somewhere," she chuckled.

He stood up and wiggled his hips. It was a sad sight that made her laugh as he said, "I still got a little motion in my ocean. You wanna roll on my pole?"

"You are a disgusting old man," she said, giggling like a schoolgirl.

He relaxed and his wicked smile turned warm. "I'm just messing with you. I try to get with a woman as fine as you, and my heart would give out 'fore you got my boxers down. I'm just happy to see you smiling. You really do have a beautiful smile. You should try using it more often."

He winked, then walked out of the room.

forty-seven

For once in her life, Lauren wasn't concerned about the next man, the next date, the next come-up. She was completely and utterly happy being a one-man woman.

That's why she almost didn't answer her cell phone when it blared and Craig's name flashed on her screen.

"Hello?" she said, deciding to go ahead and answer so she could make a few things clear. Then she was going to do as Matthew had done, press DELETE.

"Hey, sweetness," he said. "How are you?"

"Who is this?" She plopped down on her bed. She'd only been home a few minutes, to get some more clothes since she'd been at Matthew's place all week.

"So it's like that now? You forgot who I am?" He sounded offended.

Craig's impeccable, athletic body flashed through her mind, but she quickly brushed it aside. She let out an aggravated groan. "What do you want, Craig?"

"Oh, so you do know who it is."

"What. Do. You. Want?" she repeated.

"I miss you."

"You need to miss me. Miss me with all this foolishness you're talking."

He laughed. "I see you haven't lost that attitude. You know that turns me on."

"Craig, what can I do for you?" Lauren huffed. "Would you like to pick up that jewelry for your wife?"

He chuckled, like that was an in joke. "You know, that was smooth how you deflected my wife. I mean, I was telling my boy how you were the perfect mistress."

She used to take pride in those words. Now they made her cringe. The love of one good man had made her realize how bad it had been settling for that title.

"Let me explain something to you. Who I am and who I was are two different people," she began.

"Aww, dang, so Iyanla fixed yo' life or something?" He chuckled again.

"You can joke all you want, but I don't roll like that anymore." The fact that he was so flippant pissed her off.

"Meet me at the Marriott. I bet I can get you to change your mind."

She rolled her eyes. "Whatever. I won't be meeting you today or any day. Your wife is crazy."

"Don't worry about her. I got her in check."

Boy, was this getting old. "Okay, Craig, let me see if I can break this down to your jock-understanding level. What we had was fun. I enjoyed it, but it's over. You need to focus on your wife and your kids, and I'll focus on my soon-to-be husband."

That turned on the light. "Oh, so you're about to be married?"

She immediately regretted telling him that. The last thing she needed was him causing any problems.

"I'm out the game, okay. Can we leave it at that?"

His cockiness returned. "Oh, so it's cool for you to be all up in other folks' marriages, but you wanna get all righteous when it comes to your own?"

"Whatever, Craig. I have found my happily ever after. So I'm good. That's all I'm saying."

"You people with these rose-colored views of marriage crack me up," he said cynically. "Tell you what, hang on to my number, babe. I give you two years of marriage. Tops. But the first time you catch him creeping, you'll call me back."

That caused a sick feeling in her gut.

"Oh, don't tell me you're one of those who thinks he won't cheat," Craig said when she didn't say anything. "I don't know a man that doesn't."

"Say what you want, Craig. There are some men that are faithful."

"And I heard there was a blue unicorn in the mountains of Maine, but no one has seen it yet." He laughed like he'd really said something side-splitting.

"You're so not funny," she snapped. "It is possible for a man to be faithful."

"Have you met one yet? Your daddy? Your grandfather. Uncles? Friends? Stop me when I name one."

The fact that she couldn't stop him made the phone tremble in her hand. Was she being naïve to think Matthew would be faithful? When they were together before, as far as she knew, he never cheated. But they were kids.

As if he was reading her mind, Craig said, "Even the ones you think are faithful aren't. The male species wasn't meant to be monogamous. That's the bottom line."

Her father had uttered those exact same words. But Lauren refused to let the demons of her past ruin her future.

"Well, I'll take my chances," she said breezily. She didn't want to let him know that he'd rattled her. "Bye, Craig. Have a nice life." She slammed the phone down, hoping it was a stamp of closure on the past.

forty-eight

It felt so good to be in love. Really in love. Lauren would never be a fool in love like her mother was, but she definitely could see how someone could be fooled by love.

She watched Matthew watch the game, then snuggled in closer. This had to be what Heaven felt like. Lauren had forgotten what happiness felt like. She didn't realize how much she had resigned herself to playing second fiddle. How she'd convinced herself that the happiness she was feeling right now didn't exist.

But now that she was letting go and loving, she'd never felt more at peace.

She and Matthew had spent every spare moment of the last three weeks together. She'd accompanied him to formal dinners, receptions, important meetings, and networking events as he tried to solidify his nomination. He'd been there for her jewelry showcase, to comfort her with her family issues, and just to show her how to have fun. That's not to mention his unconventional sides—pottery class, wine, and painting, and of course the mind-blowing sex. Better than it had been in college. Yes, this was perfection personified.

Because Matthew's house was bigger than Lauren's condo, she had ended up spending most of her time at his place.

"I need to go home and wash some clothes," Lauren said, pulling herself up from the bed, where they'd been lounging all morning, watching old movies.

"Why can't you do laundry here?" he asked.

"Uh, because my clothes are at home."

"I think that's part of the problem."

She waited on him to crack a smile. When he didn't, she said, "Come again?"

"When is your lease up?"

She'd complained to him about her landlord and shared her desire to buy her own place. "At the end of next month. Why?"

"Because I don't think you should re-sign it."

"And where am I supposed to live?"

"Here."

"Boy, bye," she said.

"I'm serious."

She shifted on the bed, pulled out a flap of pillow lodged under her shoulder blade. "Matthew, we get along so great because I can go home and you can go home."

"Okay, but—"

"Plus, we've only been back together a few weeks."

He leaned over so his head was lying on her stomach. "But we have history. So technically, we've already been together two years and three weeks."

"Matthew, I'm not moving in with you."

"Don't write the idea off totally. Think about it. Matter of fact, come here and let me convince you," he said, pulling her down to him.

His passionate kisses were interrupted by his ringing cell

phone. Lauren snuggled his neck as he reached over to answer it. Lauren continued to kiss his chest as he said, "Hello?"

He sat up. "Oh, hey, Ingrid."

"Ingrid?" Lauren said, frowning as she stopped midkiss. Lauren sat up in the bed next to him.

"I'm so sorry about canceling on you. I honestly meant to call you back . . . No, I completely get how you think that's foul, and truthfully, it is. I should've talked to you. But it's just been crazy. Between work and . . ."

Lauren folded her arms. He was going to disrespect her and talk to this woman in front of her?

"You are completely right," Matthew continued. "I should've followed up and returned your call."

Lauren got up to leave, but he grabbed her hand to stop her as he continued talking. "I didn't call because I got back together with my girlfriend." He kept his eyes on Lauren as he spoke.

Lauren could hear Ingrid's voice through the phone. She definitely didn't sound happy.

"Yes . . . Thanks for being understanding . . . No, I think this is going to last awhile . . ." He smiled at Lauren. "You take care of yourself."

He pressed END on the phone and tossed it back on the nightstand. "Sorry about that. Had some unfinished business. No, wait." He retrieved the phone, then tapped the screen, before turning it to face Lauren. Matthew had pulled up Ingrid's name in his contacts list.

He scrolled down to the button that said DELETE THIS CONTACT. He then pressed the button, causing her info to disappear. "Now it's finished," he said as he tossed the phone on the bed and pulled Lauren toward him. "It's just you and me."

She contemplated resisting, but that sign of fidelity had touched her and she fell into his embrace. Lauren thought about her own cell phone. She needed to do a lot of deleting herself.

Lauren didn't realize that she had dozed off. She woke up to see Matthew watching the local news. The anchor was delivering some story about a scandal at another area college.

"Doggone shame. Such a talented guy brought down by his libido," Matthew said.

"Who is that and what happened?" Lauren asked as she yawned. She wasn't really interested but wanted to discuss things that interested Matthew.

"The president of North Carolina AI is in the middle of a major scandal. Apparently, two of his employees have accused him of sexual harassment. I don't know why people think they're invincible," Matthew said, shaking his head. "What's done in the dark always comes to light."

That observation made Lauren cringe. God knows she'd done dirt she hoped would forever stay buried. But her days of wallowing in the dark were over, so hopefully, she was good.

After the report, Matthew turned the TV off, then turned his total attention on Lauren.

"What?" she asked.

"I love you."

"I love you, too," she replied. If felt good to say those words with no trepidation.

"Marry me," he said.

"What?"

"I know I should give you some elaborate proposal, but I can't wait. I need you in my life. Permanently."

Lauren could feel goose bumps springing up all over. "Matthew, I don't know what to say."

"Say yes. Wouldn't you like to be the first lady of a prestigious university?"

"First lady? Really?" She laughed.

"I'm for real. Colleges are serious about the president's wife."

She studied him to see if he was playing. She was shocked to see he wasn't. "Okay, I think the whole first lady thing is cute and all, but marriage? We just got back together."

"I don't need to spend years dating someone I've already dated for years." He scooted closer to Lauren and took her hands. "It's looking good for me with this job, and I'd love to start this new chapter of my life with you. I don't have a ring, but first thing in the morning, we can go see Luigi Zheriwoski."

Lauren was surprised Matthew even knew who the famous jeweler was. "Yeah, right. He doesn't take new clients. Luigi books up two to three years in advance." It was her biggest dream to work with him, but she wasn't yet on his level.

Matthew handed her a card. "For some people he does."

Being a designer herself, Lauren had occasionally dreamed of the perfect ring, but she always thought it was just that—a dream.

The thought that she could have a ring designed by Luigi Zheriwoski sent her insides into a tailspin. "Lauren, we have a history, so this didn't just come out of nowhere. I prayed for the right woman, and God answered my prayers by sending you back into my life. I want—no, correction—I *need* you to be my wife. Lauren Robinson, will you please marry me?"

"I-I . . ."

"One day you'll fall in love so hard, marry a man, and he'll cheat on you and break your heart. Then maybe you'll understand my pain."

Lauren pushed back the familiar refrain. This man wasn't her father.

"Well?"

She wrestled with the huge tidal wave of her past. That didn't matter anymore, did it? This was Matthew, not anybody else. Finally she found the strength to say, "Yes! Yes, I'll marry you," as she threw her arms around his neck.

forty-nine

All Lauren's excitement dissipated at the sight of her friend standing at her front door, puffy-eyed and upset.

"Hey, are you okay?"

Vivian stepped to the side and let Lauren in. "No, I don't think I'll ever be okay again," she said somberly.

Lauren had made a beeline to Vivian's to share the news of her engagement. She hadn't expected to walk into this. Vivian sat down on the sofa. Balled-up tissues were strewn all over the sofa and floor. Lauren had texted after she'd done a jewelry drop-off and asked if she could swing by. Vivian had just replied, *okay*, but she'd never said anything about crying for hours.

"Okay, what's going on?" Lauren said, taking a seat across from her.

"My son is gone," Vivian cried. "He's really gone."

"Oh, wow. So they moved?"

She nodded. "My ex has taken my son to Seattle. I didn't even get to say good-bye. My evil ex talking about 'that would've just made it harder.'" She let out a loud sob. Lauren moved closer to pat her back. "My baby isn't going to know who I am in a year."

"Don't say that," Lauren said. "He'll always know his mother."

"My ex already tries to turn him against me. The distance won't help."

Lauren wasn't good at comforting, but she felt like she should do something to make Vivian feel better. "Well, you'll be able to go back and forth to Seattle and see him," she said, trying to find some light.

"Not if my ex has his way. You don't understand. He's powerful. He has money. I have nothing. I've tried to understand how I ended up here, but I just can't. I just can't." She was rambling through her tears.

"What happened? You know, to get you to this point?"

"The crazy part is, he cheated on me, but I'm the one who ended up with the short end of the stick."

"I don't understand that. How did he get custody of your son?" Lauren asked.

"I told you, he has money. Money trumps everything else! They tried to paint me as unfit. All I ever did was love that man and love my son, and he cheated, but I'm unfit?"

"Okay, don't get worked up," Lauren said, patting her leg.

Vivian dabbed her eyes. "I need a drink."

"I'll get something," Lauren said, grateful for a reason to escape. This was truly an awful problem without any hope of a solution. "What do you have in there?" she asked as she headed toward her kitchen.

"There is some Hennessy in the cabinet."

Cognac? Yep, Vivian was in a pretty bad place.

Lauren found a glass and poured Vivian a drink. She passed on fixing a glass for herself since she was planning to cut her visit short.

"Look, I've been sitting here crying all day. What's up?"

Vivian said after Lauren handed her the glass. "You said you wanted to tell me something."

Lauren tried to restrain the smile creeping up on her face. She didn't want to appear too ecstatic. "I'm getting married."

"What?" Vivian sat up.

"Yep, ever since I did like you said and let my guard down with Matthew, we've picked up where we left off, but with an intensity that's out of this world. I don't know if he planned it or not, but out of the blue he asked me to be his wife."

Vivian stared at her, her face emotionless. Lauren guessed her own sadness was keeping her from being happy.

"Wow," she finally said. "You just get it all, don't you?"

"What?" Lauren said, losing her smile. "I don't have it all. I'm just lucky."

"That's my point. You stay lucky." She took a swig of her drink. "You get the happily ever after." She shook her head like she didn't want to discuss it anymore. "Well, congrats to you."

The flat way she said this left Lauren feeling deflated. "Well, thanks. I think."

Vivian sighed. "I'm not trying to steal your joy. My son leaving is just really painful for me and I don't know what to do."

"Well, I'm sorry about everything with your son, but I'm sure it'll all work out." Lauren really was trying to be optimistic. But she could tell from the look on her friend's face, Vivian believed she'd never see her son again.

fifty

Today was going to be a bad day. Joyce felt it in her spirit. She felt it in the fact that she woke up in a fog.

She'd dreamed about Vernon last night. She'd dreamed of that day they first met, outside the diner. Only, in her dream she went her way and he went his. He told her he was engaged and she left him alone.

If only her dream had been real.

It should be against the law for a woman to love a man like Joyce loved Vernon Robinson. She loved him more than she loved herself. More than she loved her children.

There was something truly wrong with that.

She knew that now. And she knew it was time to forgive herself for all the mistakes she'd made.

Joyce threw back the covers and tossed her legs over the edge of the bed. She tried to stand, but felt dizzy and immediately sat back down. She blinked, tried to focus, and still felt she was leaning sideways. Maybe she needed to just sit for a minute. Compose herself.

Only, ten minutes later, she still didn't feel any better.

"Mrs. Joyce, are you okay?"

She heard the voice, and it sounded near, but she couldn't

make out where it was coming from. In fact, she couldn't make out much of anything.

She opened her mouth to tell whoever was in front of her that something was seriously wrong. But no words would form. It was as if her tongue had become too heavy.

The walls closed in, and everything around her went black. Joyce felt herself floating away. And then he touched her hand.

"Vernon?" she asked, surprised.

He smiled. "Hey, beautiful."

Her mouth felt pasty. "Wh-what are you doing? Where am I?"

"Shhh," he said. "I just wanted to come tell you that I loved you."

"Am I in Heaven?" She had a second thought after saying that. "Or, if you're here, am I in Hell?"

Vernon chuckled. "No. I came to you. You didn't come to me. I just came to tell you that it's not your time."

"Huh?" Joyce wondered why he looked the way he had when she met him. Why didn't he look old and gray, the way he did when she put him in the ground? And what the heck was that white glow around him?

"I just want to tell you, it's not your time," he repeated.

"I'm tired, though," she said wearily. Joyce didn't know what was going on, but she felt drained. And she wanted a white glow around herself.

"Yeah, harboring hate can do that."

"I don't have any hate," she said.

"Yes, you do. And resentment." He lightly tapped her heart. "And that boils over here and consumes you."

Despite all the grief he'd brought her, seeing him made her smile. "Since when did you become so wise?"

"I haven't. I learned things too late."

"Like what?"

He took her hand. "Like how precious you are."

They stared at each other for a minute, and then she asked the question she'd asked the day she buried him. "Why, Vernon? Why did you hurt me so bad?"

She saw true regret in his expression. "I don't have any excuse. I was selfish. Weak. There is just no excuse. You didn't deserve any of what I did to you. Instead of being there for you when you needed me, I turned my back on you."

That brought tears to Joyce's eyes. He'd said that before, but this time she believed him.

"All you did was love me," he continued.

Joyce nodded. "And I just wanted you to love me back."

He wiped away the tears she didn't know she was shedding. "I loved you. I just didn't know how to love you the right way. I loved you like my father loved my mother. And his father loved his mother."

And my father loved my mother, she thought.

Vernon continued. "I caused your pain. Me, and me alone."

"Why are you telling me this now?"

"Because I want you to make peace. All of this was me. I was deceitful. I put our daughter in the middle of this. She loves you. She needs you. Don't shut her out."

She felt a pang of regret. She'd been feeling the same way lately.

He squeezed her hand tighter. "I'm begging you. Forgive our child. I know it's hard. I hurt both of you and I pray for that forgiveness every day. But I need you to make this right before it's too late."

She wanted to ask Vernon some questions but he started fading.

"Vernon?" She struggled to sit up. "Vernon?" She squinted, trying to bring him back into focus.

"She's coming to," Joyce heard someone say.

"Mrs. Robinson, can you hear me?"

Vernon disappeared and her vision grew even more fuzzy, then cleared.

"Wh-what happened?" Joyce was lying on the floor, surrounded by a dozen people. Ernest, Pearl, and some other people were standing in the doorway, watching in utter fear.

"Am I dead?" she asked.

"No," the facility resident nurse said with a relieved smile. "You just passed out."

She and two other orderlies helped Joyce up off the floor and back onto the bed.

"Why did I pass out?" She flinched as the nurse shone a flashlight in her eyes.

"I don't know. The doctor is on the way. They'll run some tests. Did you eat this morning?"

Joyce thought for a moment. Did she? She couldn't remember.

"She didn't," Ernest announced from the doorway. "I came in here about three hours ago to see if she wanted to go eat before the kitchen closed, but she was still in bed."

Everyone looked at Joyce strangely, probably because she was an early riser. The fact that she was still in bed at ten o'clock was a shock itself.

"I know you don't like the doctor to visit," the nurse told her, "but I need you to not fight me on this, okay?"

Joyce nodded. She just didn't know. Between the passing out and her visit from Vernon, she was all too ready to co-operate and find out what the heck was wrong with her.

fifty-one

W hat is this?" Lauren waved the newspaper in front of Matthew's face. Her heart had been racing since she'd opened the morning paper and seen her smiling picture blaring at her.

"Looks like the local newspaper," Matthew casually replied. He was sitting at his kitchen table working on a budget proposal for the board.

Lauren thought he was sure doing a lot of work for a job he didn't officially have yet, but he explained that he had to show the board he was ready to handle the job.

"I know it's a newspaper," she said, waving the Raleigh *News & Observer* some more. "I'm talking about this!" She jabbed the front page of the Lifestyles section.

Matthew looked up from the budget report and flashed a smile. "That's us. Surprise."

"Surprise? Really?"

He looked confused. "Umm, I thought you would be happy. They did a feature story on us."

"I don't want a feature story on us," she protested.

"Why not? What's the big deal?" He took the paper and studied it more closely. "I think this is actually a good picture of us."

When the picture had been taken at the Congressional Black Caucus dinner last week, she never imagined it appearing on the front section of a newspaper.

"I don't understand what the problem is." He handed the paper back to her. It had been three weeks since he'd proposed. Three whirlwind weeks. As promised, they'd gone to see Luigi, the jeweler, the day after Matthew had proposed. Not only had he designed the ring of her dreams, but he'd rushed it so that they could pick it up within a week. And now she was sporting it proudly.

They'd agreed on a one-year engagement, figuring it would give him time to get settled in his new job, which everyone was confident that he would get.

"Why are we plastered all over the newspaper?" she asked again.

Matthew kept grinning. "Babe, you need to get used to it. When I become president of Carolina State, we're going to be in the paper quite a bit."

Lauren had never been one for the limelight. Especially with the life she'd led. She'd wanted to quietly marry Matthew. There was nothing quiet about this.

"You should've told me you were going to do this, because I would've told you that I don't want to do this."

"Why? Are you wanted by the FBI or something?" he joked.

Lauren cut her eyes at him.

"I'm joking. But no, really, you're not, are you?"

She flung the paper at him. "Of course I'm not wanted by the FBI. I just don't like my business all over the place."

"Well, we're a public couple now and my position is a

public position. We have an image to maintain. We will be analyzed and scrutinized. That's one of the drawbacks of the position, but it does come with perks."

"Ugh," she moaned. "You sure seem certain that you've got the job."

"I'm the most qualified. The other guy has the experience, but he doesn't have the effervescent personality like me." He closed his work, stood, and stepped toward her. "Babe, sorry I didn't tell you. I actually thought it would be a nice surprise."

She sighed, deciding it would be useless to continue arguing. "I just don't want anything messing up our happy home."

"And what could possibly do that?"

If only you knew, she thought.

"Lauren, I don't know if you understand what I do as a college administrator. It's almost like a politician," Matthew said, pulling her into a hug. "This is regulated by the board, so the position is political. Alumni have to like you, the state has to like you, the students have to like you."

"What if I don't care whether people like me?"

Matthew made a wry face. "Unfortunately, you'll have to learn to start caring."

When she didn't respond, he gently kissed her forehead. "Sweetheart, I'm sorry, I wasn't trying to upset you. I'm dumbfounded as to why it has you so upset. Are you ashamed? Do you not want people to know we're getting married?"

"Of course not." His words caused her to think. Why was she so upset? Why was she so secretive? Maybe because that's what her father had always taught her to be. But she wasn't Matthew's mistress. She was about to be his wife. A title that she needed to wear loud and proud.

"You're right. I'm overreacting."

He smiled appreciatively as he returned to his seat. She took a look at the picture again. "First lady, huh?" She finally smiled.

"The real deal."

"So does that mean I get a staff and a budget?"

"Not quite. It is the number-two HBCU in the country, but they aren't on that level yet. It's the Ivy League of HBCUs. Embrace it."

She was about to say something else when the phone rang. She grabbed her cell off the counter, glanced down at her caller ID, and let out a sigh.

"It's my mother's facility." She pressed the ACCEPT button, bracing herself for whatever this call was about. "Hello?"

"Hi, Lauren, this is Amanda, your mother's nurse. We wanted to let you know that your mother had a little incident."

That caused her to stand at attention. "What kind of incident?"

"She passed out again."

"Is she okay?"

"She's fine. She's come to. We've had the doctor check her out. They're going to run some tests. We're not quite sure what happened. It might just be exhaustion."

Or it might be cancer coming to claim her, Lauren thought darkly.

"Do I need to come there?"

"No, she's fine, but we did want to make you aware."

"Okay, thanks." Troubled, Lauren hung up the phone. The nurse sounded like everything was fine. So why was Lauren's gut telling her something different?

fifty-two

Terminal.

That was the most devastating word in the English language. That was the word Dr. Rodriguez had just uttered. That one word had completely rewritten the course of Joyce's life.

"Joyce, are you okay?" Dr. Rodriguez asked.

She nodded, unable to form any words to respond.

"So, what does that mean?" Lauren asked.

"Yeah, Doc. I know you had said it had spread, but we thought . . ."

Joyce had forgotten that her son and daughter were sitting at her side. Julian had gotten in last night, which should've told her this was serious since he'd just left. She vaguely remembered him tiptoeing into her room in the wee hours of the morning. For a moment she thought she was dreaming again. But this morning his smiling face had greeted her. Lauren had been standing next to him. And when a somber Dr. Rodriguez walked up behind them, she knew this wasn't going to be pretty. She didn't, however, know it was going to be this ugly.

"So, you see all of this black area," the doctor said, pointing to the X-ray of her brain. "This is where the tumor has spread."

"So, did the surgery do any good?" Julian said crossly.

"Surgeries," Joyce felt compelled to correct. She glared at the doctor. "I mean, why have I been enduring all of this poking and prodding and radiation and pills if I'm just going to die anyway?"

Joyce was trying to make a joke about dying, but she wasn't ready to go. Seeing this X-ray put a real time stamp on her life.

"I've always been honest with you. I've said from the beginning, nothing is guaranteed. We got eighty percent of the tumor, but the twenty percent that remained was too aggressive. I told you that it was spreading. We just didn't expect it to go this fast. And it has now wrapped around the optical nerve. At this point there's nothing we can do."

"You can't take it all out?" Lauren asked. "All of the affected area?"

"No. Such an operation would be fatal. There wouldn't be enough left for her to be functional. There really is nothing we can do about it. I'd be surprised if you made it six months," he said bluntly.

"So, I'm dying for real?" Joyce finally managed to say.

"I think your focus should be on being comfortable in these last days," Dr. Rodriguez said.

"How is a person supposed to be comfortable when they have a date with death?" she snapped.

The doctor looked at her sympathetically, then patted her hand. "Let me know if I can do anything for you."

"Yeah, you can give me a new brain," she snapped. Julian's

hand went to the small of her back. For once she wasn't comforted by her son's touch.

"Why is this happening to me?" Joyce cried when the doctor left the room. "What did I ever do to deserve this?"

She buried her head in her hands and sobbed. Julian immediately moved toward her. Lauren hesitated, but within moments she was hugging her, too.

fifty-three

Just when Lauren thought the situation couldn't get any more dire, her mother's psychiatrist delivered the final blow.

"I'm sorry; after reviewing all of the doctor's notes, that's my recommendation," Dr. Lawson said.

They'd returned from Dr. Rodriguez's office and tried to get their mother settled in the facility. It was grueling because she kept crying that she didn't want to die in that place.

Her outbursts had brought out Dr. Lawson, and once they'd gotten their mother settled, Lauren and Julian had returned to Dr. Lawson's office for this news.

"What does that mean?" Lauren asked.

The doctor sighed. "It means your mother is right. The best thing for her right now is to be with family."

Lauren instantly balked and turned to her brother. "So, do I need to get her plane ticket or will you?"

Matthew, who had met her here once Lauren called so upset, put his hand on her leg.

"Come on, Lauren," Julian said. "We need to be realistic. This isn't about us. This is about our mother and making her last days comfortable. North Carolina is her home. She has friends here."

"She doesn't have any friends," Lauren pointed out.

"Plus, I'm about to be deployed to Iraq," Julian continued.

"Tell them you can't go," she replied.

"It doesn't work like that. And besides, there is no way Rebecca can handle Mom and the twins alone."

"Oh, no," Dr. Lawson interjected. "I wouldn't suggest putting her on a plane. She can't handle that trip emotionally or physically."

Julian shrugged like that was the end of the discussion.

Lauren glared at her brother as her eyes misted.

"We got her," Matthew said, stepping in.

"No, we don't," Lauren hissed.

"I know you have your issues, but she's dying," he gently said. "Not only do you need to make things right, but you can't let her die in this place."

Lauren glared at her fiancé, but he cocked his head toward the door. "Can I talk to you for a minute?" He didn't wait for her to answer as he took her hand and led her out into the hallway.

She didn't say a word as he turned to face her.

"I need you to take a deep breath. I know this is stressful," Matthew began.

"That's not the half of it," she replied. "I don't understand why this burden has to fall on me. It's just not fair."

"Well, we know that life isn't fair," Matthew said. "Your brother is right. A military base is not the place for your mother. Plus, they have two small children. She doesn't need the stress of rambunctious toddlers."

"And I don't need the stress of a cantankerous old woman who can't stand the sight of me," she said.

"Some of us would die to spend time with our mother."

This bit of pabulum had no effect on her. "Some of you don't have my mother."

Lauren knew that Matthew had lost his mother in elementary school to a drunk driver. He'd been raised by an aunt, so obviously, his mommy issues were clouding his judgment.

"Sweetheart, don't be like that," he pleaded with her. "I can't imagine letting someone you love die alone."

Lauren motioned around the facility. "Look at all these people. She won't be alone."

Matthew continued to show that endlessly patient face he had.

"I just don't understand why this burden has to fall on me," Lauren continued as she began pacing back and forth in the hallway.

"Because there is no one else. It doesn't mean that your brother loves her any less. It just means that you're in a better position to care for her."

Lauren spun around, her eyes misting. "What about me? Does anyone care that I'm the one sacrificing? I'm tired! She hates me!"

"Your sacrifice doesn't go unnoticed. I know you think your brother doesn't notice, that your mother doesn't appreciate you, but they do."

"If I wasn't here, they'd have to figure something out," Lauren muttered.

"But you *are* here. *We* are here. This is not all going to fall on you. It will fall on *us*," Matthew said, taking her hand to stop her pacing.

While his words touched her, the mere thought of her mother living with her gave her hives. "Oh, great. Just what I need to start off my marriage—my mother living with me."

"Lauren . . ."

"I have to go."

"Where are you going?"

"I need some air. I will call you later."

Aunt Velma's house had always been a place of solace. That's why Lauren turned her BMW into the driveway of her aunt's house. She was her voice of reason when Lauren was a ball of emotions.

"You okay?" Aunt Velma asked, greeting Lauren at the front door before she could even ring the doorbell.

"No."

Her aunt stood to the side and motioned for her to come inside.

Lauren stomped past her, flung her purse on the sofa, then spun to face her aunt. "I can't do this."

"Do what? Have your mother come live with you?"

"How do you know?"

"Julian called me."

Lauren rolled her eyes. "Let me guess, he wanted you to convince me to let her stay."

"I don't need to convince you to do what's right." She closed the front door firmly. "Have a seat."

Lauren fell down on the hard sofa as her aunt took a seat in the recliner across from her.

"You and your mama about to work my doggone nerves," Velma said.

"What?" Aunt Velma always took her side when it came to her mother, so this was surprising.

"Y'all both getting on my nerves. Your mama knows better, and at this point you know better, too."

"I'm not the one with issues. She's the one that has held on to all this hate for me—"

"Yeah, yeah, yeah. You were a child when my brother

was doing his dirt," Aunt Velma said, cutting her off. "But I'm talking about now. You and your mama need to put on your big-girl panties and deal with your issues."

"Again, I don't have any issues. You're sounding just like her."

"She has issues. She chose to stay in that marriage. And I love my brother to the core of my soul, but how you let a man do you is how he'll keep doing you. The minute she showed him that his cheating was acceptable, he knew that it was acceptable. So she needs to accept her role in that."

"That's what I've been trying—"

"And you," she said, cutting Lauren off, "you need to understand that your mother was hurt and she's been carrying that demon for a long time."

"I understand that," Lauren said resentfully. "That's why I've been going there."

"But you stand in judgment of her."

That brought Lauren up short. She supposed her aunt was right about that. Lauren finally sighed. "What am I supposed to do?"

"Your mother doesn't have long. The doctors done told you. Let her come stay with you. Make things right. God doesn't make mistakes. Everything happens for a reason, even if we don't know what that reason is. Maybe He wants your mother living with you so you can find some common ground to help you both heal."

They'd given her mother six months. Maybe she could try. That way—whether it worked or not before her mother died—Lauren could say she tried.

fifty-four

Joyce needed some laughter in her life. Something, anything to help her smile. That's why she was wheeling herself down the hall to the dining room. This stupid wheelchair was aggravating, but since the nurses were worried about her getting dizzy and passing out, they insisted that she use it.

The nurse had tried to serve Joyce breakfast in her bed, but she didn't want to be stuck there. Julian was coming by to see her before he left this morning and she was praying for a miracle.

Dear God, please let my son have a change of heart.

Joyce didn't know why that prayer found its way into her thoughts. She knew that Julian couldn't take her back with him. Part of her understood that it didn't make sense for her to go live on an army base. But the other part couldn't help but hold out hope.

Joyce wanted to go say good-bye to a few people before Lauren and Matthew came to pick her up. She rolled up to a table in the rec room, where a somber Pearl and Wanda sat with a couple of friends.

"Good morning," Joyce said.

They all looked up at her, and only Wanda muttered a weak, "Morning."

"Well, I guess y'all must've heard I was leaving," she said. "That's the only thing can explain why all of you are sitting around here with puppy dog faces."

They exchanged glances that made Joyce uneasy.

"Okay, what's going on?" she said. That's when she noticed the empty seat next to Pearl. "Where's Ernest?"

Still, no one said anything. "Hello, are y'all mute today?"

Pearl gently patted her hand. Joyce instinctively pulled it away. "Somebody needs to tell me something. Where is Ernest?"

"Ernest died last night," Pearl said, her words soft and filled with pain.

"What?" Joyce said.

"Cancer won," Wanda said, her eyes getting misty.

Even though they all knew death was imminent, Joyce didn't think any of them were ever prepared.

"They found him on the floor in his bathroom. They think he'd been there all night."

Wanda shook her head. "Lord, please don't let me die in this place like that."

Joyce was speechless.

"I need to see his room," she said, spinning around in her wheelchair. It's not that she didn't believe them; she needed to see for herself in order to process that he was gone.

She rolled down the hallway to Ernest's room. Her wheelchair came to an abrupt halt in front of his door. The empty room panged her heart. The orderlies had already boxed up Ernest's belongings. On the side of the box was written "Donate."

"Why are you donating his stuff?" Joyce asked the nurse who was passing by in the hallway.

"No one wants it. That's what they told us to do," she casually said as she went about her rounds. Joyce wanted to cry as she thought about the fact that Ernest had no one who cared enough to pick up his stuff.

"Mama, are you okay?"

Joyce looked back to find Julian standing behind her. She hadn't realized that he'd walked up. Joyce nodded as he grabbed the back of her wheelchair and wheeled her away.

"I don't want to die in this place," Joyce said.

"You're not. You're leaving in two days," he reminded her.

"And I'm going out of the frying pan and into the fire."

Julian spun her chair around, a little sharper than usual. "Mama, I need you to go in with the right attitude," he said. "This is a big strain on Lauren."

"Nobody asked her to do me any favors," Joyce snapped.

"I asked her," he said firmly. "Because whether you want to admit it or not, you need her. And she needs her mother. Can you try to be her mother?"

"So you're turning against me now, too, trying to tell me I'm not a good mother?"

"You were a good mother, an excellent mother—to me." He touched her hand. "Go be a good mother to your daughter. Can you do that for me?"

Joyce didn't know why—Ernest's death, her diagnosis, her years of hurt—but suddenly, she burst out crying.

Julian immediately embraced her. "Shhh, don't cry. Everything is going to be all right."

She heard his words. She just didn't know how much she believed them.

fifty-five

Her mother was coming to live with her.

Lauren had tossed and turned all night, but she had still been unable to process that information. No, this wasn't going to work. Lauren didn't care what Matthew or Aunt Velma said, she didn't need this drama in her life. Not now. Julian had to step up at long last.

Lauren glanced at the time on the kitchen stove. She knew her brother's flight had gotten in late last night, but it was 10 a.m. and he was a military guy, so he had to be up already. As she pulled her phone out of her purse to call him, it dawned on her that maybe *he* wasn't who she needed to be talking to.

Lauren took a seat at Matthew's kitchen table and swiped her contacts to get to her brother's name. She hoped to have this conversation before Matthew returned from getting them coffee.

She pressed the home number for Julian.

Lauren waited as the phone rang.

"Hello?"

"Hey, Rebecca."

"Who is this?"

Her tone caught Lauren off guard. "Umm, it's Lauren. Julian's sister."

The hostility dropped away and her voice softened. "Sorry, Lauren."

"Are you okay?"

"Yeah, ah, um, I'm okay."

She didn't sound okay.

"Your brother isn't here," Rebecca said.

"Actually, I wasn't calling for him," Lauren replied. "First of all, how are the kids?"

"They're fine. Outside playing." Rebecca usually sounded warm and inviting, but although she didn't sound angry like she did when she'd first answered, her undertone was tense. Probably the twins stressing her out.

"Well, I won't hold you long. I just needed to talk to you about something," Lauren began. "I don't know how much Julian has filled you in on what's going on with Mama."

"Yes, he told me she was in treatment. I've called to check on her a couple of times, but I can't ever seem to catch up with her," Rebecca replied.

"Well, it's taken a big turn for the worse. And the doctors have said there's nothing left for them to do. They've only given her a few months to live. And naturally, she just doesn't want to spend her last days in that facility. So, the doctor thought it would be best if she went and lived with a family member."

Silence filled the phone. Lauren had expected that, and she started speaking quickly to convince her sister-in-law.

"I know you have your hands full, but Mama could actually be a big help to you and the twins. She really loves those boys and she'd—"

"Lauren," Rebecca said, cutting her off, "I don't know how much you know about what's going on with me and Julian."

"I know you guys have the perfect family. It's just me here. I can't take care of Mom by myself. And you know how much my mom adores Julian."

"Yeah," Rebecca harrumphed. "Because she thinks he walks on water."

"I just think it would be better if Mama went there," Lauren said.

Rebecca made a strangled sound, then said, "Lauren, Julian and I are separated."

Lauren almost fell out of her seat. "Separated?"

"Yes, and I will be filing for divorce."

"Are you kidding me? Why?" She couldn't think what could possibly be wrong in their picture-perfect marriage.

"Your brother is a cheating jerk," Rebecca huffed.

"Cheating? Not Julian."

"Yeah, Julian got y'all fooled," Rebecca said. "Everybody. His superiors, his family, his friends, they all think he's this super great guy, but he is just a low-down dirty dog."

Lauren was still trying to process what her sister-in-law was saying. Surely, this woman was talking about someone other than her brother.

"And if it's one thing I don't do," Rebecca continued, "is stay with a cheating man. It wasn't the first time, either. Fool me once, shame on him. Fool me twice, shame on me. He won't get a third chance."

Lauren was speechless. Her self-righteous brother, who had blasted her father for cheating, had turned around and done the exact same thing?

"I am really sorry to hear that," Lauren managed to say.

"Yeah, well, so goes life," Rebecca said sarcastically. "Sorry I can't be much help, but I'm trying to figure out the next step for me and my kids."

Lauren couldn't help but admire Rebecca. She thought her brother had gone and found the most timid white woman he could find, but he messed around and got someone who had more strength than any black woman she'd known.

"Well, no, I definitely understand," Lauren said. "Take care of yourself."

They said their good-byes and Lauren hung up, dumbfounded. She couldn't believe her brother had followed in her father's footsteps.

At first Lauren debated whether she should call and confront him, but she knew he had to be hurting, and they had enough going on that she didn't need to be rubbing salt into his wounds.

She'd made the decision to wait before bringing it up with him when her phone rang. Julian's number flashed across the screen.

Lauren pressed ACCEPT. "Hey," she said.

"Hey." His voice was soft, like a kid who'd just been busted at the cookie jar.

"I just talked to Rebecca," he said.

Lauren didn't say a word.

"She told me she told you."

"What I don't understand is, why didn't you tell me?"

Julian sighed. "And say what, Lauren? Yeah, you know our father who I berated all my life, I'm just like him?"

"Julian, I'm shocked. You cheated on her?"

"I can't believe I did it, either," he said. She'd never heard her brother sound so despondent. And he'd just been here and given no indication that anything was wrong on the home front.

"She said you did it twice."

Julian was sad as he replied, "I did. It was just something that happened. These women around here throw themselves at the army men, and I . . . I just messed up, Sis."

"How did she find out?"

"The first time, I confessed."

"What did you do a dumb thing like that for?" Julian had definitely not learned anything from her father. Vernon Robinson's motto had been to deny, deny, and deny some more.

"I was so ashamed of what I'd done, and she could tell something was wrong. So I came clean. The second time, I just . . . I don't know. I had too much to drink, which is no excuse, but I let Amaya—that's the woman's name—talk me into going back to a motel. But it was all a setup. Amaya had called Rebecca, hoping she'd show up, leave me, and then Amaya and I could be together."

Lauren felt like there was more to that story. Amaya wouldn't have been scheming ways to break up his marriage unless their relationship had been going on for a while. But Lauren felt like it didn't matter. No need to rehash all of the details; the deed was done, and Julian was about to lose all he had.

"Why couldn't Rebecca be like Mom?" Julian said. "She forgave Dad all the time."

"And you hated her for it. And she hated herself for it," Lauren reminded him.

"I know that," he said quietly. "I messed up. Bad. Now Amaya is threatening to go to my superiors. You know adultery is grounds for them to kick me out of the military."

And yet, you risked it all, Lauren thought.

"You'll be okay," she said. No need to beat him up, since he was doing a pretty good job of that himself.

"Please don't tell Mama. I'm begging you."

Lauren thought about his request. A year ago, it would've given her great pleasure to burst her mother's Julian-is-perfect bubble, but now she could only ask herself, what purpose would it serve? Her mother was in her last days. The only news she needed was positive.

"I promise, I won't say a word," Lauren said.

"Thanks," he said, relieved. "Look, I'm sorry I let you down."

"You didn't let me down. We both have made some bad choices in life." Just then Matthew walked into the room and Lauren smiled. "The beautiful thing about life is our past doesn't dictate our future."

As Matthew handed her her coffee and lightly kissed her on the lips, Lauren believed that statement from the bottom of her heart.

fifty-six

Matthew was right about the limelight. A girl could get used to this. Lauren was loving the perks of being the front-runner's fiancée. She could only imagine what it would be like to be the president's wife. This was where she was supposed to be. Standing proudly by her soon-to-be-husband's side. Usually she shied away from attention. But this she could get used to. Even though it was strange to her, these people were treating her like royalty.

She'd been by Matthew's side during an alumni reception this morning and Lauren had felt like a dignitary, the way everyone was catering to her.

"Told you, these people don't play about their university," Matthew whispered.

He was on point about that. Some woman who said she was Miss Carolina State in 1952 said she looked forward to working with Lauren to do their part "to take our beloved university from number three to number one."

Lauren didn't know exactly what she was supposed to do, but she was looking forward to doing her part.

Just six months ago, this all would've seemed like an implausible dream. But now she was wondering should she channel Michelle Obama or Jackie O.

Matthew gave her a kiss on the cheek as he took her hand and led her onto the stage. They'd left the reception and come straight to this press conference, where the prestigious Alumni Association was announcing its unyielding support of Matthew for the next president of the university. The vote by the Carolina State board was in three weeks, and the association wanted to go on record.

Dr. Laurence Stephens, the president of the Alumni Association, took the stage.

"Thank you all so much for coming out," he began. "To say we are thrilled to be here would be an understatement. As you know, we are very serious about our beloved institution."

"That would be the understatement," someone mumbled from the crowd. That elicited some light chuckles and a smile from Dr. Stephens.

He continued: "So you know we have vetted, dissected, discussed, and settled upon someone we think is the perfect fit for Carolina State. We hope that the board will take our wishes into consideration. In fact, we called you here today because we wanted to share with you the amazing plans that the association has and introduce the man we hope will help us in the execution of those plans."

This seemed unconventional to Lauren. Who touted the candidate in the press before he officially got the job? When she'd mentioned it earlier, Matthew said the association had wanted to go on record because the state board had a way of trying to circumvent their desires.

". . . At this time, we'd like to bring Dr. Matthew King up to say a few words." Dr. Stephens stepped aside, looking like a proud father as he motioned for Matthew to take the podium.

Matthew launched into the speech they'd worked and re-worked last night. It was brief but on point. Lauren had never been more proud.

"At this time, we'll take questions," Dr. Stephens said, once Matthew was finished.

A few reporters tossed out university-related budget questions, which Matthew answered with impeccable skill, like he'd been studying for them all of his life.

"Again, Dr. King has to officially get the job before he can lead us to the mountaintop," Dr. Stephens said, laughing as he stepped in to wrap up the questions. "So we hope the board will honor our request to award him the coveted position."

"Excuse me," a reporter in the front row said, raising her hand. "Just one more question for Dr. King before he goes."

Dr. Stephens nodded and stepped back away from the mic.

"Yes, ma'am?" Matthew asked.

She stood. "Robin Pendleton, *Carolina Daily News*. Dr. King, how do you plan to keep your impending personal drama from causing you to lose focus should you get the job?"

Matthew frowned. "Personal drama? I don't have any personal drama."

The reporter looked down at her notes, then said, "Hmmm, I'm talking about the alienation of affection lawsuit brought on against your fiancée, Lauren Robinson."

"Excuse me?" Matthew said

Lauren's mouth dropped open. Lawsuit? Matthew looked confused. Dr. Stephens looked blindsided.

"I have no idea what you're talking about," Matthew said. "And I'm sure if there is such a lawsuit, this is some kind of misunderstanding."

"No, I don't think so," the reporter said. "It was filed in circuit court yesterday. It is brought against Lauren Robinson by Teresa Brooks, alleging alienation of affection for a long-term relationship with her husband, Thomas. She's also cited," the reporter paused and counted, "one, two, three, four, five other cases that are reportedly all going on right now."

Lauren felt like she was about to pass out.

"Well, I assure you this is all a misunderstanding," Matthew began, but Dr. Stephens stepped in and took over the mic.

"A big misunderstanding," Dr. Stephens said. "But that is not what we're here to discuss, and we are out of time."

"But I think our readers would like to know because personal drama like that could affect your 'beloved institution' . . ." Her sarcasm was on full display.

"Again, thank you for your time," Dr. Stephens said, ignoring her. "And have a great day."

Of course, several reporters started shouting questions, all of which they ignored as Dr. Stephens ushered everyone out.

"So, do you have any idea what that reporter is talking about?" Dr. Stephens asked as soon as they were in the hallway. Several members of the Alumni Association, including the former Miss Carolina State, were no longer looking at Lauren like she was royalty.

"No, not at all," Matthew answered. He turned to Lauren. "Do you?"

"Of course not," she replied. If she'd known anything about a stupid alienation of affection lawsuit, she wouldn't have been within a hundred feet of a press conference.

"Do you know this Thomas person?" Dr. Stephens demanded.

A lie formed on the tip of her tongue, but she didn't let it escape. Dr. Stephens might not have vetted her past, but she had no doubt that, at this point, he would leave no stone unturned in trying to get to the truth. A lie would only compromise her.

"Yes, Thomas was a client, but I have no idea where his wife would get that something was going on."

Matthew shook his head in disbelief as the publicist for the Alumni Association came rushing in. "Oh my, this is not good. Every station is reporting on this lawsuit. Because these cases are so rare, they're running with it." He thrust some papers in Matthew's direction. "Apparently, they have texts they say are from Lauren's phone."

"Texts? Anyone can fabricate texts." Matthew perused the papers. Lauren nervously looked over his shoulder. She had to steady herself when she read the texts. They were real. Graphic and real.

"Dr. Stephens—" Matthew began.

Dr. Stephens, who was trembling with suppressed rage, cut him off. "Go home, Dr. King. Just go home and I'll talk with you later. I need to get a handle on this."

fifty-seven

One of the most endearing qualities about Matthew was his placid temperament. He very rarely got upset. Once, in college, a professor had wrongly accused Matthew of cheating and he'd gotten so angry that he'd broken a chair. But other than that, Matthew was a master at keeping his emotions in check.

That's why the sight of his veins bulging in his neck had Lauren shaking in her stilettos.

"Stop lying, Lauren. This isn't making sense," he bellowed.

They'd left the press conference and ridden home in silence. Lauren had wanted to say something in her defense. But she couldn't find the right words. Plus, the one time she'd opened her mouth, she'd only been able to get his name out before he cut her off.

"Let me just read this when I get home," he said.

Once home, he headed straight to the living room, sat down on the sofa, and began reading. He didn't say a word until he'd finished the entire six-page document.

"Explain," he demanded.

"I-I don't know what that's about. I told you that."

Matthew shook his head. "So you want me to believe that

some random woman just picked you out to file legal papers against you with no proof, no grounds. Nothing. That's your story and you're sticking to it?"

Lauren didn't know what she was thinking. She hadn't read the lawsuit, but she doubted that this case was going anywhere, especially now that the media had gotten wind of it.

"Matthew . . ." The doorbell rang before she could get her sentence out.

"Hold on," he said, agitated as he got up to answer. He looked out the peephole and a pained expression filled his face. "It's Dr. Stephens."

Matthew opened the door. "Good evening, Dr. Stephens. Please, come in."

Lauren figured they'd be hearing from Dr. Stephens, she just didn't know it would be this soon.

"We need to talk." He glanced over at Lauren. "Alone."

"Yes, of course," Matthew quickly said.

Dr. Stephens didn't bother acknowledging her, which sent a sick feeling into Lauren's stomach. "I'll give you some privacy," she said, stepping out of the room.

Lauren stopped just around the corner so she could hear the conversation.

"This . . . this is not good," Dr. Stephens began.

"We are just as shocked as you," Matthew replied. "We are trying to get to the bottom of that lawsuit."

"Can you get to the bottom of this while you're at it?"

Pregnant silence filled the room, then Matthew said, "Where did this come from?"

It took everything in Lauren's power not to rush into the living room to see what Dr. Stephens had handed Matthew.

"It was emailed to me and other board members right after the press conference. It's a list of powerful married men that your fiancée has apparently had affairs with."

"I-I don't understand." Matthew sounded flabbergasted.

"Look, I wish that we could keep personal lives private, but in the position you're about to occupy, there is no such thing as a personal life. And a scandal like this can keep you from getting the votes you need."

"It can't be true. None of this can be true."

"I don't know whether it's true or not. If it's not, you need to find the source of these allegations and nip them in the bud. The board is voting in three weeks. Such impropriety will en-sure that they go with another candidate." Dr. Stephens's voice gained a spark of anger. "I've fought hard to get you this posi-tion. There are men all over the country that would love to be in your shoes. President of Carolina State is a coveted position. It is the only HBCU where our president makes over five hun-dred thousand. We cannot have it brought down by scandal."

"But . . . well, there has to be more to this story."

"Unless the story is a blatant lie, I'm not interested in talking about it. One thing you'll learn about me is that I don't pussyfoot around. You'll have to pardon my bluntness, but if this is true, you have some hard decisions to make because no matter how much you love someone, you can't turn a ho into a housewife."

That was it. Lauren couldn't help it. She took a step for-ward and stood in the entryway. Both Dr. Stephens and Mat-thew looked in her direction. She expected Dr. Stephens to mutter an apology, but he just glared at her like she was dirt. "I'll be in touch," he announced before walking out the door.

Lauren felt some kind of way about Matthew allowing that man to talk about her like that, but she knew now wasn't the time for that discussion. "Matthew, I'm sorry."

"Too late for sorries." His jaw was tight as he handed her the paper that Dr. Stephens had just given him. "Guess you don't know anything about these guys, either, huh?"

Lauren felt faint as she read the paper. She knew how much he wanted this job.

"I need you to help me understand what's going on." He walked over to the bar to fix a drink. "Now the board is getting emails listing all the married men you've been with. This is like a bomb to my candidacy. You really pissed someone off."

"Matthew, I swear I don't know what this is about." Her stomach was in complete knots. "Obviously, someone is out to cause havoc in our lives." She glanced back down at the email. The headline read, "Carolina State's Finest." Under that was a picture of Lauren and Matthew, then the words, *I wonder if he knows all the married men she's slept with.*

Listed on the paper was 80 percent of the men she'd been seeing. Who knew all of this and how?

"This is some garbage," she said.

"First the alienation of affection lawsuit. Now this. What's really going on?" The look in his eyes told her that he was still hanging on to hope that this could all be explained away.

"I have no idea!"

"So you don't know these men?" He grabbed the paper and read some of the names. "Thomas Brooks, Craig West, Lewis Cole, David Yen."

Lauren stopped him. "This is some bull. David Yen is my dentist!"

Matthew didn't seem persuaded. "What about the rest of them. Cornell Jacobs, Felix Seawood?"

Lauren was still trying to figure out who in the world could have connected all of these dots. Not one of them knew the others existed.

"So, again, someone just randomly levels these charges against you and just randomly makes up names?"

"Someone is intent on ruining me. On ruining us." Lauren's mind raced as she tried to make sense of this. Teresa, Thomas's wife, must be behind this since she filed the lawsuit. But how in the world did she know all the other stuff?

"Maybe it's one of your ex-girlfriends," Lauren said.

Matthew ran his hands over his head like he was seriously considering that possibility. "I wonder if Carla would do something like this."

"Who is Carla?"

"She's an ex that didn't take our breakup too well."

"You've never told me about her."

"Have you told me everything about everyone you dated?" he said, glancing down at the paper. "This is all just too much. You know what, maybe you should concentrate on your mother and let me figure this out. Lauren, I have really worked hard to get to this position, and I need a minute to process the fact that it could all be crashing down."

No way could she come clean. The lie that she originally stated came barreling out. "I don't know who these men are. I don't know why someone would spread these vicious lies about me."

Yet an inner voice was asking: How would she be able to start over when she was always forced to lie?

295290290 ReSHONDA TATE BILLINGSLEY

Matthew didn't believe her. "I'm tired of the lies, Lauren. I need to know what's going on. I have a lot at stake, and I can't solve this problem if you're not honest with me."

"I don't know why someone is doing this," she replied. That was the truth.

"Are you cheating on me?"

"No," she said. "Absolutely not." She was still thinking through her options. This mess seemed like it was only going to get worse, so she needed to come clean. At least, somewhat clean. "I may have messed around with a married man, but it was before you and I got together."

Okay, so she couldn't make herself come all the way clean.

"What do you mean, you may have? Either you did or you didn't."

"No, I mean, I did."

"Did you know he was married?"

Another lie almost came out, but she slowly nodded.

"Is it the guy from the lawsuit?"

She nodded again.

"Wow. Okay. So this is his wife doing all of this?"

"I don't know," she said.

"It has to be," he said with finality. "And that means, we need to have a conversation with him and her. Are you still seeing him?"

"Absolutely not," she said. "That's why I don't understand this." She couldn't bring herself to tell Matthew that she didn't know which wife it was.

"We've got to get this under control. Our image is everything. The public is scrutinizing me and, by default, you."

"Well, I didn't ask to be scrutinized," she snapped.

Matthew wasn't dealing with attitude at this point. "Look, I'm not trying to upset you. We just have to get to the bottom of this. My job is on the line here. Not only is the presidency at risk, but I could lose my job altogether because the board isn't going to want any of this bad publicity. There's no telling what this woman has up her sleeve next. I just want us to nip this in the bud before it gets out of control."

Lauren didn't know why she was snapping at Matthew. It wasn't his fault that she'd messed with the wrong woman's husband and now, someone was out for revenge.

Matthew paced back and forth.

"Look, Lauren. Maybe you shouldn't go to the dinner with me tonight. Maybe you should just stay here and get everything ready for your mother."

Lauren's feelings were hurt, but she couldn't do anything but say, "Okay."

Although she wouldn't go to the dinner, she wasn't staying home. Lauren was about to get to the bottom of this because she'd be damned if this woman—whoever she was—would ruin the life she was planning.

fifty-eight

Joyce couldn't believe how much she missed that snaggle-toothed man. She didn't realize it, but Ernest had provided her only joy in this place. If she were to come back and visit anyone, it would've been him.

The memorial service for him today had been beautiful. Joyce loved how the staff had come together to put on a beautiful reception. They even had a slide show featuring Ernest in several of his comical moments. In each picture she didn't see the face of someone dying. She saw the face of someone choosing to live.

"Nice service," Pearl said. Even though the reception was held at the facility, they all had dressed up in proper mourning attire.

Joyce nodded. "I just wish I'd gotten the chance to say good-bye."

"We all do," she replied. "Unfortunately, that's the thing about life. We don't know how to embrace the joy until it's gone."

Lily, one of the more quiet patients, spoke up. "I'm going to call my sister today. I don't want to die with regrets."

Pearl said, "That's what Ernest used to always say. Live so you die with no regrets."

Regrets. Joyce had lots of those. Yet she could spend her last days making things right with Lauren. She didn't want to die with regrets.

Wanda said, "On another note, I saw that mess with your daughter."

Joyce cut her eyes in Wanda's direction. Only her messy behind would bring up a topic like that at this time of mourning.

"Alienation of affection?" Wanda continued. "Ain't that that thing that woman sued that *American Idol* singer for?"

"I don't know. I don't get in folks' business like that. Maybe you should try it," Joyce retorted.

"Hmph, and here I was thinking she was an angel for always coming here to see you," Wanda sneered. So much for them bonding over Ernest's death. She was back to her old ways.

"You don't know anything about my daughter," Joyce said flatly.

"Seems like I know she screws other folks' husbands," Wanda replied with a chuckle.

"You must be trying to join Ernest in the afterlife," Joyce growled. She was using a wheelchair but she wouldn't hesitate to get out of it if necessary.

Wanda waved her off. "How she gon' get mad at me because she raised a loose child," she told Pearl.

"Wanda, now isn't the time," Pearl said, also disgusted.

Joyce debated arguing with her, but decided it wasn't worth the effort. "Bye, Pearl," she said, spinning around and wheeling off. She couldn't wait to get away from this place.

fifty-nine

Lauren couldn't believe how in a matter of hours, her life had taken such a drastic detour. Dr. Stephens wasn't playing. Her past had come back with a vengeance, and now the man she loved was going to pay the price.

Lauren wished she were at home with Matthew, working this out, not in Target buying supplies to make her mother comfortable. Lauren still wasn't feeling the idea of settling her mother in Matthew's place, but she knew he was right about it being the best place for her, especially now that she knew everything that was going on with Julian.

Julian.

She was still shocked that her brother—who grew up despising what his father had done—had turned around and done the exact same thing.

Vernon Robinson had really messed his kids up.

But Lauren was determined to stop focusing on the past, and worry about the present.

That's if she still had a present with Matthew.

"Well, if it isn't Raleigh's resident ho."

Lauren spun around to come face-to-face with Dana, her ex-lover Craig's scorned wife.

Judging from her look of contempt, Dana no longer bought their story. "You know, my gut told me not to believe that cockamamy story you gave me about Craig buying jewelry for me and a spa day," she continued. "But you were so convincing and I thought surely, this woman wasn't so low to lie for my husband. And yes, I wanted to give my husband the benefit of the doubt," she said, sneering at that notion. "I guess that's what you were counting on, though. Of course, his other long-term side chick outed him." She laughed at the expression on Lauren's face. "What, you thought you was the only one? Hmph. Well, the other side chick busted him when she informed me that she was HIV-positive." She gave Lauren a measuring look. "Have you been tested? I have, since you know we were all screwing each other."

Lauren gasped and almost fell over backward. HIV? She and Craig had used protection, but nothing was foolproof.

The look on Lauren's face made Dana bust out laughing. "Ha. I'm just kidding about the HIV, but it could've happened. And well, you just never know, so you might want to check that out."

Lauren stared at Dana in disbelief. "Really? Who does that?"

"Yes, really. I should've let you keep wondering, but I'm not low-down like you."

Lauren shook her head. "That is the most childish thing I've ever heard."

"Don't try to judge me," she snapped.

Lauren didn't know what to say. Number one, she wasn't in the mood for this girl. Number two, this was exactly why she only messed with powerful men, because she didn't do ghetto drama. Craig had wooed her with his rugged good looks and near-perfect body.

"Whatever. I don't know what you're talking about, so excuse me." She tried to step around Dana.

Dana moved in her way to prevent Lauren from going around. "Nah, I don't think so," she said. "You know, I saw the press conference." She folded her arms across her chest. "Alienation of affection, huh? I wonder if we can make that a class-action lawsuit. Maybe we can take an ad out in the Sunday paper." She motioned in the air. "If Lauren Robinson screwed your man, please call 1-800-KILL-THAT-THOT and join our class action lawsuit."

Lauren glared at her. "I'm not even going to dignify you."

Lauren tried to step around again, but this time Dana put a hand on her shoulder.

Lauren glanced down at Dana's hand. "If you don't get those Klingon nails off of me . . ."

Dana stepped in her face. "Then, what?" A momentary silence hung between them. "That's what I thought. How long were you screwing my husband?"

Lauren wanted to tell Dana everything she did that Dana didn't, but she'd left that part of her life behind her. She didn't need another scorned wife in her life right now.

"Look, I don't know what you and Craig have going on. I haven't seen him since you came charging me up that day in the hotel."

Dana folded her arms. "I don't believe a thing you say."

"And I don't care what you believe. Your issue shouldn't be with me. It should be with your husband," Lauren said.

"Hmph, speaking of husband, you still gonna have one? I

went to Carolina State. And I agree with what they're saying on social media. We don't want a president that can't tell his wife is a ho."

That stung. But Lauren was determined not to show it. "Look, little girl. You have no idea the hell I have been through. And as you know, stuff in my life is already jacked up. What's one more murder charge?"

That made Dana step back. People often mistook her prissy nature for weakness. But she was two seconds from snapping.

"Now, if I were you, I'd go home and check my husband, because I'm sure you didn't put him out. And by the way, tell him to lose my damn number and stop texting and calling me. Now, move your ghetto ass out the way before they have to call for a cleanup on aisle two."

Dana glared at her hard, but she did step to the side.

Lauren composed herself and strutted to the front to pay for her items. She was so sick of these men and their wives. Someone was out to ruin her, but Lauren doubted that Dana had the brainpower to set her up. Who in the world could it be? As she paid for her purchases, she made a decision. Screw what Matthew said about leaving this alone. She was determined to get to the bottom of things and end her personal drama.

Lauren paced back and forth across the plush carpet of Thomas's downtown office. The receptionist was giving her the side eye, and Lauren could tell the woman couldn't wait for her to leave so that she could get on the phone and gossip with her friends about the raving lunatic who had just demanded to see her boss.

As Lauren wore a hole in the Berber carpet, she couldn't help but think that maybe showing up here wasn't such a great idea. But it was too late for regrets. She was here now and she wasn't leaving until she talked to Thomas.

"Ms. Robinson." Thomas appeared in his office doorway, wearing a classic Armani suit, which must have cost three thousand dollars. He plastered on a fake smile, no doubt for his secretary. "Come on in."

The secretary smirked at the two of them. Any other time Lauren would've given her one right back, but today she was on a mission.

"What the hell is wrong with you?" Thomas said as soon as the door was closed. "Why are you showing up at my office like this?"

"Alienation of affection? Really?" Lauren waved a copy of the lawsuit in his face.

"You think I want this?" he said, lowering his voice. "This is bad for business. My wife is losing her damn mind. And here you come giving her more ammunition. There is no telling what kind of spies she has around here."

"I thought you had your wife under control. That's what you always tell me."

He huffed, his Ivy League education taking a backseat to his hood upbringing. "Look, I got enough drama. I don't need you trippin', too."

"I don't need this," she shot back. "I'm about to get married."

Thomas stared at her. "What?"

"Married."

"So, what does that mean for us?" His whole tone had changed.

She flung the papers at him. "Are you freaking kidding me? There is no *us*. Your wife is suing me."

"My wife is crazy. I figured since I'm headed for divorce court now, you and I—"

It was Lauren's turn to be shocked. At no time had Thomas acted like he expected anything other than a booty call.

"You figured I'd be sitting around waiting on you? It doesn't work like that, Thomas."

He held his hands up. "Whoa. Who are you and what have you done with my Lauren?"

"You don't have a Lauren. You have a woman that stroked your ego and told you what you needed to be told at that time. She was your side chick." Uttering the words made her cringe.

He stepped forward and tried to hug her. "Well, now she can be my main chick."

Lauren pushed his arms back. "I don't want to be your main chick. I want you and your crazy-ass wife to leave me alone."

He looked wounded after his advance had been repelled. "She's trying to get ammunition, that's all."

"By suing me? And stalking me?"

"Stalking?"

"Yes."

"Oh, no. She might've filed the lawsuit, but she would never stoop to stalking. She'll try to take us both down, but not harassment."

"Oh, that makes me feel so much better," Lauren quipped.

"Look, just lie low. She's just mad because she found the hotel bill for our trip to Paris. All this will die down soon."

Lauren glared at him in disgust. "Thomas, we didn't go to Paris."

He paused. "What?"

"No, asshole. That was your other side chick."

"Oh, dang." He stepped closer to her again. "Well, that's beside the point. All of that will die down. She's moving forward with the divorce, talking about she has enough to take me for half." He had the audacity to laugh. "It's cool because it's only half of what she knows about."

What was she thinking when she hooked up with this man? "Just get your wife in check." The last thing Lauren needed was her name dragged through the mud. Not at a time like this.

"I think we need to go away for the weekend," Thomas said smoothly. "Let's go to the Caribbean, get our heads together."

"I think you need to get your wife together." Lauren stormed toward the door. "Make this go away, Thomas. You claim to be such a big shot, make it go away."

"So, can I call you later?" he called out after her.

"You can go to Hell and lose my number."

She stomped out of his office, past the nosy receptionist, and back outside to her car. Once inside, she fell back against the seat and rubbed her temples. She still didn't know how Teresa found out all that information.

Lauren felt her stomach churning as she imagined how long the list could turn out to be.

sixty

Who wants to know when they're going to die? Definitely not Joyce. She would've much preferred that death stole in at night and took her that way, because this way was Hell on earth.

When Lauren arrived to pick her up this morning, Joyce was intent on greeting her with a smile and a positive attitude. But the cancer had other plans. She'd woken up to excruciating pain. The nurses had given her meds that had alleviated the agony some, but her head was still throbbing.

"Come on. Stand up," Lauren said.

Joyce kept her face stoic as Lauren and Matthew helped her into the wheelchair. Her daughter had done well with this one. He was so charming and attentive, and it saddened Joyce when he'd told her on the ride home that he and Lauren were together for two years in college.

She had known so little about her daughter's life.

"Thank you," Joyce told Matthew as she eased out of the car and into the chair.

"Come on in," he said, wheeling Joyce through the front door of his spacious ranch home. "The nurse has already gotten your room set up for you."

Lauren had told her they'd hired a nurse. They were going

all out to make her life comfortable . . . before she died. Truth-fully, Joyce didn't think that would be long. She felt weaker by the day, and the bouts of blurry vision and extreme exhaustion were becoming a regular occurrence.

"Is there anything I can get you?" Lauren asked once they were inside.

"No, I'm fine." Their relationship was so strained that for once, it made Joyce sad. What had she done to her baby girl to create this distance?

Lauren busied herself, no doubt trying to ease the uncom-fortable tension that hung in the air.

"What's this?" Joyce asked when she noticed a bag of pic-tures on the dining room table. She wheeled over and placed the bag in her lap.

"Nothing," Lauren said, racing over to pull them out of Joyce's grasp.

"No, I want to see them," Joyce replied, tightening her grip around the bag.

Lauren stepped back, defeated. "Aunt Velma gave me those to make copies."

Joyce pulled out several of the pictures. A smile crossed her face at the baby pics of Lauren and Julian. She stopped when she got to a tattered black-and-white photo of Lauren.

"Oh, I remember this picture." Joyce pulled it out. "I had just bought you this lavender ruffled dress. I had a grown-up ver-sion of it. And we wore it Easter Sunday when you were five years old. Only you wanted to wear yours every Sunday thereafter."

Joyce laughed at the memory, even though she expected a bad one to overtake it. When it didn't come, Joyce managed a smile. Maybe, just maybe, her last days could be filled with nothing but the happy memories.

sixty-one

She dreamed of Vernon last night. Only in this dream, she wasn't sick. They were happy. Her whole family had gathered for Thanksgiving.

Vernon and Joyce were old. They were sitting on the porch, holding hands as children played in the front yard. Then Julian and his wife appeared. Behind them were Lauren and Matthew. They were all together.

That dream was what Joyce wished her reality could've been. But just like there was no happy beginning, there would be no happy ending.

She opened her eyes when she felt the wetness on her face. "What are you doing?" she asked as Lauren ran a towel over her forehead.

"You're sweating really bad."

Her voice felt weak and she coughed. Lauren helped her mother into a sitting position.

"Here, sit up, so you can take your medicine."

She poured two pills into Joyce's hand and handed her a glass of water. Joyce eased the pills into her mouth, then took a sip of water to wash them down. She didn't bother asking what they were for.

"Thanks," she said, handing her back the glass.

"Is there anything I can do to make you more comfortable?" Lauren asked.

Tears sprouted into Joyce's eyes as she stared at her beautiful child. She took her daughter's hand. "Lauren, I know that I haven't been the best mother. But I can't leave here without you knowing . . ." She looked down, finding herself on the brink of a huge chasm. She'd never uttered these words before. ". . . without you knowing how sorry I am."

Lauren looked like those were the last words she ever expected to hear.

"Mama, don't worry about any of that. The sickness has you talking delirious."

"I'm not delirious. I'm dying." She clutched Lauren's wrist, wanting her to know this was for real. "Your father came to me in a dream. He begged me to forgive you. And he wants you to forgive him, too."

"Forgive him for what?" Lauren said, uncomfortable.

"For putting you in the position that he did. For being the catalyst that destroyed our relationship." Joyce didn't know why, but a part of her wanted Lauren to say their relationship was not destroyed. "I'm so sorry, honey. I love you with all of my heart. I don't know what day will be my last, but I don't want to leave without you knowing that. And well, I need you to forgive me, too. I don't want to die with us like this."

Lauren was not as moved as she'd hoped. "Mama, stop saying that. I forgive you and you're going to get better." Joyce didn't know whether she meant that or if she was just saying it because she thought Joyce needed to hear it. Either way, those words warmed her heart.

"Thank you for letting me spend my final days here and

not in that god-awful place," Joyce said. No sense in arguing about whether death was imminent, because they both knew that it was.

"You're going to be fine." Finally, what Joyce had said was sinking in, and Lauren looked grateful. "I know we're not really praying people, but maybe we should try," Lauren said.

"Maybe that's what's been wrong," Joyce mumbled, feeling a pang of sadness that she had let women drive her not only out of church, but out of her relationship with God. "But I'm no longer delusional and I believe my time is up. And honestly, I'm ready. I'm tired and I'm ready." She tightened her grip on her daughter. "The only thing I want is to see you marry that man because he's a good one."

"You'll see us," Lauren assured her. "You'll be around next year."

Joyce tsked. "I might not be here next week." A wild notion came to her, but before she could stop herself, she said, "I know this is a lot, but can you move the wedding up? I want to be there to watch you get married. I've missed so much of your life."

Lauren frowned. Joyce knew the request caught her off guard.

"Move it up? I don't know if that's something we can do." Lauren's eyes shifted downward. "Honestly, I don't know if there's even going to be a wedding."

Joyce patted her hand. She didn't know why she expected her to do something so drastic. Joyce needed to just be happy Lauren wanted to look after her. It was selfish to make that request when her daughter had so much on her plate. "I understand."

Suddenly, she felt drained by the conversation. She had never felt so weak. But she had to ask how Lauren was. She hadn't talked to her about the lawsuit, but Joyce could tell that it was weighing heavily on Lauren.

"How are you doing, you know, with everything that's going on?" Joyce asked.

She shrugged. "I'm making it. Matthew is really upset."

"He's a good guy. He'll come around."

"I hope so."

This was one of the first conversations Joyce had had regarding her daughter's personal life in a long time, and that both saddened Joyce and made her happy.

"I'm going to sleep now, okay?" Joyce said, worn out.

A look flashed on Lauren's face, like she thought if Joyce closed her eyes, she wouldn't wake up.

"I'm fine. I won't die in my sleep," Joyce said, her voice low. She said a quick prayer that her words would be true.

sixty-two

Her fiancé had lost his mind. Apparently Matthew had overheard Lauren's mother's request to move the date up. And without consulting with her, he'd gone in when Joyce awakened from her nap and told her that they would indeed move the wedding up.

"Why would you tell her we can do it?"

Matthew shrugged. "Because we can. We can give her that."

"Matthew, we have a lot going on. The board vote, the lawsuit, all this drama . . ."

Lauren expected Matthew's mood to immediately shift, but she was surprised when he said, "I prayed about it. What God has for me is for me."

She wished that she could have his faith. If the tables were turned, she'd still be mad. So the fact that he was not only no longer furious, but willing to marry her early, made her heart swell even more.

"What did I do to deserve you?" she asked.

He pulled her close. "I could ask you the same thing. I'm hopeful that everything will work out and they'll still give me the job."

Lauren prayed for that, too. She didn't see how Matthew would still want to marry her if he didn't get the job.

"Are you sure you want to move this up?"

"Our wedding day will be about us. Saying I do. Whether we do that now or six months from now is not going to change anything. So let's give your mother this slice of happiness."

Lauren was touched by the way he was always thinking of others.

"Besides, everything happens for a reason. This could actually work out well. This way I could be married, and it'll send a message about this whole lawsuit. So the more I think about it, it's a brilliant idea."

As bad as she wanted to marry Matthew, Lauren didn't see how she could pull off a wedding in a couple of weeks. "I just can't—"

"Get Vivian to help you. We already said we weren't doing anything elaborate. We can go to the courthouse if that's easier."

Lauren balked at that idea. "I am not getting married in a courthouse."

"Call Vivian. She'll help."

Lauren finally gave in. Kissing him, she promised, "Okay, let me start planning my wedding."

It was obvious as soon as she picked up the phone, Vivian would be in no mood to plan a wedding.

Lauren had called her a few times to check on her after her son left, but she kept sending the call to voice mail. Lauren had been trying to give her time to come out of her depression.

But so far she hadn't. Which is why she was surprised when Vivian picked up the phone.

"Yeah?" she said.

"Hey. It's Lauren. How are you?"

"Fine," she said, sounding completely unfine. Lauren made a note to herself that when she got through with this drama with Matthew and everything with her mother, she needed to take Vivian away for the weekend.

"Maybe I should call you later," Lauren said.

"Naw, I'm good," Vivian replied. "What's up?"

Lauren hesitated, debating whether she should ask. But who else would she get to help? No one.

"I was trying to see if I moved the wedding up, do you think you'd be able to help me plan something really quickly?" Lauren said. "My mother wants to see us get married."

"I don't understand."

Lauren filled her in on everything that had been going on the past two weeks—her mother's diagnosis, moving in with them, and her request to move up the date.

"Wow, that's noble," she said.

"I know. I'm going to let the bitterness and anger go."

"That's easier said than done," she mumbled.

"Yeah, I know. But I finally found my happy."

"I'm glad you have. At least somebody has."

"Your happiness is coming."

"Naw," she mumbled. "I'm good. I don't need another man. He'll just cheat on me like the last one."

Lauren uttered words she never thought she'd say: "You know, not all men are bad."

"They aren't, are they? Because you sure found a good

one." Her tone was condescending, but Lauren wasn't going to let her mood be ruined.

"You're right about that."

Vivian sounded put out, but she said, "All right. Let me know what you need me to do. As a matter of fact, I'll start looking for a place for the reception."

Lauren hadn't expected such a quick response. "Oh, wow. Thank you, girl, you're a lifesaver."

"No problem. I have no life anymore. I may as well help you plan yours."

Lauren ignored her negativity, just grateful that they would be able to pull this off.

sixty-three

Who would've ever thought that this moment could actually happen? Joyce watched her daughter model the long snow-white dress with the intricate lace train. She was an absolute vision of loveliness.

"Umm, I don't know." Lauren studied her reflection. "I mean, it's nice, but it's kinda old-timey."

Joyce wanted to tell her the one before made her look like a cheap hooker, but she was determined to stay positive. God was smiling on her today. Even though she was extremely tired, she was feeling better than she had in weeks. Lauren had wanted her to stay home, but she desperately wanted to help Lauren pick out her dress. Joyce had missed so much, and sickness was not going to make her miss this. In fact, Joyce felt in her heart that God was letting her hang on long enough to take part in her daughter's wedding.

"I think this one is gorgeous," the saleswoman said.

"That's because it's the most expensive," Lauren joked.

"Don't worry about costs," Joyce said. She didn't have a lot of money, but what she had left, she wanted to share with her daughter.

"Mama, you don't—"

"Let me, please?"

She was grateful that Lauren didn't continue arguing. After everything that had happened, they would be together for the most joyous occasion of her daughter's life.

sixty-four

Lauren couldn't believe that they had pulled this off. They were holding a small, intimate ceremony at a church that they rented out, since they didn't have one of their own.

Both Matthew and Lauren agreed that that would be their first order of business—finding a church home.

Lauren looked over at her mother, grateful that Matthew had convinced her to do this. She didn't look good. In fact, she looked weaker and frailer than Lauren had ever seen her. But she was putting on a good face, though Lauren could tell by the look in her eyes that she was in pain.

It had taken about two hours to get her dressed this morning. She wouldn't let Lauren help, but Aunt Velma had swung by.

"I wanted to give you something," Joyce said. She shifted her walking cane to the side—she had flat-out refused to use the wheelchair—then handed Lauren a wedding ring, which hung from a small gold chain. "This is the ring your father gave me." Joyce fingered the metal band. "I debated giving this to you because, well, honestly, I didn't want to jinx you. But this circle symbolizes the lives we created, along with you and your brother. And that, in and of itself, is priceless. So here's your something old."

Lauren took the necklace and put it around her neck. She leaned in and kissed her mother on the cheek. "I'm glad you're here. Thank you."

"I'm so glad to be here." Her smile was strained. She turned to the nurse attendant who'd come along to assist. "Can you help me out, please? I want to take my seat."

Lauren was going to walk down the aisle by herself, which was fine with her because her father was there in spirit. The only bridesmaid she had was Vivian. And that was fine, too.

"So, are you ready?" Vivian asked.

Lauren turned to her friend with a big smile. "I am. I am so incredibly happy." She stopped short as she noticed Vivian's red, swollen eyes.

Lauren frowned. They were close, but not close enough to shed tears. "Why are you crying?" Lauren asked.

Vivian's face turned mean. "You're so happy, huh?"

"Yes, I never thought this day would come. I'm not just happy, I'm blessed."

Vivian let out a pained chuckle. "Blessed? How ironic. You ruin all of these marriages, but God still blesses you. How crazy is that?"

Lauren stared at her friend in disbelief. Surely, Vivian was not going to start tossing around judgment on today of all days.

"Vivian, I don't know what your problem is, but the love of my life is waiting to marry me, so—" Lauren stopped abruptly when she saw Vivian pull out a small-caliber handgun and point it directly at her.

"Wh-what are you doing?" Lauren gasped, eyeing the chrome pistol.

"You think I'm going to let you have your happily ever after?" she hissed.

"Vivian, what are you doing?" Lauren asked, in shock.

"I'm doing what I have been carefully planning for the past year." She held the gun firm, utter contempt across her face.

"I don't understand. Why are you doing this?"

"You have no idea, do you?"

Lauren knew that Vivian was going through bouts of depression, but had she snapped as well?

"You are nothing but a conniving little whore!" Vivian cried. "You destroy people and then don't give them a second thought!"

Lauren took a step back and held up her hands like she was in some movie. "Vivian, I don't know what's going on, but I'm going to need you to calm down and put the gun away."

Vivian released a pained laugh. "Have you ever bothered to ask my son's name?"

"Huh?"

She jabbed the gun in Lauren's direction. "I said, have you ever bothered to ask his name?"

"What does that have to do with anything?"

"His name is Cornell Jacobs, *Junior*. I'm Vivian Harold Jacobs."

Lauren froze.

"Yeah, you know Cornell, *Senior*. Very well. You screwed him on a regular basis. But you know, even after I found out about you, I was willing to forgive him. But he told me you made him realize what he was missing and he wanted out. And because he had the money, he took my son with him." Her words were venomous.

"Vivian, I-I thought you were my friend," Lauren stammered.

She laughed harder. "Friend? Skank, you're not deserving

of any friends. I hunted you," she said slowly, piercing every word. "I tracked you. I followed you to hot yoga and then I befriended you. At the time I didn't know what my intentions were. I just needed to see the woman that destroyed my life."

"I don't understand."

"Neither did I. And I wanted to understand. I *needed* to understand. And then, I got to know you and I watched you callously tear down one marriage after another."

"So, you were just . . . Wait." Lauren had a sudden flash of Vivian in her bedroom standing near her nightstand. She'd had an uneasy feeling, like Vivian had been snooping, but she'd been so preoccupied with her mother that she'd let it pass. "Did you give that information to Teresa Brooks? Send it to the board members at Matthew's school?"

Vivian smiled proudly. "Only a whore keeps her men in her datebook."

That explains so much, Lauren thought. The day Vivian used her bathroom, she must have ducked into Lauren's bedroom and stolen her planner.

"What did you hope to get sending that information?"

"I want you to suffer! Like I'm suffering." Tears streamed down Vivian's face. Lauren's eyes darted around the room. Hopefully, the wedding planner or someone would come looking for her. "Vivian, just let me go and we'll forget this ever happened."

"I'm not a bad person," Vivian said, gun still pointed, like she was talking to herself. "All I wanted was to please my husband, be a good mother. But women like you keep it from happening. Women like you give husbands the false idea that the grass is greener when you digging with hoes."

Lauren debated whether she should lie and claim igno-rance, but this was a calculated plan. Obviously, Vivian had planned everything down to the last detail. Lying would only make things worse.

"Please? Just let me go. I'm about to get married." Lauren's voice cracked.

"Do you think I sympathize with you?" Vivian said, cock-ing the gun. She looked like a madwoman. Strands of hair had been released from her perfectly coiled bun, as if she'd been pulling them loose one by one. Black streaks ran down her face from the mascara, and it looked like she'd purposely taken scissors and cut the sleeves off her dress. "I know you don't think I'm about to let you have some happily ever after."

Lauren measured the distance to the door. She could run, but Vivian would get a few good direct shots to her back.

"Vivian, you can still see your child. You won't be able to see him in jail," Lauren said, deciding to reason with her rather than run.

Her voice shook. "His daddy has already poisoned him against me, trying to make him think I'm crazy, and now my own son doesn't want to be bothered with me. I. Have. Nothing."

Lauren knew there was no reasoning with Vivian. Maybe a harsh dose of reality would help her. "Your husband was leaving long before I came into the picture," Lauren said.

"That's bull!" she screamed, jabbing the gun in Lauren's di-rection again. "All marriages have their problems. What women like you do is you magnify them. You flash freaky sex, you're nice to them . . . because you only have to see them for the couple of hours that you're screwing them. You don't have to see them and watch them leave their drawers in the middle of the floor.

You don't have to take care of a child, the house, then try to frig-gin' make them feel like a king when you're utterly exhausted. You just whip in, all made up, screw our husbands, whisper sweet nothings, then go on back to your life." She began pacing as she rambled. "I contemplated how I could make you pay. I even thought about seducing Matthew. But here's the tripped-out part: you got a good guy. And every time I watched you with Matthew or listened to one of your ridiculous stories, I seethed inside because you don't deserve a good guy. You deserve to suffer like all the women you've made suffer."

Lauren decided she would have to take her chances and make a dash for the door. She was just about to do it when the door swung open.

"Lauren, baby. I left my clutch . . ."

Joyce's words trailed off when she noticed the gun pointed at her daughter. "What is going on?"

"Go away," Vivian spat.

Instead, Joyce slowly walked into the room, and stopped right in front of Lauren. "My God, what are you doing?"

Vivian jabbed the gun with one hand, while wiping her face with the other. The move only smeared her mascara more. "Look, old lady. This ain't your business. Go away."

Joyce ignored her, pushing her weight on the cane to help her stand erect. "Lauren is my business."

"Mama, she's right," Lauren said, trying to edge in front of her mother. "Vivian and I are just talking. Just go."

But instead of moving, Joyce took a step closer to Vivian. "This doesn't look like talking to me. Put that gun down."

"Do you think I'm playing?" Vivian yelled. "I'm not afraid to use this!"

Joyce wagged her finger. "My daughter is getting married today. You get out of here with this foolishness before we call the police."

That caused Vivian to get even more agitated. "I'm not playing! I will shoot both of you."

"Mama, move," Lauren said, trying to push around her mother.

The strength with which Joyce held her back was surprising, especially considering how frail she'd been this last week.

Joyce narrowed her eyes at Vivian. "Young lady, put that gun down now."

"I'm not afraid to use this!" Vivian said.

Lauren knew she had to defuse the situation because Vivian seemed to be slowly losing it. But before she could act, Joyce raised her cane like she was about to strike Vivian.

"I told you—"

"Mama, no!"

As soon as the words left her mouth, there was a loud pop. Then unearthly silence.

Joyce's back hunched and she fell to the ground.

"I-I wasn't trying to shoot her!" Vivian said, immediately dropping the gun in terror. "Oh my God. Oh my God!"

"What have you done?" Lauren dropped to her mother's side. "Mama!" She lifted her mother's head and placed her hand over the bloody spot in her stomach. Was she really about to watch her mother die in the same manner that her father had? "Nooooo! Mama, hang on. Please hang on." As Lauren eased under her mother, trying to provide a cushion, the blood seeped onto her white-beaded gown.

Vivian was sobbing, muttering something about not

"meaning to shoot her." But her words were becoming jumbled. All Lauren could hear was the life coming out of her mother's body.

"Get some help!" Lauren screamed. "Somebody help us!"

The door swung open again and the wedding planner stood looking in shock. "Oh my God. What happened?"

"Get help! Call 9-1-1!" Lauren screamed.

The wedding planner took off.

"I'm s-sorry I was such a bad mother," Joyce whispered.

"No. I'm sorry. I'm sorry for everything I did," Lauren cried.

"F-Forgive me."

"Shhh, Mama. Just hold on."

"F-Forgive me," she repeated.

"I forgive you! Now just be quiet. Help is coming." She rocked back and forth as tears streamed down her face.

A small smile spread across Joyce's face. "Thank you. Tell Julian I love him, too . . . I'm coming, Vernon."

As Joyce's eyes slowly closed, a smile crossed her face, and Lauren let out a piercing scream.

epilogue

There is nothing like karma. She'd rained down on Lauren with the wrath of a scorned goddess, leaving her life in shambles.

After they put Joyce in the ground, Dr. Stephens delivered the disastrous news that despite the fact that Teresa Brooks had dropped her lawsuit—rumor had it her husband paid her off—the board was offering the presidency to someone else. The devastation on Matthew's face was heartbreaking.

"Everything happens for a reason," Aunt Velma told Lauren after Matthew broke the news. She didn't understand why a man as deserving as Matthew should miss out on his dream.

Vivian had been arrested for shooting Lauren's mother. But she was in a mental facility, so there was no telling whether she'd get better. Of course, after the shooting, Lauren and Matthew didn't move forward with the wedding. And now, two weeks later, Lauren doubted that they ever would. Marriage was obviously not in the cards for her, she figured.

"Good to see a smile on your face," Lauren said as Matthew walked into the den.

"I have reason to smile. Florida Union heard that Carolina State passed on me, and they want to make me an offer." He sat next to Lauren on the sofa. "So, if you're willing, I'd like to still get married and move to Florida."

She looked at him in disbelief. "You want to still marry me?"

"Nothing would make me happier."

He didn't have to tell her twice. Nothing would make her happier, either.

"Yes, I'll marry you!" Lauren planted kisses all over his face. She didn't know why she'd been given another chance. But she was grateful just the same. She was going to take the good from her parents' marriage and toss away all the bad. Her happily ever after was here and she didn't plan to ever mess that up.

A Note from the Author . . .

When I first came up with the title for this story, *The Perfect Mistress* was the perfect fit. But I almost changed it. After all, as a married woman of twenty years, I didn't want anyone thinking I thought there was even such a thing as a "perfect mistress." But the title fit this story perfectly. As I normally do, I wanted to tell a story that went beneath the surface . . . and in this case, show how the things we do as parents—good and bad—lay the foundation that shapes our children. THAT'S the bigger story here. At no time when Vernon was gallivanting around town, daughter in tow, did he stop to think of the seeds he was sowing into his own child. And the branches that would flow from that deception.

That's why I write. Yes, I want to entertain you with a good story, but I also want to make my readers think about their own choices and reflect on the consequences that are often extensions of the decisions we make.

Of course, I would not be able to do any of the things that I do without the support of a network of people who support, encourage, and uplift me both personally and professionally. God has truly blessed me with an awesome team.

The coach, the top dog, the man who pushes me, my husband, Dr. Miron Billingsley. You've been on this journey since

I began. Thank you for holding it down, pushing me, loving me, even when I rolled my eyes at your constant "shouldn't you be writing instead of watching *Scandal*" admonishment. My three beautiful children, Mya, Morgan, and Myles. Thank you for your patience and understanding. And for keeping me grounded by sending me texts, telling me things like, "When you get off the red carpet, can you come take me to Target for a posterboard?"

To my sister, Tanisha Tate. You've been there since before Day One . . . since we were kids and I was making up stories on you for entertainment. If God told me to design the perfect sister, I would design you. Thank you for everything, especially carrying the load of caring for Mama. I am eternally grateful.

To Victoria Christopher Murray, my business partner, my writing partner, and my very dear friend. This book wouldn't be what it was if it wasn't for you. Thank you for putting your own projects on hold to help me work through the dynamics of this book. Amazing doesn't even begin to describe you. (Have you ever thought about mentoring people?) ☺

To one of the dearest friends a person could ever ask for, Pat Tucker. Distance doesn't diminish how eternally grateful I am for your friendship. It has been an honor taking this literary journey with you.

There are so many others in this industry who have been a tremendous support . . . I'm almost hesitant to name names. But special thanks to my other business partner, Jacquelin Thomas, and also Nina Foxx, Eric Jerome Dickey, Kimberla Lawson Roby, and Lolita Files. To Tiffany Warren, Rhonda McKnight, and Renee Flagler . . . thanks for the convos that keep me from jumping off a cliff some days. ☺

To my Brown Girls Books family: Jason, Princess, Pam, Norma, Kimyatta, Brianna, Lasheera, Michelle, Angela, Damita, Richelle, Gina . . . thank you so much for all that you do. To our amazing author partners . . . I'm so honored to be affiliated with you! We're truly changing the game!

And to my dear, dear, FOREVER friends—who buy every single book, even if they don't read them. Clemelia, Jaimi, Raquelle, and Kim . . . you have had my back since I was a telemarketer in college having you listen to my spiel every other day so I could get credit. It's so great to have friends who understand when you don't keep in touch like you should, but when you do, are able to pick right back up like you just spoke yesterday.

As usual, a tremendous thanks to my agent, Sara Camilli, my phenomenal editor, Brigitte Smith, my publicist, Melissa Gramstad, and the rest of my family at Gallery— thank you for believing in me! Big thanks to Sheretta Edwards for all of your help in making my writing life more manageable. Yolanda Gore, thank you also, for, well, everything.

I also have to give a huge thanks to all of those who made my movie dreams come true. For *Let the Church Say Amen,* thanks to Regina King and Reina King for your commitment to the project and staying true to the book. To Queen Latifah's Flavor Unit, BET, Bobcat Films, and all the talented actors and crew . . . thank you for bringing my work to the screen! To the phenomenal cast, including Naturi Naughton, Lela Rochon, Brely Evans, Trav, and Hosea Chanchez, you rock. But then, I'm sure you already know this. To my TV One team . . . especially fellow Houstonian, D'Angela Proctor, looking forward to big things!

Thank you to all the book clubs that support my work. I hate naming names, but I wouldn't be where I am were it not for your support, so special thanks to Neo-Renaissance Book Club, Sistahfriends, Christian Fiction Café Book Club, Sisters Who Like to Read, Readers of Delight, Sistahs in Harmony, Cush City, Black Pearls Keepin it Real, Mahogany, WOW, Brag about Books, Women of Excellence, Savvy Literary Ladies, Mocha Readers, Characters Book Club, Tabahani Book Circle, FB Page Turners, African-American Women's Book Club, Women of Color Book Club, Zion MBC, Jus'Us Book Club, Go On Girl Texas 1, Bookclub Etc, Pearls of Wisdom, Lady Lotus, Soulful Readers of Detroit, Brownstone, Agape Book Ministry. (If I left you off, charge it to the head . . . because the heart is eternally grateful.)

Thank you to all the wonderful libraries that have supported my books, introduced me to readers, and fought to get my books on the shelves. Thank you also to Yasmin Coleman, Pilar Arsenec, Hiawatha Henry, Curtis Bunn, Gwen Richardson, Orsayor Simmons, King Brooks, Lisa Paige Jones, Sophie Sealy, Radiah Hubbert, and Jurrell Ahmad Fullerton.

And I know this may be a bit much . . . but when you have a circle of friends and supporters, you want to show your gratitude, even to your cyber friends. So a great big virtual hug and a real life thanks to my Facebook friends/supporters: Naturopath Cecie, Tonia, Heather, Sharmel, Jackie, Linda, Ernest, Shirley, Sharon, Gloria, Pam, Tracy, Nelvia, Phyllis, Erika, Robbie, Leslie, Ashara, Nita, Jetola, Bettie, Cassandra, Renee, Marsha, Shawn, Deb, Michelle, Kathy, Jackie, Sheryl, Candace, Tyra, Alisha, Theresa, Lisa, Carla, Kendria, Josie, Denise, Ina, Chevonne, Dasya, Monique, Gina, Ina, Tracey,

Raquel, Marcena, Cheritta, Maleika, Christie, Sylvia, Deborah, Demetria, Cebrina, Lolita, Tyra, Jetola, Cindy, Joanna, Maurice, Juda, Cecelia, Deborah, Shawn, Lachelle, Vonda, Marth, Chenoa, and Sherryle. I know there are so many more, but I think my copy editor will start cutting right about here, so this is for all those I forgot! Big, big thanks also to: _____. (Write your name here!)

Lots of love and gratitude to my sorors of Alpha Kappa Alpha Sorority, Inc. (including my own chapter, Mu Kappa Omega), my sisters in Greekdom, Delta Sigma Theta Sorority, Inc., who CONSTANTLY show me love . . . and my fellow mothers in Jack and Jill of America, Inc.

And finally thanks to you . . . my beloved reader. If it's your first time picking up one of my books, I truly hope you enjoyed it. If you're coming back, words cannot even begin to express how grateful I am for your support. Thank you. From the bottom of my heart.

Much Love,
ReShonda

the
PERFECT
MISTRESS

ReShonda Tate Billingsley

INTRODUCTION

Lauren Robinson wanted a simple life, and a simple life meant no strings. If love always led to infidelity and heartbreak—like it did with her cheating father, Vernon, and scorned mother, Joyce—then the best thing was to never become someone's wife. So Lauren took a cue from her dad and never expected anything from the married men she dated, who had oblivious wives and plenty of money to spoil her with. But when ex-boyfriend Matthew King comes back into her life—the first and last man to ever break Lauren's heart—she begins to question whether she's really happy.

Joyce Robinson didn't know what she had done to deserve the life she was getting. Not only had she lost both parents to disease, she lost her husband, Vernon, too—to a vengeful, gun-toting mistress who would not accept him leaving her. Worst of all, her teenaged daughter, Lauren, had enabled him to destroy their family. Now, dying of brain cancer and stuck in a facility, Joyce is trapped—not just by her disease-riddled body, but by an embittered heart, a cold facade, and an unresolved anger toward her now grown-up daughter. Will she be able to make peace with Lauren—and her choices—before it's too late?

TOPICS AND QUESTIONS
FOR DISCUSSION

1. In *The Perfect Mistress,* we're introduced to two parallel narratives of mother and daughter, Joyce and Lauren. What are your initial impressions of their relationship?

2. It's clear Lauren loves her father deeply, and when he suggests that she might lose him if her mother ever discovered his extramarital relationships, she definitively decides never to tell a soul out of that fear. How does his threat of leaving manifest in her behavior, both as a child and as an adult?

3. When Joyce leaves to stay with her parents after Vernon cheats on her, her father insists that she stay with Vernon, saying the only thing that's unforgivable is physical violence, and that anything else can be worked through. What do you think of this statement? Can anything be forgiven, or should it?

4. Vernon tells Lauren that humans weren't created to be monogamous and that she'll understand when she's older. When Lauren asks her father if he'd be okay with Joyce having boyfriends the way he has girlfriends, a "look of sheer horror" (p. 87) sweeps across his face. He tells her that it's different for men and women. Is it? If so, how?

5. What is the pivotal moment when Joyce decides Lauren has committed the ultimate betrayal against her? Why do you think it was so easy for Joyce to blame and hate Lauren for what had happened?

6. Lauren ended her two-year relationship with Matthew in college because she believed he was cheating on her. When he comes back into her life, however, she is surprised by how happy she is to see him. What do you think are the real reasons why their prior relationship ended?

7. When Matthew and Lauren are discussing a high-profile sexual harassment scandal in the news, Matthew comments that it's a shame such a talented guy is being brought down by his libido. What's problematic about that statement? Besides the obvious differences between an affair and sexual harassment, what are other reasons why someone would stray apart from a dissatisfied sex life?

8. Time and again, people in Joyce's life comment on how Vernon was such a great father but a lousy husband. Do you think he was a great father? Why or why not?

9. Vivian tells Lauren that she's contributing to the "destruction of the black family" (p. 163) by having affairs with married men. Do you agree with her? Why or why not? If there were no women with whom men could have affairs, would their relationships or marriages be perfect otherwise?

10. Joyce says to Lauren, "It was bad enough that you stole his heart from me, but then you turned around and watched him give it to other women" (p. 223). What do you think she means by this? How does this statement reveal Joyce's true feelings?

11. Lauren reminds Joyce during Julian's staged therapy session that she was just a child when her ultimate "betrayal"

took place and thus is entitled to forgiveness, and that her debt is paid. What is Joyce's response to that? Why do you think Joyce dismisses the "just a child" excuse?

12. Several people have to remind Joyce that Lauren deceived her mother because she wanted the approval of her father. Why do you think Joyce feels so hurt, even decades later, by Lauren's secret?

13. Lauren's mother makes the ultimate sacrifice on Lauren's wedding day by attempting to apprehend Vivian, who was threatening Lauren's life. What are the parallels between Joyce's and Vernon's last few moments on earth?

ENHANCE YOUR BOOK CLUB

1. Do you believe the adage "once a cheater, always a cheater"? With your book club, discuss what it means to cheat (Is it cheating when it's physical? Is it cheating when it's emotional?), whether or not someone can change, and if you'd ever enter into a relationship with someone whom you know has cheated on others in the past.

2. Visit www.reshondatatebillingsley.com and select another Tate Billingsley title for your club's next book. Have the group individually rank the characters in both books from best to worst (or favorite to least favorite). Take turns arguing your case!

3. A number of films tackle the topic of infidelity and the dissolution of a family. With your book club, select a film that centers on the woman—whether she's the cheater or the scorned—and have a movie night. (Don't forget the popcorn!) Afterward, discuss its parallels with *The Perfect Mistress*.